She arched a delic

"I am the woman who [...]
marriage. I'm also addressed as Mrs. Walker. I
am the woman who has shared the loft with you,
whose bosom you have slept upon." She curled up
her fists and pressed them against his chest. "That
makes you my husband."

"Not the one you deserve. I'm—"

"Mine."

"No."

But he was hers—whether he ought to be or not
didn't change the reality.

Oh, hell. He cupped her cheeks in his hands then
came down upon her lips, kissing them hard.

Author Note

Do you love stories of redemption? They are among my favorites.

To see our heroes and heroines face their demons and come out better for it is deeply satisfying. To see them turn from an ugly past, to walk in the light of love, is at the heart and soul of courage. In *Wed to the Texas Outlaw*, Boone Walker must fight ruthless criminals. But none of them is more difficult to conquer than the guilt he harbors over his own past. His road to redemption might be a darkly troubled one, were it not for Melinda Winston walking beside him, lighting his path with her unshakable trust. I hope you enjoy this story of darkness to light, of desperation to joy and new beginnings.

May the spirited Melinda Winston charm you. May the outlaw Boone Walker steal your heart.

CAROL ARENS

WED TO THE
TEXAS OUTLAW

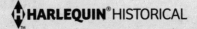

Recycling programs
for this product may
not exist in your area.

ISBN-13: 978-0-373-29871-6

Wed to the Texas Outlaw

Copyright © 2016 by Carol Arens

All rights reserved. Except for use in any review, the reproduction or
utilization of this work in whole or in part in any form by any electronic,
mechanical or other means, now known or hereinafter invented, including
xerography, photocopying and recording, or in any information storage
or retrieval system, is forbidden without the written permission of the
publisher, Harlequin Enterprises Limited, 225 Duncan Mill Road,
Don Mills, Ontario M3B 3K9, Canada.

This is a work of fiction. Names, characters, places and incidents are
either the product of the author's imagination or are used fictitiously,
and any resemblance to actual persons, living or dead, business
establishments, events or locales is entirely coincidental.

This edition published by arrangement with Harlequin Books S.A.

For questions and comments about the quality of this book,
please contact us at CustomerService@Harlequin.com.

® and TM are trademarks of Harlequin Enterprises Limited or its
corporate affiliates. Trademarks indicated with ® are registered in the
United States Patent and Trademark Office, the Canadian Intellectual
Property Office and in other countries.

Printed in U.S.A.

Carol Arens delights in tossing fictional characters into hot water, watching them steam and then giving them a happily-ever-after. When she is not writing, she enjoys spending time with her family, beach camping or lounging about a mountain cabin. At home, she enjoys playing with her grandchildren and gardening. During rare spare moments, you will find her snuggled up with a good book.

Carol enjoys hearing from readers at carolarens@yahoo.com or on Facebook.

Books by Carol Arens

Harlequin Historical

The Walker Twins

Wed to the Montana Cowboy
Wed to the Texas Outlaw

Cahill Cowboys

Scandal at the Cahill Saloon

Linked by Character

Rebel Outlaw
Outlaw Hunter

Stand-Alone Novels

Renegade Most Wanted
Rebel with a Cause
Christmas Cowboy Kisses
"A Christmas Miracle"
Rebel with a Heart
Dreaming of a Western Christmas
"Snowbound with the Cowboy"

Visit the Author Profile page at Harlequin.com.

In loving memory of Jim Reed, who never left home
without his pocket full of dog treats.
Brother, we will always remember you
as a best friend to man's best friend.

Chapter One

Buffalo Bend, Texas, October, 1883
In the courthouse of the Honorable Harlan J. Mathers,
located at the rear of the Golden Buffalo Saloon

"Mr. Walker, do I have at least your partial attention?"

The edge of impatience in the judge's voice snapped Boone Walker back to the here and now. He shifted his gaze from the woman seated beside his lawyer to the matter at hand.

"Beg pardon, Your Honor." From his seat on the elevated defendant's chair, Boone tried to direct his full attention to the proceedings but it wasn't easy with the piano player on the other side of the thin wall practicing the tunes he, no doubt, intended to perform this evening.

To Boone's mind it sounded jarring and cheap. Even though he'd lived a tawdry life on the run from the law, he didn't care for the irritating sound.

"Keep in mind that we are determining your future," the judge declared, glaring at him from under bushy gray brows. "The decisions made here might grant you your freedom."

He doubted that. Even if Judge Mathers personally handed him the keys to his prison cell, he couldn't imagine that he would ever really be free.

Public opinion had branded him an outlaw and that stigma would follow him forever; a dirty shadow that the brightest day would not diminish.

A gust of October wind blew a hail of yellow and red leaves past the courthouse window. Public opinion or not, he wouldn't mind having these cuffs off his wrists so that he could gather a pile of autumn's glory, toss it up and watch the leaves fly where they might and land where they pleased.

In spite of the judge's admonition, his attention returned to the woman. The public at large had not been admitted to this hearing. Other than a few curious faces peeking through the dust-smeared window, there was only him, an armed guard, his tenderfoot lawyer and the lady.

And she was clearly a lady, as pretty as they came. She leaned forward in her chair, watching intently while Stanley Smythe paced and presented his case. Her eyes crinkled in concentration, a fine line creased her forehead nearly to her hairline. But it was the slight parting of her lips that intrigued him and kept his attention returning to her when it should be on the outcome of these proceedings.

Why was she here? He was certain he didn't know her. The women he had been acquainted with his whole life had not been ladies—beginning with the wife of the man he had shot all those years ago.

"Let me present to you a boy, Your Honor." His lawyer, Stanley Smythe, swept his arm dramatically toward Boone. The little man stood as proudly as his five-foot-and-about-three-inch frame would allow. "Imagine, if you will, the boy Boone Lantree used to be before he crossed paths with a certain kind of woman. What chance did he have against that cunning taker of innocence? A scarlet woman to the core? And she, along with a vagrant known to be intoxicated at the time, the only witnesses to the presumed crime, other than the defendant's brother."

"I've read your letter, Mr. Smythe, and might I point out that Mr. Walker is no longer a defendant but a convicted murderer?"

"Wrongly convicted, as you will see once I have presented the facts."

The woman bobbed her head vigorously in agreement. A dislodged curl at her temple bounced with her nodding. Apparently the pretty stranger was aware of Smythe's facts. He couldn't imagine why she would be, though.

Couldn't imagine why the young lawyer had taken a shine to his case, either.

He'd never even met the man until yesterday. But five months ago, the one-year anniversary of his conviction, he'd received a letter from Smythe asking to represent him in having his verdict overturned.

Since then they had corresponded by mail and he'd learned that the fellow wanted to make a name for himself.

Didn't explain who the woman was, though. The lawyer's wife maybe, but trying to picture them together... well, it didn't seem likely.

"Let's get on with it, then." Judge Mathers waived

his hand to the empty room. "I've got a jury trial coming up at one o'clock and I could use my noon meal before I get into it."

"Yes, indeed," Smythe agreed with curt a nod. "Picture, then, our young innocent, his pockets full of earnings from his first payday working as a janitor for the general store. A meager amount to be sure, but the boy's own for the spending. Now imagine a grown woman with her rouged cheeks and swaying hips seeing the boy and figuring him for an easy mark. She flirts with him, his eager young heart takes a tumble."

As he recalled the event, it wasn't his heart that reacted so much as his—but after a few moments of Martha Mantry's flirting, it was true that he had fallen under her spell. And it had to be said that he had not known Martha was married.

"Our boy believes the woman has taken a shine to him just as he has to her. So he follows her to her room, full of eager innocence—a lamb to the slaughter, if you will—unaware that Elliot Mantry, the deceiver's husband and partner in crime is hiding in the closet, waiting to steal every cent the boy worked so hard to earn."

The lawyer did put a nice spin on things. Boone's money had been hard-earned—it was just that he'd meant to give it to Martha after she had relieved him of his virginity. He wouldn't have minded his empty pocket in that event, but having the money stolen rankled even after all these years.

Harlan Mathers yawned while glancing at the clock. This was not a good sign. Boone would feel more encouraged had the judge appeared to be interested in his case.

"Put yourself in young Boone's place, Your Honor. We have all been that age at one time."

This line of argument seemed to intrigue the woman. Her lips parted another half inch while her blue eyes blinked wide. She glanced back and forth between Smythe and Mathers.

"Let's get to the hammer and nails of the subject, shall we?" Mathers drummed his fingers on his desk. "My noon meal won't stay warm forever."

Lunch didn't seem a half-bad idea to Boone, either.

"I'm merely setting the scene." Stanley Smythe smoothed his tweed vest with trim, slender fingers and squared his shoulders. "So the events that followed will be in perspective."

"It's clear enough, Mr. Smythe. A boy who had no business bringing his money to town lost it to a pair of con artists, got drunk and challenged one of them to a gun fight. Elliot Mantry, who was also drunk, may or may not have been reaching for his gun. His widow, watching from the window, says that he was not. The facts were confirmed by a fellow who could barely stand or speak."

"That is the story that convicted my client. But as you know, the woman did not testify to this in court because she was serving time for continuing her treachery against other children. Boys who ought to have grown to be the pillars of society, the rocks upon which law and order depend. But instead, because of Mrs. Mantry, they were led down the path of depravity. Like young Boone, here, they have been forced into a life they would not have chosen."

Being caught up in Smythe's story, some of it true and some far-fetched, he nearly forgot the woman with Smythe until she sniffled and dashed a tear from her eye.

"May I speak, Your Honor?" she asked.

All of a sudden the judge didn't look so bored. His face lit up and he was all smiles, and she, pretty dimples flashing, smiled back.

With a rustle of feminine-sounding cloth, she stood then folded her dainty gloved hands demurely in front of her.

He'd like to see the man who didn't swallow every word the enticing creature had to say.

Boone would decide later if he believed her or not. Years ago he had believed everything Martha Mantry had told him and look where that had gotten him. Over time he had discovered that women could be skilled at getting what they wanted by flashing a comely smile or a swishing a pair of rounded hips.

Just what was it that this one wanted?

"I would simply like to ask that you look at your own past, Your Honor, or at your own grandchildren, if you are blessed." Miss Every Man's Dream wrung her fingers. "Even little girls are born with a spoonful of mischief. The only difference between Mr. Walker and myself is a bit of good luck."

That and the fact that she had not likely ever put her lips to a bottle of whiskey or carried a gun on her hip thinking the world was as easily conquered as the dust under her boots.

"And here is something to consider…did you realize that Boone Walker has a twin brother?" She arched a pair of prettily shaped brows. "At first, this might not seem to relate to Mr. Walker's situation, but upon reflection you will see that it does. The boys' parents named them the same name. Boone Lantree and Lantree Boone. I ask you, sir, what kind of parents name their children the same name? Lazy ones, I say, and uncaring—the boys were doomed from the start by the very people who were supposed to nurture them."

She sure as shooting wasn't describing his folks. They were not lazy or uncaring. Ma and Pa had named them for their grandfathers. By giving him and his brother both of the names, no one got offended.

Since he didn't know what the woman was up to, and she seemed to be on his side, he didn't correct her. Probably should, though. It wasn't right to let Ma and Pa's memory be sullied. Every day it ate at him; how he'd caused them grief over the years. They had gone to their rewards many years back from fevers, he'd come to find out. He always wondered if they died believing the things said about him.

"A twin, you say?" The judge leaned forward on his elbows. "If the parents were so neglectful, what became of Lantree Boone Walker? What has he done with his life?"

The woman sighed, looking sorrowful.

Did she know Lantree? His brother had always been a square shooter, always the responsible one.

He ought to have asked his lawyer about Lantree, but never had. Too much of a coward, he guessed, to come face-to-face with what his running must have cost his twin. Even given their opposite personalities, he and his brother had been close growing up. Right up until the day Boone had run, leaving Lantree cradling the body of a dead man.

Smythe did mention that it was Lantree who was paying his fees. He did know that little bit.

"He's a hardscrabble cowboy, branding, roping, cussing." She shook her head in what he saw as exaggerated sorrow but the judge seemed too smitten with her pretty pout to notice the insincerity.

She was truthful about the cussing, though. His brother did cuss. "Hell and damn" as he remembered it. The phrase was his brother's one claim to wildness.

He doubted that Lantree had changed that much over the years. Must be that the woman was trying to show that because of Ma and Pa, neither of them had had a chance at growing up respectable.

Hell, being a cowpoke wasn't so unrespectable, not like being an outlaw was.

"Lantree Walker was the only other reliable witness to the shooting," Smythe declared. "His testimony at the time was that it was a fair fight, maybe even favored Mantry since he was a man coming against a boy, but the widow's words held sway. Young Boone, fearful to his bones, had run away, as children will do.

"I could not help but be appalled that, at my client's trial, Lantree Walker's original testimony was not presented. All we heard were the written lies of a convicted thief and child exploiter along with the deranged memory of an inebriate. Clearly, Lady Justice wept on the day that Boone Walker was convicted."

"Just so," the woman added with a quick glance in his direction.

Boone didn't know who this "innocent child" was they kept talking about. It sure hadn't been him. He'd been born wild and only become more unruly over the years. On that long-ago day that he'd taken his money to town, Lantree had taken his, too. But his brother had put his in the bank.

While they'd been born twins, identical to look at, they had never been peas in a pod.

"I'll need some time to sleep on what's fact and what's not." The judge stood, stretching his back. "We'll meet tomorrow, ten o'clock sharp."

The woman took a deep breath and let it out slowly. She gazed at Boone as though his fate was of some importance to her.

She nodded and then turned with a swish of that fancy womanly fabric. The scent of roses followed her. That was pleasant, given that he hadn't smelled a rose in some time.

He watched her bustle twitch to and fro while she walked toward the big set of doors that led to the street behind the saloon. When she pulled the door open, a flurry of leaves blew inside.

Who in tarnation was she?

Stanley Smythe waived his fork as he spoke to Melinda Winston across the table in the dining room of the Inn of the Golden Buffalo. She could not truthfully say that she knew what the lawyer was going on about…in fact, she could not even say that she actually saw him.

While she did a fair job at stabbing her lunch with her fork, even chewing a bite now and again, she was fairly consumed by her first impression of the black sheep of the family.

No matter how she tried, she could not get Boone off her mind. How could she when she had spent the better part of the two-week journey to Buffalo Bend wondering what he would be like?

Would a condemned man seem different than any other? Would evil intent glint from his eyes? Or would he have the same demeanor as an innocent man?

And, having listened to Lantree's recollections of

what had happened that long-ago night, and having been spellbound by the lawyer's presentation of an innocent boy wronged, she did believe that he ought not to have been convicted. While there was no denying that he had killed a man, it was clear as raindrops that it had not been in cold blood.

Still, it wasn't the first murder that had folks shivering in their beds at night. There were reports of many other heartless crimes, each one more wicked than the next.

This morning in the courthouse, she had studied Boone long and hard. During that time, she did not feel evil lurking behind his eyes.

Melinda, having a well-favored face and figure, had, of necessity, developed a keen sense of male integrity. She had come to read men as easily as she read books. She'd had to. If she succumbed to every sweet talker who presented his suit, she would be in sorry shape.

Yes, within Boone she did see a troubled soul, one who carried a great deal of guilt. But she had to agree with Lantree, and with Stanley, when they insisted that Boone was not who the tabloids portrayed him to be.

Seeing Boone earlier, cuffed at the wrists and chained at the ankle, had been disconcerting.

Boone looked like her cousin by marriage…identical in every way. She'd had to blink several times to remind herself that it was not Lantree sitting on the defendant's chair.

After all the years the brothers had spent separated, one would expect some differences but as hard as she had stared, she hadn't been able to spot them.

One would think that the brother who spent his life as a healer and a protector would look vastly different from the one who spent his life, if the stories were to be believed, in crime and debauchery.

They did not, and this confused her.

Both men wore their blond hair long, just grazing the shoulder. Identically, they peered out at the world from under slightly lowered brows.

Upon deeper inspection, though, she had been able to see the difference in the souls of the men looking out of those lake-blue eyes.

Until recently Lantree's expression had seemed slightly haunted by an unkind past. Not anymore, though, since he had married her cousin, Rebecca.

Boone's expression did not seem haunted so much as jaded, as would be expected having lived his life among the seedy and corrupt.

"You are my responsibility, after all."

"I b-beg your pardon?" Melinda stuttered, ashamed that her attention had wandered so completely from what Stanley Smythe was saying.

"I promised your cousin that I would take care of you. While you've done a fair job of pushing your food about your plate, you've eaten only four bites."

"Have I?" He'd counted them and knew there were four? She didn't even know that. It was hard to decide whether that was a comfort or an intrusion of her privacy. Not that dining in a public restaurant was private, but still, what she did or did not eat was her own business.

"You have. And before you decide that it is none of my concern, may I remind you that I argued against you coming to Buffalo Bend?"

"You did, Mr. Smythe. Quite vehemently." She took a bite to appease him and, because now that she was paying attention, the food was quite good. "I was nearly forbidden to come."

The wide, fancy doors of the dining room swung open and Judge Mathers charged through them. His expression looked stormy. Perhaps he was one of those men who turned grumpy if their meal was delayed. She and Smythe had left the courthouse after the judge and were now nearly halfway through their meal.

"After acting as your guardian these past weeks," Smythe declared, returning her attention to him once again. "I've got to say that *forbidden* is not a word that you hold in high esteem."

It was true. As a word *forbidden* was akin to a bull's red flag. Once the bright temptation was waived, all one could do is charge after it.

It had been this way ever since Mama had changed. A mischievous adventure now and then helped Melinda forget for a moment that it used to be Mama who laughed at unreasonable rules, Mama who led her girls in lifting their skirts and dancing a playful, half-scandalous jig.

Sometimes, a half-scandalous jig made Melinda forget that it had been Papa who'd stolen Mama's joy and left her bitter.

He had always claimed that Mama was the prettiest wife of them all...that Melinda was the prettiest little girl. Clearly, that had not been enough to guarantee his love.

Watching Stanley stab an innocent piece of steak repeatedly with his fork, she could only smile and do her best to appreciate the lawyer's efforts on behalf of her family. He really was a dedicated fledgling lawyer.

"Well, someone needed to represent the family." She paused to thoroughly chew two bites so that Smythe need not fear that she would starve. "With baby Caroline only five months old, Rebecca would not consider taking her on a long trip…and Lantree would never consider leaving them without medical care…so here I am."

"Indeed." He sighed, his slim shoulders sagging in his finely tailored suit. "But I'd like to say again that I am perfectly capable of presenting Mr. Walker's case on my own. That it would be an easier task if you had remained safely at home."

"None of us doubt your ability, Mr. Smythe, or your dedication to our Boone."

"'Our Boone'? You only just set eyes on him a couple of hours ago."

"As true as that may be, family is family and that is precisely why I'm here."

And it was. Grandfather Moreland had taken her to his heart as though she was one of his own. And she was Rebecca's own, who was Lantree's own. This made Boone Melinda's own as much as anyone else's. For all that he was a stranger, family stood by family.

"A quest for adventure is the more likely reason," Smythe pointed out, "but here you are. I ask that you not make it difficult for me to return you safely to the waiting arms of your kin."

While she considered a way to rebut that statement, which was difficult because it was partly true, a young woman crossed the dining room then sat in a chair across the table from the judge.

She looked as thunderous as he did.

"I'm quite family oriented," Melinda said to the lawyer, but she couldn't help casting a sidelong gaze toward the judge and the woman. "My cousin's husband's brother's future is far too important to leave to strangers."

"You are more of a stranger to him than the woman who cleans his chamber pot. It was evident that Boone spent the better part of our hearing wondering who you were."

"I'd like to meet him, put his mind at rest, let him know his family cares."

"Pregnant! How could you make such a blunder?" the judge snapped a little too loudly. Several heads swiveled toward the table where the pair glared at each other.

"Is she his wife, do you think?" Melinda whispered to Smythe.

Smythe shrugged. "He looks like he blames her for it. If she was his wife, he'd be taking some of the responsibility. Judging by her age, I'd guess she's his daughter, poor girl."

Melinda did not openly gawk, as many were doing, but from the corner of her eye, she noticed the judge glare at his cooling meal.

For all that she resisted staring, her ears were not so discriminating. They heard what they heard, and that was the judge saying something about counting both her and her husband out and wanting the advance money back.

"That's good news," Smythe murmured. "At least the girl is married, so whatever the trouble, it can be dealt with."

They ate in silence for a moment, as did the rest of the diners.

"I want to meet my cousin." She reminded Stanley Smythe, setting her fork down on her plate.

Her guardian's expression hardened. He slid his glasses up his nose. If he'd had more hair, she guessed it would be standing on end.

"I'll tell him who you are but I will not have you associating with criminals."

"Once you've worked your magic, he'll no longer be a criminal."

"As your temporary guardian, I forbid it."

She clenched her fingers around her fork.

"I understand," she said with the most distracting smile she knew how to give. "I leave that to your judgment."

"You do?"

"Of course."

His gaze at her was less than believing and she couldn't blame him for that. She did, indeed, have every intention of meeting Boone Walker.

She owed it to Rebecca to discover everything she could about their relative.

Boone reclined on a cot in a cell at the Buffalo Bend sheriff's office, his head cradled in his arms and his elbows jutting out. The space, dimly illuminated by a lamp that shone under the crack of the deputy's office door, was a sight better than his prison cell back in Omaha.

He watched a dusting of stars through the barred transom set high on the wall that faced the alley. Damned if they weren't prettier than the finest jewels.

Wind whistled through the slats with a chilly moan. The cold that rushed in wasn't comfortable but that was a small sacrifice for a breath of fresh air.

Because he'd spent much of his life living in the open and on the run, the thing he had missed the most over the past year of incarceration was fresh air.

Locked up, there had been days when the scent of a hundred prisoners's sweat and stale pee permeated the prison walls like smoke trapped in a flue. Made a man want to puke.

If, somehow, his dandy little lawyer managed to get his sentence overturned, he'd never again so much as bend a rule that might jeopardize his freedom.

He placed one hand on his chest, over his heart.

"I vow it on my—" he nearly said "honor" but remembered he was short on that virtue. "Hell, I just vow it."

He'd endeavor to be as reformed as any man could be. As righteous as Lantree had been on his best day. As good as Ma used to pray he would be.

Thoughts of his brother had haunted him over the years. One time he'd even snuck back to the home farm. From the look of things he'd been about five years too late. All that was left of the place was half of the barn and the outhouse minus its roof.

He would have visited the cemetery but it was near sunup and the protection of darkness had begun to fade. And in all truth, he hadn't wanted to know if Ma and Pa were there. Hadn't reckoned he could face the dawn if he saw his brother's grave.

That would have meant that it was too late to beg his forgiveness, if there was any to be had. But now he knew that Lantree was not in that cemetery.

That meant he had lived years hearing the ugly stories about Boone Walker. Did he believe them?

Hell's curses, even if he didn't, how would he ever face Lantree given all he had done to break his brother's heart? Maybe one day he would write, try to make amends, then again, maybe it would be better not to. It might be for the best if he just continued to be a memory, one that probably faded with each passing year.

Something hit the wall near the window. A mischievous kid tossing a rock, he reckoned. Getting a thrill out of riling a killer is something he, himself, might have done as a know-nothing youth.

Damn if that character flaw hadn't helped get him where he was today.

Hell, he'd been drunk when he'd shot Mantry. And full of himself. He'd been sure as moonrise that he'd get his money back; have the fellow groveling at his feet in apology.

He'd learned a thing or two since then, not that it made him any less of an outlaw.

Over the years he'd done some things just to get by. Most of them he was ashamed of, but he'd never killed again. At least he didn't have that sin on his conscience.

A pebble sailed between the bars of his cell window and landed on the floor with a thud. Best to ignore it until the kid got bored and went home. No doubt, tomorrow he would be bragging about how he riled the beast and gotten away with it.

With Halloween only a couple of weeks away, maybe Boone ought to leap up, holler and rattle the bars, give the kid a real story to tell his friends.

While he thought about it, the pelting quit, so he resumed his admiration of the stars.

A few moments later he heard scraping outside then a pause and then more scraping. It sounded as though something was being dragged across the dirt toward his window.

Quietly he scooted from his cot and crouched beside the wall below the transom. He'd heard stories of vigilantes delivering warped justice through unguarded windows.

"Mr. Walker?" a feminine voice whispered. "Mr. Walker, are you in there?"

Startled, he looked up. A pair of beautiful eyes blinked in the dim light. Even from down here he could see that they were as blue as daybreak.

He stood, slowly meeting her gaze.

"Oh, there you are." Strands of wind whipped hair crossed her mouth. She puckered her lips to blow it away. "Why were you on the floor?"

He took a big step back. Had to. Because, stranger or not, the urge to reach his hands through the bars, cup her face and kiss that puckering mouth was strong.

It had been some time, a good long year, since he had lain with a woman, which might explain the feelings she stirred up, even with only her face in view.

"Who are you?"

Clearly she was the woman from the courthouse…the lady. But who was her guardian? What kind of man let a sweet-looking thing like her just slip out into the night?

"Who let you out?"

"Let me out?" Her brow wrinkled, looking puzzled.

"Who is supposed to be making sure you don't run afoul of some low life in the dark?"

"Oh…well, that would be Mr. Smythe, your lawyer."

"He gave you permission to go out unaccompanied?"

"Naturally not. The man is dedicated to my safety. But just now he's asleep. It's a wonder anyone else is, though. His snoring is rattling the walls. Who would have guessed such a small person could create such a ruckus?"

"Who would have guessed that a lady would not have the sense to stay inside after dark?"

"Really, Boone, I've lived the past several months in

the wilds of Montana. I can't imagine that crossing the street from the hotel to here can hold any more danger than that."

Who was this woman who felt she could call him by his given name when they had not even been introduced? Was she someone from his past that he'd forgotten?

Not the hell likely.

"You're standing half a block from two saloons. Men of low morals stagger down this alley all night long."

"I doubt that. I've been out here for nearly half an hour trying to get your attention. I've yet to see a single low-moraled staggerer."

"You're looking at one, miss. I suggest you get back to the hotel and let Smythe think he's doing his job." He sure hoped that his lawyer was better at presenting his case than he was at watching over pretty little misses. "Who are you, anyway?"

"That's what I came to tell you. And since Mr. Smythe has forbidden me to speak with you, I had no choice but to come over after dark." She curled her fingers around the transom bars. Her fair hands were velvety-looking now that he saw them without gloves. "In Stanley's opinion, ladies should not engage with criminals."

"I can't help but agree."

"Naturally, I pointed out that after he pleads your case, you will, in fact, no longer be a criminal."

"May I ask why you so all-fired care?"

"Because that is what family does. They care."

Family? He reckoned that in spite of the woman's beautiful face, she must be deranged.

He and Lantree had been the only children of only children. Couldn't recollect that there had ever been anyone but Ma and Pa and the two of them.

"You wouldn't know me, of course, but I'm your cousin...of sorts. Melinda Winston."

"Miss Winston, I don't have any cousins. Go on back to Smythe. I'll watch until you get safely inside the hotel. I can see the front door from here."

A great gust of wind tilted Miss Winston sideways but she caught her balance.

"This stack of crates isn't as sturdy as one would hope," she said with a laugh. "You didn't used to have cousins, but now you have me."

He didn't know what to say about that so he remained silent, listening to the wind knock something against the side of a building and the drunken laugher of a couple of fellows leaving the Golden Buffalo Saloon.

It was more than a little alarming to hear them coming in this direction.

"I see that this is confusing for you, Boone, but would I be calling you by your given name if I was not related to you?"

"I get the feeling that you are a lady who does as she pleases when she pleases."

"Well, yes, that is true." Her smile indicated that she reckoned it to be a virtue rather than plain willfulness. "And that's why I've come to tell you about Caroline."

"Caroline?" He didn't recall a Caroline in his past. He didn't like to think that he'd forgotten but...

"Your beautiful baby niece."

His heart constricted. He felt gut-punched.

"Lantree's got a daughter?"

"And a wife—my cousin, Rebecca Lane Walker. That makes me your cousin and I'm here because they can't travel with the baby being so young."

The men's laughter grew louder. There was an edge of nastiness to it that made Boone's skin prickle.

"We'll talk, but later." The drunks had noticed her. There was but one conclusion they would come to about a woman standing on crates in the dark speaking to a convict.

"Hey, lady! I've got a quarter." They'd reached the conclusion even quicker than he thought they would.

"Better run. I'll see that you get across the street safely."

She stepped off the crates, took four steps then spun around, her brows arched in question and the wind whipping her skirt.

"I don't see how you can when—"

"Get!"

The men picked up their pace. He watched her run for the safety of the hotel but not quickly enough. Her pursuers were only steps behind.

Boone stooped, snatched up the pebble that she had tossed through his window. He fired it at man in front and hit him square in the back of the head.

The fool dropped cold. The other drunk tripped over him. They both rolled around in the dirt.

Hell, who would have guessed that all the practicing at skipping stones that he and Lantree had done as children would turn out to be so useful?

Melinda Winston, her skirts flapping, reached the safety of the hotel door. With her hand on the knob, she turned, flashed him a smile then, oh damn, she winked.

Heaven help Stanley Smythe was all he could think.

Chapter Two

Melinda closed the door to her hotel room and leaned against it, her breath coming fast and hard. Those men had nearly latched onto her skirt.

What a lucky thing that the fellow in front tripped and brought his friend down with him. There was more than her safety at stake.

The last thing she wanted was for Boone Walker to think, as every other man did, that simply because she was a female she was not able to look out for herself.

Still, she could only admit that even Rebecca, her comrade in adventure, would agree that this pursuit had been a close call.

She would feel guilty forever if something happened to make Stanley Smythe feel that he had failed as her guardian.

Had it not been for him finally agreeing to let her come along, she might be at the ranch right now, counting cows. As much as she loved Moreland Ranch and everyone living there, it was isolated.

How would she ever meet the one man destined to be hers? In the time she had lived there she had entertained three possible suitors. One looking for his third wife, the next a good friend and contemporary of Grandfather Moreland's and the last…well, to be frank, he was not at all interesting.

Someday she would like to return to the mountains, live near Rebecca and Lantree. She could not imagine raising her children any place but near her cousin.

But, if there were to be children, there needed to be a husband and she was not likely to find him milling around with the cattle.

With her breathing restored, she crossed the room to peer out the window. The men who had chased her were just now getting to their feet. The swifter of the two rubbed the back of his head. His drunken companion glanced around as if confused.

Well, all was well that ended well. And a close call was only that. Close. As it turned out, she had been quicker and luckier.

And the risk had been well worth it since she had been able to make the acquaintance of her new cousin, to let him know that he was an uncle and he had his family's support.

Standing beside the window and protected by the darkness, she unbuttoned her dress and stepped out of it. The men below shuffled back to the saloon and went inside.

Dry, gusty wind blew up clouds of dust. The streetlamp below her window illuminated the grains as they whirled and swirled.

She plucked the pins from her hair then reached for the hairbrush on the dresser beside the window. While she brushed the day's tangles out, she thought about Boone.

How could she not? The man was a puzzle.

He was handsome, like his brother, and yet not at all like his brother. The features all added up to mirror images, but when she looked at Boone, there was a little flutter in her belly.

He made her feel edgy and uncomfortable—but at the same time fascinated.

That didn't happen when she looked at Lantree. At least not after the first glance, because by the second glance she'd known that he was meant for Rebecca and the flutter had vanished and never returned.

Maybe the flutter would be gone for Boone, as well, once she thought things through. Once he was not so mysterious, her heart might settle back into place.

She stared at his transom window. From where she stood, it was just visible through the rising dust.

It ought to be that Boone was as different from his twin as dusk is to dawn. One a healer, one an outlaw. An angel and a devil.

Or that might not be true at all.

After the brief time she had spent with Boone, she wondered if in his heart of hearts he was more like Lantree than it first seemed. Perhaps he, too, might have been upstanding had his life not taken such an ugly turn.

Recalling their conversation, he had been concerned for her safety.

What sort of a soul lived inside Boone Walker? The hardened criminal that life had made him? Or had something of the boy survived the hard life…maybe that person would resurface once Stanley won him a new future.

She set her brush aside and plaited her hair all the while staring at the transom window down the alley.

What was he thinking about at this moment? She could not help but wonder. No doubt he wanted to know more about his family. She hadn't had the time to tell him anything except that his brother was a father.

In the event that he wasn't freed by tomorrow night, she'd go back and tell him the rest. About Moreland Ranch and how his brother had become a doctor, about how deliciously in love he was with his wife.

Melinda sighed. Where was the man who would be deliciously in love with her?

Oh, it was true that men were in adoration of her left and right. They put her on a pedestal, admired her but did not lift a foot to climb up after her. There must be a man somewhere who had hands big enough to yank her off, to love her even when she stood on solid ground.

Where was the man who would look past her face to really see her? The one who would love her down to her soul, who would want her with all her faults and virtues? The one who would never leave and still want her when she was old and her beauty faded?

Where was that man? She wanted to know.

A movement caught her eye. Boone's face appeared between the transom bars. Moonlight reflected off his handsome features.

She thought he was gazing up at the stars but from this distance it was hard to tell.

Perhaps he was watching…her.

His hand lifted into view. He waved.

Feeling a flush from her hairline to her toes, she waved back.

A serious flutter that may or may not be gone by ten in the morning twisted her insides in a way they had never been twisted.

This was disturbing since she wanted that feeling to be for the man she married. It was unlikely that Boone, given his past, would even consider a wife and family.

And…who was he really? Maybe he was the dastardly outlaw of the broadsheets and not the hapless boy that Stanley presented him to be.

Quite honestly, she had no way of knowing for sure, even though she was very good at reading people. Was it possible that she felt a kinship to him because he looked like Lantree, whom she loved, or was she drawn to him because he was exceptionally handsome? If that were the case, she would be like her own hordes of suitors, infatuated with an image.

My word!

She backed away from the window, flung herself on the bed and waited for her nerves to settle or for morning to come.

Morning came first.

By ten o'clock the next day the wind had quieted. The courthouse door was left open to let in the sun-warmed air of an autumn morning.

The sounds of wagon wheels and commerce rolled past. Scents from a nearby bakery drifted in. Boot steps fell heavy on the boardwalk then faded into the distance.

Boone listened to the noise in an attempt to keep his heart from beating out of his chest and his shirt from becoming soaked with nervous sweat.

Apparently, Judge Mathers didn't want to hear more formal testimony. First thing upon entering the courthouse he had ordered Smythe into his chambers and shut the door.

His lovely "cousin" had leaped from her chair when the slender lawyer disappeared.

Her pacing was putting him on edge. The swish of fabric feathering around her ankles made his insides itch. The sound of the guard's boots tapping on the floor echoed from one wall to the other when he wearily shifted his weight.

Life was funny when one man in a room could be tied up in agitation waiting to see where his future would go and the other so bored he risked drifting into a doze.

Melinda Winston suddenly stopped pacing and approached Boone at a quick pace. She had her mouth open, apparently ready to say something, when all of a sudden the guard came to attention and blocked her way.

She blinked at him; she flashed dimples.

"I would take it as a kindness if you would let me speak to my cousin," she said in a voice as sweet as any he'd ever heard.

"I'd like to oblige, ma'am, but it's against the rules."

"Oh, of course," she sighed with a lift of her bosom. She shrugged then turned to walk away. Suddenly she spun around. "It's just that I have family news. Would it be acceptable if the three of us sat on this bench with you in between me and Mr. Walker?"

"Don't know that there's a rule against it but—"

"I'd be ever so grateful."

Had she practiced that batting of the eyelashes? He'd wager a hundred dollars that she had. She was skilled; he'd have to give her that. He'd wager another hundred that the deputy didn't know he was being reeled in, a fish flopping on a hook.

"I reckon it can't do any harm, as long as the two of you keep your distance."

"Thank you." She gave the deputy's forearm a quick squeeze then sat on the bench. "You are a true gentleman."

Bedazzled, the man could only nod.

Boone sat on the left side of the lawman. By damn, the fellow was preening.

Miss Winston, with her hands folded in her lap, leaned forward so that she could peer at him around the guard.

"What I didn't have time to tell you last—" She stopped suddenly. Apparently she didn't want it known that she had snuck out in the dark of night. "Last time we met, is that Lantree is more than—"

"This is a mockery of every legal standard!" Stanley Smythe's voice penetrated the wall. He reckoned even the saloon keeper could hear the ruckus. "I will not stand for this."

That didn't sound promising for his future. Melinda cast him a quick frown.

Long silence stretched in which he could only guess the judge was speaking in a quieter tone. The clock in the courthouse seemed to tick louder all of a sudden… with a longer time between each swing of the pendulum.

Even the deputy turned his head in the direction of the judge's chambers, listening.

"My client should walk free on the merit of his own innocence and you know it."

More silence, except for the clock that grew ever louder.

Melinda stood and turned toward the door with her hand at her throat.

Oddly his mind conjured the sound of his brother's voice saying, "Hell and damn!"

"No! This is highly irregular. I will not permit it."

Boone stood and faced the judge's chamber. So did the deputy.

All at once the door flew open and Judge Mathers strode out, his robe flapping like the black wings of doom.

"A situation has come up, Walker," he announced. He didn't sit at his podium but he did pick up his gavel and point it at him. "If you help me out I'll set you free."

Didn't sound so bad to Boone, but his little lawyer bristled.

"My client refuses. I insist that you release him without putting him through this farce."

Melinda tipped her head to the side, the fine line etching her forehead reaching her hairline.

"May I speak, Your Honor?" Boone asked. "I reckon I ought to know what kind of help you need and why it's got Mr. Smythe in a tizzy."

"Not a tizzy, but a bout of righteous indignation!" Smythe marched across the room and stood in front Boone with his hands on his hips, looking for all the world like a bristled bantam rooster protecting his oversize chick.

It was damn hard not to admire the man.

"You may speak, sir."

"Sir" coming from a judge…it made his neck tingle.

"What kind of farce are we considering?" Not that it mattered much if it earned him his freedom.

"I'm in a bind."

The judge set down his hammer and stepped down from his polished podium. Crossing the room, he gripped Boone's shoulder and looked up, holding his gaze along with his future.

Whatever the judge wanted, Boone couldn't imagine refusing, short of murder, that is. He was well and done with that in this lifetime.

"I want you to capture an outlaw gang. If you do, you are a free man."

"Mr. Walker." Smythe, who had been pushed aside by the judge, elbowed his way back in. "I advise you to refuse. You ought to be a free man, by your own merits. The judge has no right to include you in his dangerous schemes."

"It is within my power to set you free or to send you back to the penitentiary."

It didn't matter what Smythe felt about the right and wrong of the situation. Boone knew that in reality, Mathers did have the authority to decide his future.

"How many outlaws in this gang?" he asked. Not that it mattered. He was not going to turn down his single chance to be a free man.

"Last we knew, six. Shouldn't be a problem for a man of your…talents, shall we say?"

Rumor had cast him as a cold-blooded killer and the judge must believe it, otherwise he would not have offered him this opportunity. No one knew that the one killing he had committed had not been in cold blood. Liquor and ignorance had been running hot in his veins that night.

But he did know outlaws. Had run with them most of his life.

"I'll take the job, Your Honor, in exchange for my freedom."

He only hoped that it would not be in exchange for his soul. It was hard to imagine how he was going to round up six outlaws, possibly hardened killers that folks believed he was, without bloodshed.

Smythe let out a resigned sigh. "I'll have this written up, everything neat and legal."

The judge nodded, his expression satisfied, then turned toward the podium and started up the steps. He pivoted suddenly.

"Oh, and you'll need a wife."

Surely the judge was making an absurd joke.

Melinda cocked her head at him, searching for any sign of mirth.

Unfortunately all she could detect was satisfaction dashed with a pinch of smugness.

"A wife?" Boone gasped.

Poor man, trading one shackle for another.

From outside on the boardwalk a woman's singsong voice drifted inside. She was reciting a child's ditty and doing an off-key job of it.

"How the hell am I supposed to capture outlaws and protect a woman while I'm doing it?"

The judge shrugged away Boone's concern. "I had a deputy and his missus set for the job, paid them a pretty penny of taxpayer money, too, by way of a bonus. Yesterday I was informed that the wife is in a family way and now they've backed out of the deal."

"I'll get things done quicker on my own," Boone declared, his complexion looking blanched. "Where in blazes would I get a wife anyway?"

How odd that Boone cast her a brief sidelong glance. No, perhaps not. No doubt he had only been breaking his stare-down with Mathers.

"A wife is a must, my boy. Everything has been ar-

ranged for you and the missus to pose as homesteaders—
it's the only way to draw the criminals out. This particular
gang goes after settlers."

"I'll settle as a single man."

Mathers shook his head. "No, that won't do at all. A
wife gives the impression of vulnerability."

"That may be, but where the blazes do you think I'll
conjure up one?"

The singsong voice stopped suddenly, to be replaced
by footsteps pattering into the courthouse.

Suddenly a smile shot across the judge's face. "Ah,
here she is now!"

"Back out while you can, Boone," Smythe urged.
"We'll take your case to a higher court."

Melinda sat hard on the bench. Even the guard
groaned under his breath.

Boone's bride-to-be had hair the color of cinnamon,
lips the hue of ripe radishes and a crimson gown that
barely covered anything.

"Miss Scarlet Cherry—" the judge inclined his head
toward Boone "—meet Boone Walker, your intended."

"Oh, my, my," Miss Cherry purred, but even that was
off-key. "It's the outlaw in the—" Scarlet Cherry stroked
nicotine-stained fingertips over Boone's wrist "—flesh."

This would not do. No, not in a thousand years. This
woman was to be Rebecca's sister-in-law? Baby Caroline's auntie?

If only Lantree were here. He would intervene with
a lecture about the risk of venereal disease.

In spite of the fact that Scarlet Cherry's name had
everything to do with red, her face was pale, lined and
sickly looking. No doubt she had a dreaded illness.

Wish as she might, Lantree was not present. No one

from the family was here to take Boone's side...no one but her.

What was she to do? She might argue against this marriage all day and night but, with his freedom at stake, Boone would go along with this scheme in the end.

Truly, who could blame him for that?

Still, there must be something that she could do to prevent this injustice.

She covered her face, thinking, trying to figure a way out of this mess...other than the obvious one.

Peeking out from between her fingers, she saw the harlot press her beleaguered charms against Boone's arm. He stared down at her with a frown.

"Miss Cherry," Boone said while disengaging his arm. "As much as I appreciate your willingness to help, I'll do this on my own or not at all."

"Good day to you, ma'am." Stanley plucked Miss Cherry's sleeve and hustled her out the open doors of the courtroom.

My, but that was a relief. The very last thing she wanted to do was report that Boone had been forced to marry that brightly hued woman.

As far as Melinda could tell, Boone was a man who could capture the outlaw gang all on his own. He had a hard, worldly edge to him that his brother did not have.

Truly, all Boone had to do was cast the outlaws the scowl that he was currently giving the judge and they would put themselves in irons.

"It's a wife or a jail cell, Walker. The choice is yours."

"That is no choice at all!" Melinda leaped to her feet, feeling the injustice to her bones.

"It's the one he's got, young woman. Perhaps you

would like to volunteer for the assignment…grant this outlaw his freedom."

The challenge had been laid at her feet…and it was not as though the idea had not been making her stomach churn for the past fifteen minutes. Could she really make such a leap without running outside and losing her breakfast?

Marrying a stranger, no matter that he didn't quite feel like one because of Lantree, was beyond bold. It was life-changing and perhaps the most foolish thing she would ever do.

But in the end, family stood up for family. It was the way love worked. Lantree loved his brother and Rebecca loved Lantree. Melinda loved Rebecca and they all loved baby Caroline, therefore—

"Perhaps I would!"

Her mind reeled; she could scarcely find her breath. With three words she had changed the course of her life. In all, though, she was not sorry she had risen to Mathers's challenge even if she had to resist the urge to run outside and be sick.

Honestly, there was nothing else to be done.

Judging by the loud objections of Stanley and Boone, they were not well pleased with her decision. Indeed, her ears rang with Boone's curses and Stanley's bellows of outrage.

Mathers was grinning, though. It occurred to her that maybe he had brought the harlot here simply to goad her into volunteering. When one thought about it, Melinda would make a far more believable homesteader than Scarlet Cherry would have.

Yes, indeed. All she needed was a couple of sturdy brown dresses and she could play the part to perfection.

"I'd like to speak with you for a moment, Boone." Her quiet statement silenced the profanity. "Over in the corner."

She led the way toward a bench in the rear of the room.

Boone followed, then the guard and, after him, Stanley. Only Mathers remained near the podium, hands in his pockets. Rocking back on his heels, he looked like the cat who'd swallowed the canary.

"Gentlemen, I'd like a word with Mr. Walker in private," she said with a nod at her escorts.

"I'll allow it," called the judge.

With a scowl at everyone, Stanley Smythe followed the guard to the far side of the room.

"Miss Winston, have you lost your mind?" Boone whispered before they had even taken a seat on the bench.

"You've been speaking to my mother?" She laughed as she fluffed her skirt on the bench. Couldn't help it because she clearly heard her mother's voice in her head. She had heard the disapproving tone too many times growing up to not hear the familiar voice in this moment of upheaval.

"This is hardly a laughing matter, ma'am. Mathers isn't talking about acting married, he'll have us hogtied in a second."

"Judge Mathers?" She stood and turned toward the podium. "What if we simply acted as though we were married? It would accomplish the same thing."

"It would accomplish your reputation being ruined. I'll not have that misfortune darkening my career. No, no, indeed. It's marriage or prison."

She sat back down.

"We're strangers." Boone rubbed a hand over his face. She heard his palm scrape the rough stubble of his beard, the chain of his handcuffs jingle. "Why do you want to help me?"

"Because we aren't strangers at all. We may have only just met, but through Lantree, Rebecca and Caroline we are family…forever bound."

He stared at her, his brows lowered while he shook his head in apparent denial of the facts.

Well, no wonder he was in a sullen state. He was being put in a completely unfair situation.

Yes, indeed, and hadn't he spent the better part of his life the victim of an unfair situation?

"Your Honor?" Melinda stood again. "Once Mr. Walker fulfills his mission and you grant him his freedom, can our marriage be annulled?"

"Under a certain condition."

She sat down, arching a brow at her reluctant relative. "There, you see? Once we meet the condition, everything will be as it was before, except that you will be a free man."

"Not worth the risk."

"But it is! Do you know how much your brother has worried about you over the years? How he's watched the Wanted posters, praying that you hadn't been captured or killed, hanged even?" She caught his hand and pressed it between her palms. "Boone, you owe it to Lantree to fight for your freedom."

"With you as the ammunition?" He snatched his hand from hers. "Woman, are you insane?"

Chapter Three

"While it's true that I'm overwhelmed by this hornet's nest we've landed in, I'm quite lucid. I understand what I am doing."

"I'm in a hornet's nest. You are not."

The woman smiled at him as though they were not about to jump hand in hand off a cliff. Hell's curses, there was a twinkle in her eye.

"You're making light of a serious situation. The danger is as real as razor's edge. Think for a minute…your family will be devastated if something happens to you." He'd shake some sense into her if his hands weren't shackled.

"Our family, Boone. Believe me when I say that you are an important member—you can't know how much you are loved."

He might be able to dismiss what she was saying if her demeanor had not become suddenly serious. As intently as he looked into her eyes, there was no trace of the woman who could clearly get anything she wanted with a smile. "Your absence has been hard on your brother. You owe it to him to do whatever you need to do to come home."

As true as that might be, he could hardly risk Miss Winston's safety to accomplish it.

"Besides," she said, "they will have every confidence, as I do, that you are fully able to protect me. And might I point out that I am far from a withering violet. I am well able to care for my own safety."

That statement just went to show that the lovely Miss Winston didn't know a hill of beans about what she was getting herself into.

The woman looked as delicate as a porcelain doll. If she'd ever even been in an outlaw's presence, he'd eat his hat.

"My brother hasn't seen me in half a lifetime. He can't know what I will or won't do."

"Maybe not, but, Boone, I know."

"No." He stood. It wasn't worth the risk. "You don't know a damn thing about me."

The walk across the room to the judge felt like twenty miles uphill.

"I appreciate the offer, Your Honor, but you know as well as I do that the risk to Miss Winston is too great."

"It's a damned shame, son."

"It's a damned outrage!" Smythe actually shook his fist at Mathers.

While it might not be an outrage, it was a damned shame. He'd come so close to freedom, had nearly been able to taste it. Sleeping in the open and being able to go wherever the wind blew him had been within his grasp. He'd been only a decision away from being able to see his brother again.

That was the worst of it, he reckoned. Not seeing Lantree.

"You're right, Smythe. It is an outrage." Mathers

turned from the lawyer to pin Boone with a hard gaze. "If you choose to spend your days behind bars, that's no one's tragedy but your own. But those folks living in Jasper Springs? Well, they live in fear every day. You'll keep Miss Winston safe by your decision, but their daughters don't dare to even go into town. The young men are at even more risk. Why, just last week— well, if you aren't interested, there's no point in reliving the tragedy."

"Please, Boone," Melinda said from somewhere behind him. "This is bigger than us. What's a temporary marriage when lives are at stake? I'll never sleep another wink knowing I could have helped and I didn't."

He ought to slap himself in irons since no one else seemed to want to, but what Mathers had just revealed pierced him through the heart. He understood more than most the damage that a criminal could do to a green boy.

He'd been those boys, going to town and having their lives ruined. Maybe Melinda was right about this being bigger than they were. What was a temporary marriage—or his freedom to choose his destiny for that matter—in relation to the lives of the people in that town?

Mathers might believe that the champion he was sending to battle was the killer who could round up an outlaw gang as easily as a cowboy herded cattle, but that was not the case.

He was no more than a dime-a-dozen criminal.

But he reckoned he could at least have the courage of Miss Melinda Winston.

And if he did get the pair of them out of this still breathing, he'd be a free man. Maybe he'd go to Montana and meet his baby niece.

"I'm uneasy about this, but I'll take the job." Even while he was speaking, he prayed that he was not making a mountain of a mistake.

Mathers clapped him on the shoulder. "Let's get the pair of you hitched, then."

Melinda rose from the bench at the back of the room. She strode toward him without hesitation. The confident smile on her face made him wonder if, in spite of the fact that she looked like a rose petal, she had a backbone of iron.

His own gut was doing backflips. He reckoned he couldn't force a smile if his future depended upon it— well, hang it, now that he thought about it, it did.

Mathers nodded at the guard who unlocked the handcuffs and took them off.

The ceremony was finished three minutes after Melinda took her place at his side.

Chances were this was not the romantic wedding that a woman like her would have dreamed of, but if he kept her safely through this, she could have that next time, when she married for real.

When the judge said he could kiss his bride, Smythe stepped between them with an exaggerated shake of his head.

Melinda extended her hand and he shook it. The deal was sealed.

"You're free to go, Walker."

Go where, was what he wanted to know. He hadn't a dollar to his name. Only the folks in this room knew him to be a free man.

It was an odd, nearly uneasy feeling to know that he could simply walk out the courthouse door and not be stopped by the deputy.

"Keep low for a day or two. Folks will wonder. We'll meet at the livery, day after next, 4:00 a.m. on the dot."

"Since we are married, it would be appropriate for you to stay with me," the blue-eyed innocent declared.

"Not as I live and breathe." Smythe snatched Melinda by the elbow. "I'll escort you to your room, miss."

Stopping at the door, Smythe turned back to shoot him a glare. "I don't approve of this, not by a mile. Still, things are what they are. You will lodge with me. Miss Winston will emerge from this ordeal unharmed and a maiden still."

He answered Smythe with a nod.

Keeping his cousin, or rather his wife, safe, would be his first obligation. Capturing outlaws and protecting a town? He'd do that but only as long as it did not endanger Melinda.

If he failed to return her safely to the family, his freedom meant nothing.

As far as the maiden business went, he'd never bedded a maiden and he could only admit that the idea intimidated the hell out of him. A man had a responsibility to a virgin. Bedding the innocent meant pledges, vows of undying love. Not false vows, either, but sincere and from a committed heart.

That was one thing he could set Smythe's mind at rest about.

At four in the morning, the moon sat fat and full on the western horizon. Boone watched its slow decent as he walked from the hotel to the livery.

Buffalo Bend slumbered peacefully. This far into October, even the crickets had gone silent. The heels of his boots clacking against the wooden boardwalk sounded like shots in the night. In a moment folks would be peering out their windows.

He reckoned he didn't need to fear that any longer. Still, old habits died hard. He leaped off the boardwalk and walked down the middle of the road where the dirt muffled his steps.

Sometime during the night Smythe had packed up his belongings and gone without even a farewell. It only made sense that with this job finished, he was on to the next case that might make him a name.

It was just a shame that Boone had never had the chance to thank him for all that he had done.

From half a block away, he spotted a light shining from under the livery door. He hoped there was a fire in the stove, as well. Nights had turned cold enough that a man could see his breath.

He went inside without knocking, figuring he would be expected.

A man shoving a log into the stove, turned. He nodded.

"Boone Walker?" the fellow asked.

Boone nodded back.

"Frank Spears. Owner of this livery." Spears slapped his hands on his pants, dusting off the splinters. "They say you're a killer."

"Folks like to talk."

"Don't mean any offense by it." Spears crossed the livery and extended his hand. "You'll need all the meanness you got to get rid of those vipers in Jasper Springs."

Boone let the heat seep into him, gathering it for the time he'd be on the trail again. Maybe someday he'd have a hearth of his own, four solid walls.

A new life was opening up to him; one never knew

how it would end up. A roof over his head and a fire seemed—

"Got a brother in Jasper Springs. A niece, too. I only hope you can help them."

"Sounds like Mathers has told you everything."

"He hired me to get the wagon loaded. Things were all set for the married couple, but it looks like a bit of good luck for you that they quit."

"Time will tell, but I reckon this beats a life term."

"There's the wagon over in the corner, loaded with most of what you'll need to set up housekeeping. I'm sending my best team to go with it."

"I'll do my best to return them to you."

Spears nodded, quiet for a moment. "You sure you're a killer? I don't see it in your eyes."

"That I am...but only the one time and both of us were drunk."

"It'll sound strange, but I'm disappointed to hear it."

"I've been a thief since I was in long pants, if that eases your mind."

"Some, I reckon. Say, I don't hold a man's past against him. I needed a fresh start myself, once. And don't worry about the return of the wagon and horses. They're yours—just—if you'll keep my kin safe."

Generosity on the part of strangers was not something he was used to. While he stumbled around in his mind thinking of a proper way to thank him, the door creaked open.

Mathers and Miss Winston—Mrs. Walker, rather—stepped inside.

His wife's cheeks were blushed pink from the cold. It hit him all of a sudden how glad he was that his bride was not that Cherry woman.

"I've written up a few things," the judge said, by-passing any sort of cordial greeting. "There's a map to Jasper Springs, a bit about the outlaws, the parts you and your wife will play. Oh, and you'll need cash." He handed him a roll of money wrapped in a rubber band. Hard to tell how much, but it seemed to be a good sum.

"Good morning, Boone." Melinda's smile might as well have been sunrise, it was that bright and cheerful. "I hope you slept well."

"Best I've slept in some time." He hadn't expected to, but he must have since he hadn't even noticed Smythe take his leave. "You look refreshed."

"It must be married life." She shot him a wink and he sucked in a breath.

"Where's Deputy Billbro?" Mathers asked, glancing around.

"Just went out to relieve himself. He'll be along as soon as he smells folks in the livery."

"Everything you need to know ought to be in here." The judge handed the stack of papers to Melinda.

"One more detail…" Harlan Mathers dug around in his coat pocket. "Here it is. Don't put it on until you make an arrest, your settler roles would be compromised."

"It" was a deputy's badge, bent and tarnished, but a symbol of law and order none the less.

What Boone wanted to do was dump it in the dirt. That badge had been his enemy for too many years.

He tossed it in the air, caught it and then put it in his coat pocket.

"Send me a wire now and again to let me know how you're progressing."

Without warning, the door opened again.

Boone had to blink to make sure he saw right.

There stood his lawyer dressed for adventure, from his stiff-looking new Stetson to his denims and his barely scuffed boots.

The new get-up made him look an inch or two taller. Even his strides seemed longer.

"Stanley?" Melinda's eyes widened. "What are you doing here?"

From the far side of the door a mule brayed.

"That will be Weaver, my mount. As to what I'm doing here, isn't it obvious?"

"Can't see that it is," Boone said.

"I made a promise to bring Miss Winston home, safe and sound." Stanley said. "I'm beginning to regret that vow but I did make it."

"Stanley, I'm sure my husband is equal to the task."

The little lawyer chuckled under his breath while shaking his head.

"Well, I'm for my bed," Judge Mathers declared.

"Not quite, sir," Smythe said. "I'll see the signed papers granting my client his freedom."

"I'll gladly sign them, just as soon as the job is finished."

"I'll have that written in pen and ink. What is there to say that you will not re-arrest him once things are wrapped up?"

"What's to say he won't take his freedom and head for the hills?"

"I say he won't," Melinda declared. "I vouch for him."

Why? She didn't know beans about him.

"And I bear witness that Mathers has agreed to sign the document," Spears added.

It seemed, with the details arranged and the vouching finished, it was time to leave the warmth of the livery.

Spears hitched the team then strode to the livery door. He opened it and stuck his head out. "Billbro! You finished with that pee?"

Seconds later an animal nosed his way into the livery.

"My word," Melinda exclaimed and scuttled closer to Boone. "Is that a wolf?"

"As far as anyone knows, Deputy Billbro is only half wolf." Judge Mathers petted the canine between the ears. "You'll be glad he's along once you get used to him."

There were a lot of things that Boone was going to have to get used to. The dog probably being the least of them.

For one thing, his wife was clinging to his arm, seeking protection.

He'd never been responsible for anyone but himself. All of a sudden there was a woman, a town and very likely a lawyer who needed to be watched over.

He'd better start getting used to the dog-wolf, since he was going to need all the help he could get.

Sometime during the wee hours of their first night on the trail, Melinda sat up suddenly from her bedroll. She gazed past the embers of the dying fire feeling uneasy.

One difference between Melinda and her husband of a day was clear already.

He looked quite comfortable sleeping under the stars while she preferred peering out at the night from behind a window in a bed piled high with feather blankets.

Darkness throbbed beyond the shrinking glow of the campfire. She could nearly imagine that nothing existed in that blackness…or that everything did. What was there to say that a wolf or even a bear wasn't lurking behind a tree? A cougar poised on the limb over her head?

She would feel better if the deputy was awake. The great hairy dog-wolf lay at her feet snoring, but not as loudly as Stanley was.

The lawyer dozed between her and Boone; a human buffer. Surely the noise he made alerted every predator within a mile. Another log on the fire might help ward them off.

She hadn't even made it to her knees to get a log before the dog lifted his snout and Boone cracked open an eye.

"What's the trouble?" he asked, propping up on an elbow.

"It's too dark to sleep."

"I reckon it's not the dark keeping you awake." He nodded toward Stanley.

The dog stood, stretched, sniffed the air then resettled his large gray body alongside her leg. He plopped his heavy head on her lap, seeming so content that she would believe he had gone back to sleep if it wasn't for his nose twitching this way and that.

"It's always darkest and coldest about now," Boone said. "But it'll be sunup soon."

"I guess you've slept in the open many times."

He nodded. "A body becomes accustomed to the fresh air and freedom. I'll admit, those nights in prison were hell on earth. I'd take a wild beast over some of those inmates any time."

"I'm sorry you had to go through that."

"It wasn't anything I didn't deserve." He gazed up at the stars, silent for a moment before looking back at her. "Melinda, thank you for what you did. I should have said so earlier but with all the travel there wasn't time to talk."

She laughed softly. "And my guardian did keep us apart as much as he could."

"Dedicated of him." His smile twitched up on one side. This was not Lantree's smile. Mischief lurked in the turn of Boone's lips.

"Well intentioned, I suppose, but he hasn't even given us a moment of privacy so that I can tell you about your brother."

Boone blew out a low whistle. "There's a part of me that's afraid to know. He's got a baby and a wife, though, so I reckon he must have turned out all right."

"He's all right now, but he did go through hard times."

"Because of me, do you mean?"

"Oh, he worried about you, certainly. But his hard times weren't to do with you, Boone." She petted the dog's head, curled her fingers into his warm fur. "Before Lantree married my cousin, Rebecca, he was engaged to another woman. At that time your brother was a doctor, a very good one, too. Well, there was an epidemic, a lot of folks died under his care, his fiancé's family among them. She blamed him—he blamed himself. She ended the engagement, and very bitterly.

"Poor Lantree ran away, from his career and himself. He was in a hard way when Rebecca's grandfather found him and gave him a new career as foreman of his ranch. I believe that Grandfather Moreland—he's not really my grandfather but that's how I feel about him so that's what I call him—gave your brother much more than a job. What he gave him was a new life. Lantree found healing at Moreland Ranch. Now he's a cowboy and a doctor."

"And a proud father?"

"He couldn't be otherwise. Baby Caroline is the sweetest little thing you could ever hope to see. She's only five months old, but already she looks just like her daddy…and you."

"I'll be damned." Boone looked pleased, smiling in a way she hadn't seen until now.

"You'll see that for yourself soon."

He was silent for a moment, gazing at the glowing coals and the fingers of flame darting from the crumbling logs.

"We ought to talk about this marriage—set some rules," he said at last.

"If you like." Dratted rules. They tended to chafe at her. Especially since they tended to put unreasonable restrictions on her behavior. If Boone took his job as her husband too seriously, he might try to control her.

Just like Mama when she'd lost her sparkle and shackled herself, and her young daughters, with society's every little directive.

"Our wedding could not have been the one you dreamed of." He arched a brow.

Naturally not. What woman could possibly dream up such a wedding? But it did have to be said that it was adventurous. And there was no denying she was intrigued at the idea of being a wife, of having a man of her own, even for a short time.

"I just want to make it clear that you won't miss out on the one with all the frills and fancies because of me. I promise that I won't compromise you."

She felt the blush staining her neck and face but in the dim light he would not see it. Really, he had no way of knowing that in the deep hours of the night she had entertained intimate thoughts of him.

What wife would not? Boone Walker intrigued her in ways that no man ever had. Even men she had known for quite some time.

"That goes without saying," she said demurely, but

there was that in her that stuffed down a sliver of disappointment. If a woman was to be compromised by such a man, it could not truly be called a compromise.

Prudent women might call her a fool for feeling such stirrings for a stranger—a reportedly dangerous stranger—but Rebecca would not. Rebecca knew that Melinda was an astute judge of character.

"I won't make unreasonable claims upon you, unless we are playing our parts."

"I do appreciate your restraint." She tried not to smile.

He nodded, sighed even.

"I'll protect you with my blood if it comes to it. I just ask that you respect my decisions when it has to do with your safety."

The last thing she wanted was his blood on her conscience. She had come to restore him to his family not take him away.

"I will do my very best," she answered more somberly.

"Well, then." He offered his hand, as though to seal the conditions of their agreement. "I believe we'll have a good marriage."

He might not think so if he knew how the press of his palm on hers made her stomach flutter.

"Good night, then." She withdrew her hand, scooted down beside the dog and closed her eyes.

Sadly, no matter how tightly she squeezed them shut, she could not hide from a niggling suspicion.

It was not impossible that there might be something between her and Boone and it wasn't Stanley Smythe.

Chapter Four

Sitting on a grassy incline that overlooked a fresh-running stream, Boone savored the last breath of warmth from the fading day. He shuffled through the handwritten notes that Mathers had supplied.

It wasn't comfortable reading about the town and its trouble because, in his time, he'd caused a fair share of trouble. He'd been the outlaw they feared.

Hell, he'd become more than that. Common outlaws could be found on every saloon corner, but his reputation had snowballed until he was seen as a monster.

And all because of bad timing.

Until the day he'd robbed the saloon in Dry Creek, he'd been as common as any other thief. That day, with his pockets comfortably sagging with cash, he'd gone out, passing a man going in. That man, reportedly angry at finding the coffers empty, had killed four people, women among them.

The killer was as common-looking as beans. Boone was tall; he had looked threatening that afternoon. So it's him they remembered…him they gave the blame to. Word spread that the pair of them were partners. After that, fear and a natural love of gossip attached many sinister stories to him. Some of them actually happened, just not by his hand. Others were born of ripe and idle imaginations.

Reaching into his shirt pocket, he withdrew the bent badge Mathers had given him and rubbed his thumb over the tarnished metal.

Holding this symbol of law and order in his hand, knowing that he would one day pin it on his vest, made him feel like an imposter. This business of upholding law and order was the last thing he'd ever imagined he would be doing.

Never expected he'd be anything other than a two-bit criminal.

He'd been a novice at crime, though, compared to the outlaws he would be facing.

The sun sat low and bright over the horizon. It was only an hour before sundown. They'd reach Jasper Springs by noon tomorrow.

That didn't give him long to figure out a way to round up six bloodstained souls. He'd have a better shot at it if he had the meanness in him that his reputation said he did.

All he was, was a survivor. He reckoned that would have to do.

A rustle of petticoats approached from behind. Melinda sat beside him, a blanket drawn across her shoulders. Funny how it smelled as if she'd brought a handful of sweet-smelling flowers along with her.

"I'd like to read those." She pointed to the papers he held.

He shook his head. "It's not fit reading for a lady's eyes."

Eyes that had been as agreeable as sugar suddenly narrowed at him. "If that lady's life depends upon knowing what she is up against, it is fit reading."

She wouldn't find it pleasant, but he handed them over.

A gust of cool wind rustled the pages in her hand. She pressed them to her bosom. He tried his best not to notice.

For a long time she was silent. A delicate line creased her forehead while she read.

Was she seeing his face when she read about the outlaws? That alone would be enough to make him feel guilty about his past, even though it was not as black as she must think. Funny how a man wanted his wife's respect. It didn't matter that he barely knew her or that she wouldn't be his wife for long.

"Six King brothers in all," she sighed. The blamed wind tugged at the paper. She pressed it to her chest again. The way the pages flapped against her bosom made it impossible not to think about—hell's curses— unsuitable things. "What will we do?"

"'We' will not do anything." He shot her a severe frown but she did not react to it. "This is all on me. The one and only reason you are here is for show."

With a delicate arch of her brow, she questioned him.

"Let's see…" She tapped her finger on the paper on her breast. He turned his gaze to the water rolling by, staring at each ripple with dedicated concentration. "There's Efrin King, the oldest, known as King Cobra. It says here that he's a greedy soul, in love with money and power. Then we have Buck King—King Diamond Back. He's second by birth and they say that he is jealous of Efrin. And what about Lump King? King Horny

Toad is simpleminded, quite evil nevertheless. I've got to say, that one worries me, Boone. You can't think to take on this whole family alone?"

"Look, I know you want to help. Seems to be in your nature to. But this is dangerous business. The only way of coming out of it whole is if you do what I tell you to without question."

"I reckon you can handle Olfin—King Hornet." Blamed, if the woman hadn't just ignored him. "It's says here he's not as bad as the others, just sort of goes along."

He should have refused to involve Melinda in this, at least more forcefully than he had. Here she was, as determined as a bee collecting pollen, to put her nose where it didn't belong.

"I welcome your ideas and that's as far as it goes." He shot her the frown again. "Anything besides that, you'll only be in my way."

"If it weren't for King Copperhead, Leland, I'd take to my bed and cover my head with a dozen quilts. But what do you intend to do with someone who, it says right here, is charming and at the same time the most deadly of them all? Of all the brothers he takes the most pleasure in violence. Did you see this, Boone?" She shoved the paper in front of his eyes. "He delights in it!"

He was silent because he didn't rightly know what he was going to do. Not with Leland or any of them.

According to the plan, they, as homesteaders, were supposed to look weak, victim-like. To his mind that was no plan at all.

Smythe, who had been collecting firewood, dumped his load beside the circle of stones Boone had set out for the night's campfire.

With his strides crisp and his back straight, the lawyer

crossed the clearing then wriggled down between him and Melinda. The dog-wolf followed but turned aside to snuffle through the brush, his tail wagging and resembling bristles on a worn broom.

Mathers had seemed to feel the beast would be helpful. But so far his disposition seemed mild; they hadn't heard so much as a growl out of him.

"You are my charge," Smythe said to Melinda. "I won't have you putting yourself at risk."

"As your husband, I say the same."

Melinda gave them both a sincere smile, a lovely one, in fact. "I would never dream of being a burden to you, Stanley. Or, Husband, of putting you at unnecessary risk."

Odd that her apparent compliance didn't ease his concern a whit.

"Still, I can't help but wonder, Boone, what you will do about the youngest, Bird King, who calls himself King Vulture? It says right here that he is unpredictable." She jabbed her slender finger at the words on the page. "Apparently charming one moment but the next nearly as wicked as Leland."

"Sounds like they consider themselves royalty," Stanley said.

"According to Mathers, they rule the town, even make other folks call them by their last name first. 'King' So-and-so." He took the papers from Melinda and handed them to Smythe. "The only law that's observed in Jasper Springs is at the whim of the Kings. Says here they hanged a boy barely out of the schoolroom for trying to defend his sister from Horny Toad. Doesn't say what happened to her."

Silence stretched for a time, broken only by the chirrup of crickets, the croak of frogs.

Suddenly there was a tussle in the shrubbery. Branches cracked and leaves scattered.

Billbro trotted out with a limp rabbit in his jaws. He set it before them.

"Good. One of us is a hunter," Stanley observed. "We won't starve."

Riding down the main street of Jasper Springs, the wagon wheels laboring over the rutted road, Melinda thought the town must have been well cared for at one time.

Flowerpots decorated the raised boardwalk. A banner advertising a long-gone Fourth of July celebration was strung from one side of the street to the other. Looking past the banner, toward the end of Main Street, she saw a fountain gurgling in the town square.

Sadly, Jasper Springs now resembled a ghost town more than anything else. Those pretty flowerpots were cracked, growing weeds, the banner faded and tattered. The spring-fed fountain sounded lovely but no one was around to enjoy it. It would be easy to imagine that no one lived here any longer.

At least there were trees to soften the dreariness of the place. Dozens of them grew around town, their fall colors bright and beautiful. What a satisfaction to know that the outlaws did not control everything.

Melinda adjusted her drab bonnet and tried to fluff her brown dress. Sadly, no amount of encouraging could make the homespun fluff.

She reminded herself that she was not here to look

her best but to pose as a homesteader's wife. To appear dutiful, hardworking and, most of all, vulnerable.

That is what her new husband must believe she is, if his hesitation to let her read about the Kings was any indication.

"Humph!" He would need to learn that she would not wither at the first sign of trouble.

Stanley, sitting beside her, the team's reins gripped in his smooth, lawyer-like hands, looked at her in question.

"It's nothing," she said, even though it was. If a man was going to rely upon a woman's help, he had to respect that she could actually help.

Boone rode in front of the wagon, sitting tall on Weaver the mule. A rifle lay square across his thighs. To her mind, he looked far too commanding to be a meek farmer, even given his humble mount.

Far too handsome, as well.

As if reading her thoughts, her admiration of the masculine image he presented, Boone twisted in the saddle.

It felt as if he looked past her eyes and into her mind, saw himself the way she saw him: bold, well formed, commanding. A smile tweaked one side of his mouth. He arched an eyebrow.

She held his gaze for an instant then quickly glanced away. For all the good it did now. No doubt he felt the heat of her blush all the way from here.

Deputy Billbro kept pace with the mule, sniffing the air and learning things about the place that mere humans were unable to perceive.

"Where is everyone?" she asked softly. It was too quiet. A muttered voice might be heard for a block. "It's midday. You'd think folks would be about."

All of a sudden Weaver brayed. The sound echoed

all over town. A curtain swayed at the window of the bank but then fell back into place. A baby cried but was quickly silenced.

Jasper Springs was not deserted, after all; it only seemed so.

Boone reined in the mule. Stanley halted the wagon beside him.

"We'll visit the mercantile for supplies," Boone said. "Make our arrival known."

Melinda wiped a spot of dirt from the wagon bench and smeared it on her cheek to make herself look weary, which she was not.

"Slump your shoulders, Boone. No one will believe that a man of your size is a weakling."

He arched a brow but did as she asked, but really, it didn't help much. He was a fine, strapping man and there was no hiding it.

Stanley slumped his shoulders, too, but it didn't make a difference, not that she would ever point that out.

The dog didn't need to act dusty and matted, he was naturally that way.

Early this morning they had discussed Mather's plan, how they would give the appearance of easy victims to attract the interest of the Kings. This would not be easy for Boone. She had noticed him chafing at the idea even from the first mention of it.

Stopping in front of the mercantile, Boone hid his rifle in the back of the wagon, then helped her down. His big hands cupping her waist did not feel anything but strong.

No, and neither did his arms as he set her effortlessly on the ground. It would take some doing to make him appear vulnerable.

"I'll need to act the nag," she whispered in his ear. "Will anyone recognize you?"

She worried that someone might have seen his Wanted poster. If they did, the scheme would be exposed.

He shrugged. "Probably not. It's been some time since that broadsheet's been spread about. Folks forget."

Chances were, that would be true of most men, but Boone was quite tall, his face striking in its handsomeness and, to her mind, unforgettable. Her cousin, Rebecca, liked to call Lantree her big blond Viking. Naturally the same could be said of Boone.

"Come along, brother Stanley," she said with a wink at her pretend sibling. "Let the theatrics begin."

"I wish you'd take this more earnestly, Miss Winston," he chided.

"That's 'Mrs. Walker.' I know you're worried about me, but between you, my husband and the deputy, I could not be safer if I were locked in a vault."

Boone led her up the stairs of the boardwalk. She gazed down at her scuffed boots, at the sad sag of her faded brown skirt while she gathered the inspiration to play her part.

The painted sign beside the mercantile door indicated that they had come during business hours but the door was locked.

Boone rapped on the wood.

"You'll have to pound harder than that," Melinda said in a raised voice while she rolled her eyes.

Her homesteader husband frowned. She hoped that he remembered that she was only acting at being a nag. "I declare, you've grown weak from all that alcohol. Soon as we settle into our homestead, I'm burying the bottle."

Boone actually gasped.

"Here, let me do it." She nudged him aside then pounded her fist on the door. Maybe she ought not to have flashed him a smile.

All at once the door opened and they were greeted by a scowling man with a drooping mustache that hid his lips.

"Don't you know to stay off the streets, today of all days?"

He hustled them inside, cast a cautious glance at Billbro, then shut the door and shoved the bolt closed.

"Looks like rain by sundown, but I can't see why that should keep us off the street now," Boone commented.

"Take off your hat indoors, Mr. Witherleaf." Melinda cast her husband a scowl then turned it on Stanley. "And you, too, brother. Don't behave like a heathen."

Her "relatives" looked startled by her bossiness when they ought to be acting as though her bitter tongue was commonplace. Later on, some lessons in role-playing would be in order.

Still, she would have to allow the men some leeway. Clearly, they had not grown up as she and Rebecca had, always trying to keep one step ahead of Mama's restrictions and at the same time avoid undue punishment.

"You're new to town." The storekeeper wagged his head long and slow.

"I'm Boone Witherleaf. This is my wife, Melinda, and Melinda's brother, Stanley."

The name Witherleaf had been assigned by Mathers and could not have been more absurd. In Melinda's opinion, calling Boone "Witherleaf" did nothing to diminish his natural aura of power.

Perhaps her nagging would seem more effective if he would hang his head lower.

"You always neglect to introduce the dog." She knelt down and snuggled the big hairy head against her bosom. "Billbro is as much a part of the family as you are."

Boone coughed.

"We're taking over the old Ramsey place," he said to the merchant.

"The Ramsey place? If you want my advice, you'll turn tail and run."

"Why would we?" he asked. "And why should we stay off the streets?"

"I reckon you'll find that out soon enough. I'm Edward Spears, by the way. This is my store, for what it's worth anymore."

"A pleasure." Boone extended his hand in greeting, so did Stanley. "Might you be the brother of the livery owner in Buffallo Bend?"

"One and the same."

"Oh, he's a fine man." Boone nodded his head. "Well, I reckon we'll need dry goods and a few tools, grain for planting."

"This time of year?" Spears asked. Melinda suspected that he was smirking under his massive mustache.

"Please excuse my husband. He's a greenhorn through and through." She stood. Hands on hips, she faced Boone. "I told you, planting is done in the spring."

"You'll need firewood, though. Trees are scarce out that way. And a gun. I notice you aren't carrying, but if you're set on staying you'll need one."

"If you really think it necessary." Boone shrugged. "I reckon I'll purchase that, as well."

Actually there were a dozen weapons packed at the bottom of the wagon.

It was good to see Boone handle the weapon Spears placed in his hand as though it were a live snake.

Mr. Spears had yet to say why they should be off the streets today more than any other day. Clearly, everyone else in Jasper Springs was of the same mind.

Boone withdrew a large roll of money from his pocket, making sure the storeowner got a good look at it.

"I'll take the dog outside for a moment," she announced.

Naturally, she would be forbidden to do so, but her intention was to find out why.

"I wouldn't, ma'am. Not without protection."

"Why ever not?"

"Olfin King was buried today."

"I'm sure that's very sad." She touched her throat, pretending that it was. But, really, that meant one less outlaw to be a threat to Boone. What a shame that according to the notes, Olfin King was the least villainous of them all.

"I reckon not so sad. You can bet the folks of Jasper Springs are celebrating behind their bolted doors. After you've been here a while, you'll understand why."

"That seems coldhearted," Stanley observed.

"What happened to Olfin King?" Boone asked.

Yes, to her mind, that was an important bit of information.

"He got himself shot in the leg a few weeks ago. The doc tried to heal it but infection set in. The Kings buried Olfin this morning. Hate to say so, but I reckon it won't be long before we'll be burying the doc."

Melinda felt her stomach turn. She slid closer to Boone; the need to be near him natural and not a bit of show in it.

The danger involved in what they had undertaken hit her fresh. Boone's big, solid presence helped to sooth the jitters skittering along her spine.

With an arm around her shoulders, he tugged her close. He squeezed his fingers, sending a message. No matter what, he would be here to keep her safe.

While she was, in most instances, able to see to her own safety, she leaned into him, took comfort in his large, Viking-like presence.

For all that she felt heartened. She knew that Boone felt the pressure of the situation. This close, she could see his jaw grinding with tension.

"We'll be on our way, then, just as soon as we've loaded the wagon," he stated.

"I wouldn't settle on that land if I were you. The Kings see it as their own. Won't be pleased that you've taken it over."

"Pleased or not, they have no legal right to it," Stanley pointed out.

"Well, you'll find that they do what they want to whenever they want to do it. And a sorry day, too, for anyone who stands in their way."

She felt Boone's muscles tense. Glancing up, she saw his expression harden.

Boone dropped his gaze, stooped his back. Clearly he was striving hard to hold on to the character of Witherleaf. Behind the playacting, she suspected he was smoldering not withering. Just now, on the inside, Boone was probably as meek as the outlaw portrayed in his Wanted poster.

"My family and I—we'll keep this gun handy." He turned it over in is hand. "Once we learn to fire the blamed thing."

One could only guess how much force of will it took for Boone to frown over the gun in puzzlement.

Leaning closer to him, she was grateful that she knew the truth. That he was bigger and stronger than any man she had ever met, and that he held her safely under the protection of his well-muscled arm.

Boone shut the door of the mercantile behind him and straightened to his natural posture since no one was on the streets to see. The bolt on the far side of the door slammed into place, but so far, the only threat seemed to be from the purple-black clouds roiling on the western horizon.

As much as he wanted to get a look at these outlaws, to find out what he was up against, he wanted even more to get Melinda securely behind the four walls of the homestead house.

He would have it out with the Kings, but not while Melinda was with him.

No sooner had he lifted her onto the wagon bench than a volley of gunshots echoed at the edge of town. Whistles and shouted curses could be heard even above the din of galloping hooves.

"Apparently the royal family has arrived," Melinda stated.

He would feel a hell of a lot more comfortable if her voice held at least the hint of a tremor.

"You ready, Stanley?" she asked.

"I am, as long as you stay in the wagon and act meek."

Melinda sighed. Boone cringed.

He could only admire her courage, but it would make his job of protecting her a hell of a lot easier if she actually was a meek little thing, eager to abide by his rules.

Of course, she wouldn't fascinate him half as much if she were.

"Whatever happens, don't move from here." He thought to remind her that this was an order from her husband but— "Please, Melinda. I've got to keep my attention on those men. I can't do it if I'm worried about you."

"Be careful, Boone." She squeezed his shoulder then slipped into her part. Covering her mouth with both hands, she managed to look instantly petrified.

Five Kings circled their mounts around the fountain in the town square, looking like a swarm of angry, evil bees. One by one, they spurred their horses, each toward a different part of town, shouting curses and shooting bullets into the air.

The rider cantering down Main Street seemed shorter than the others, with a portly belly and a spare chin.

All at once a door opened and a tall, willow slip of a woman stepped onto the boardwalk. Without taking note of her surroundings, she locked the library door behind her.

She must have been unaware of the arrival of the Kings because she spun around merrily singing "The Battle Hymn of the Republic."

"Trudy Spears!" the rider cried out.

Spurring his horse forward, the man raced toward the boardwalk. The young woman dropped the load of books she carried. Her key skittered across the wood planks.

"Been thinking about you, girl!"

Miss Spears dropped to her knees, scrambling across the pages of the open books and reaching for the key.

Boone felt the weight of the new gun in his pocket. How careless of him to have not loaded it before he'd stepped out of the store.

To complicate the matter, if he came to Miss Spears's aid, laid flat the devil dismounting his horse, he would not be believable as a bumbling homesteader.

From the looks of it, this King wouldn't be much of a scrapper were he caught without his weapon.

Not that he didn't look menacing. He had an expression about him, as though the thoughts behind his eyes didn't go too deep. It was as if he had lurid imaginings that he didn't know to keep hidden. Even his drooping lower lip had a perverted smirk, although Boone was pretty sure he was not intentionally smirking.

This one had to be Lump King, the simpleminded brother—the one with degenerate tastes.

Melinda made a noise; a fearful keening. Boone suspected this was her attempt to draw King's attention away from the girl. Melinda, or any of them for that matter, might not have existed for all the creep noticed.

From a block to the north Boone heard one of the Kings shout something about gutting and filleting the doctor.

"Trudy, you ripe little plum. Won't no locked door keep ole Horny Toad from poking around under your skirt." The man's eyes glistened. Drool dampened his disgusting mouth.

Apparently, Lump King was so caught up in his lechery that he didn't seem to notice the growl building in Deputy Billbro's throat.

There was nothing Boone wanted more than to slam the "King" to the ground and punch the daylights out of him.

But, curse it! He was a helpless homesteader, a ripe victim.

"Sir!" he said mildly, even though his temper was flaring hot. "I believe the lady wishes to be left alone."

Lump turned in surprise, as though the voice had suddenly vaporized out of the air.

"Mind yer own business," he said, walking toward the woman and scratching his crotch. He swiveled his gaze back to Trudy who had, at last, found her key but now could not open her door because her hand was shaking. "Me and Trudy, we got some—" he thrust his hips in an obscene gesture "—mating to do."

Melinda grew suddenly silent.

Boone rushed the man.

Stanley bolted across the road and up the steps. He snatched the key from Trudy Spears's fingers, unlocked the door and pushed her inside ahead of him.

Boone sensed more than saw the dog leap into the wagon and place his large body in front of Melinda, wolfish hackles raised.

He slammed Lump square in the spine. The man fell belly-first into the dirt and let out a piggy-like squeal. Boone plucked the gun from his holster then tucked it into the waistband of his own pants.

Smelling flowers, Boone glanced behind him. Melinda stood a few feet away holding a length of rope. She tossed it to him.

He tied up Lump's hands then yanked the kerchief from his fat, sweaty neck and bound his mouth with it. Jerking him up from the road, he shoved him over the horse's saddle then secured the outlaw's wrists to the saddle horn.

It disgusted Boone that being bound and gagged didn't keep Lump from staring at Melinda in a greasy, speculative way.

"Look my wife's way one more time and I'll slice off your skin. Feed it to the wolf." Maybe he ought to put on his badge, send at least this one to face justice, but there was a message that needed sending.

Hell's curses, he never had it in him to be timid in the first place.

"Tell your brothers that Boone Walker's in town—they are dethroned." He wasn't sure whether his name meant anything to Lump King or not. His expression was as blank as his emotions probably were. "Giddy up!"

At his shout, the horse bolted. Couldn't tell where the animal might run to, but the further the better. Eventually the disgusting King would end up back home. Even if he didn't remember the message, the rope and the missing gun would speak loud enough.

Only one thing mattered at this moment: getting his own to the safety of the homestead before the storm hit. The one in the sky and the one he'd just created.

Chapter Five

The first storm, the one with raindrops pelting his shoulders, hit when they were pulling into the yard of the homestead.

Looking at the house from a hundred feet away it appeared to be a sturdy place; the walls solid and the glass windows unbroken. Even the barn seemed to be in decent repair.

There was a tree in the paddock, but just the one, and it was a scraggly looking thing with only a few withered leaves to witness that it was October.

The terrain surrounding the homestead consisted of low rolling hills, dried and brown. Seeing an approaching enemy might be difficult.

Tomorrow, come rain or high water, he would look for ways to make the property more secure.

It might need to be a fortress after he'd dumped Mathers's well-devised scheme onto the dirt of Main Street.

Life sure had an inconvenient way of derailing plans.

But after seeing the Kings firsthand, after witnessing the true depravity of their natures, it had become clear that a passive farmer would not attract their attention as quickly as a renowned outlaw would.

Given the threats they had hurled at the doctor, there was no time for playacting. The sooner their attention was focused away from the healer and toward Boone, the better.

The trip from Jasper Springs to the homestead was not a long one, an hour and that with a heavily loaded wagon. An easy ride by horse might take half an hour, an all-out run a good bit less.

According to Mathers's notes, the homestead was located equal distance between town and the outlaw ranch, the property lines abutting on the northern boundary.

Raindrops dribbled off his Stetson to rat-a-tat-tat on his coat.

Beside him, Melinda had fallen asleep wrapped in an oilcloth. He knew the exact moment that her head fell against his arm because the scent of damp flowers wafted up. How did she manage that? To smell like flowers even under unlikely conditions?

"Looks like a primitive sort of place," Stanley said when they pulled up to the front door. "Not like what Melinda will be used to."

"A shack is primitive." Four solid walls to keep out the rain and the wind was sanctuary. A site more than what he was accustomed to. "This'll do fine."

It bothered him some, that the lawyer thought his wife would look down on a place that to him was a step away from paradise.

No reason that should bother him, though. She was only his wife in name and that for a short time. What she thought or didn't think was only a passing concern.

The only obligation he had to Melinda Winston-Walker was to take her home alive and unharmed.

And to get her in out of the rain.

Tucking the tarp more securely around her, he gathered her in his arms and stood. The wagon creaked. Melinda stirred, blinked her eyes open.

"I'll—" she yawned "—walk." She could only be half awake the way her words came out slurred.

"You'll fall. Rest your head, Mrs. Walker."

She sighed. Her eyes fluttered closed. He reckoned she was asleep the way her weight went limp in his arms, her breath slowing to the shallow rise and fall of slumber.

"I'll bring our goods inside before they get soaked," Stanley said, dismounting his mule and scaling the back of the buckboard.

"Appreciate it."

Carrying Melinda didn't take more effort than hefting a sack of potatoes, even when he shifted her weight to one arm to climb down.

Stanley shot him a frown. Chances are he didn't care for Boone laying hands on his charge.

Boone carried his wife up the porch steps and unlocked the door. He carried her over the threshold of the small house, oddly disappointed that she slept through what genuine newlyweds would consider romantic.

Hell's curses, he'd better keep in mind that they were not genuine newlyweds.

It looked as if the place had been abandoned in a hurry. There was firewood stacked beside the hearth in the main room and a book lying open on the floor. A loaf of stale bread was on the table, only half of it sliced. A pot of rancid-smelling something or other set on a stove so new-looking that it could hardly have been broken in.

From what Mathers had written, the home hadn't been abandoned for long when he'd rented it from the fleeing owners for the purpose of bringing the Kings to justice.

The only bedroom had a bed, a lady's vanity and a big, overstuffed chair. On the wall was an off-kilter needlework that read Home Sweet Home.

The house looked more than adequate to him but according to Smythe, Melinda would find it lacking.

Even though Melinda was his wife, Smythe was better acquainted with her.

There were women who put on fancy airs along with satin and lace. He hoped that she was not one of them. For the short time that she was with him, she would need common sense and a stiff backbone.

Pretty manners and a winning smile wouldn't keep her safe from what they would be facing. Those frilly clothes she usually wore would only get in the way.

But there was no denying that even wearing a plain brown dress, her only adornment the raindrops sprinkling her hair, dotting her face, Mrs. Walker was dazzling.

Maybe Smythe was wrong about her being too good for this house. It would be a shame to have such loveliness tainted by an overgrown ego.

Melinda sighed in her sleep. One corner of her mouth lifted in a smile. Pink and dewy, her skin looked like a flower petal.

He didn't get the sense that she was proud. Wrongheaded in her sense of adventure, yes. Also, she seemed skilled at getting her way. In this, his young bride made him uneasy.

He sat in the chair, settled her weight in his arms. The lady sure could sleep.

Outside, the wind increased, drumming rain against the window. Cold air rushed into the room from the open front door. No doubt Smythe was getting soaked. He ought to get up and help, but that would mean putting Melinda down. He'd never held an honorable lady in his arms before and might not get the chance to do it again.

Odd, how he wanted to tighten his grip and keep her safe from everything.

Besides, the bed was not yet made up. He could only admit to be glad of that because once he put her down he'd have to quit studying her pretty face. He wasn't quite finished doing that.

"Smythe," he called softly when he heard something scraping the floor. "Make up the bed with those linens packed in the trunk, won't you?"

The lawyer poked his head around the door, his hair dripping water down the scowl lines creasing his mouth.

"While you sit there holding Sleeping Beauty?"

Boone stroked a smattering of raindrops from her nose, then her cheeks with the pad of his thumb. Couldn't help but smile.

"That about sums it up."

When he glanced up, Smythe's scowl had vanished, replaced by an indulgent smile. "She's a sound sleeper."

Boone nodded. The sleep of the innocent, he reckoned. That was something he had not experienced in many years.

Smythe rooted through the trunk, found the sheets and pronounced them dry.

When he finished making the bed he lit a fire in the small bedroom hearth.

"Lay her on the bed. I'll see to her comfort," the lawyer said.

"As much as I like you, Smythe, I'm her husband. No one will see to my wife's comfort but me. Keep the door open if it makes you feel better."

"As much as I appreciate that, Walker, I'm the one sworn to her well-being."

"Not anymore."

Smythe cast him a hard look from behind his rain-spotted glasses. "Melinda deserves your respect."

"She's got that and more. I'll defend her with my life if it comes to it."

Smythe nodded. "I expect nothing less. I'll see to the animals then rustle us up some supper."

The door closed and Boone nearly laughed. A couple of days ago the dedicated lawyer would have said he'd "prepare a meal" or something of the sort.

He had not been making that up about liking Smythe. How could one not admire a fellow so dedicated to dedication?

He'd also not been making it up about being the one to see to his wife's needs. While he might not be a husband in the normal way of things, it did fall to him to care for her in the ways that he could.

From what he knew of her so far, Melinda Winston-Walker would need watching over.

He lay her down on the bed and removed her shoes. He unbuttoned the cuffs at her wrists then the pair of buttons at her collar.

It was hard not to stare at her face. She was uncommonly fair. She brought to mind a delicate porcelain doll.

He pulled the quilt up under her chin. When he did, his knuckles brushed her throat. She didn't feel like a porcelain doll, not by a mile.

That little bit of bare flesh was warm, as soft and as alluring as any woman's he had ever touched.

No, that was not quite true. Melinda, even while sleeping, was more arousing than a skilled temptress.

He picked up her hand to put it under the quilt but held it for a moment, gazing at the fair, unlined skin.

As tempting as it was at this moment in time to let his mind wander, there was no hope that this marriage could ever be more than what it was meant to be.

She was a lady, he an outcast. Their only bond a temporary arrangement.

But he'd never forget that for a time this rare and beautiful woman had been his wife.

Now that Melinda was no longer a homesteader's wife, but an outlaw's instead, it would be appropriate to bury the dull brown gown in the bottom of her trunk and dress the way she was accustomed to.

Then again, it was raining hard and had been all night long. Outside there was mud, mud and more mud. Anything she wore was bound to become dredged in it.

This plain garment would be more easily laundered than yards of lace.

At breakfast this morning Boone had instructed her to remain inside where it was warm, dry and comfortable.

What, she could only ask, was comfortable about watching through the parlor window while the pair of them went from the front window to the door to the back window, getting soaked to the skin while they devised a plan for securing the house?

Nothing is what. Especially after she had finished putting on a pot of soup to simmer after she'd mixed dough for biscuits.

Deciding what to wear when the choice was obvious was a tedious task, as was listening to the drum of the rain on the roof and the distant hammer of nails into wood.

Out in the barn, Boone and Stanley were now building shutters to fortify the windows. That didn't seem like an overly difficult task, one that only a male could do.

Billbro whined and scratched at the door.

"You'd need a bath that would take days if I let you out there."

She had never seen a beast such as this one allowed inside a house.

"Besides, Boone says you need to stay inside and protect me from every ill wind. Did you know that ill winds do not blow upon ladies on pedestals? You are right. It's nonsense. We are going out. If the rain melts us, so be it."

She shimmied out of her petticoat and her warm stockings. Respectable underclothes be hanged when it came to laundering mud from them. With a shimmy and a wriggle she put on the brown dress then tugged on the scuffed boots.

After knotting her hair in a simple bun, she motioned to the dog.

"Come along, then, let's see what's happening."

Together, they ran the hundred feet to the barn. They became soaked in an instant but burst through the barn door feeling invigorated.

Apparently the joy she felt at running through the crisp, clean rain was not shared by the men.

Standing behind a worktable they had constructed,

they scowled at her, Boone holding three nails between his lips and Stanley with his hammer halfway to burying one in a piece of wood.

"I've come to help."

Boone spit out the nails. Stanley's aim missed the mark.

"Go back inside, Melinda," Boone ordered. "There's nothing you can do here."

"I see a lot of wood needing to be nailed." Yes, indeed, there were a number of boards that used to belong to the wagon lying on the floor alongside a bucket full of nails.

"Have you ever nailed anything?" Boone asked.

"I've not had the occasion to but, really, how hard can it be?"

"Harder than one might imagine," Stanley said. He gave her his hammer and a nail. "Give it a try."

"Stanley!" She took the tool but clung to his hand. "You've got blisters! They're bleeding."

The little man shrugged, nodded his head. He didn't say so, but she guessed that he was proud of his wounds.

"They need cleaning and bandaging," she said, setting the hammer down. "I've seen less than this fester and require amputation."

That grim prediction didn't make him look any unhappier.

"Go into the house and have some soup. I'll be along shortly to tend to it."

"It's time to eat, anyway," Boone said. "We'll be up as soon as I see how easily my wife can hammer a nail."

The challenge had been cast. How she wished she had some experience at driving a nail.

As soon as Stanley shut the door behind him, Boone said, "Let's see you bury that nail."

The glint of male superiority in his eye was annoying. Just because she had never done this did not mean that she could not. How hard could it be? Just aim the hammerhead and plunk, in would go the nail.

Billbro yawned then circled his damp, furry body down onto a pile of straw.

She picked up the hammer again. Boone stood at her back. He was close enough that she could smell his masculine scent, feel the heat of his chest pulsing against her back even though they were not touching.

His breath, warm and moist, huffed against her nape. All on their own, the fine hairs stood up. She almost wished that she had not worn a bun—almost, but not quite.

Quickly, before he could thoroughly distract her, she picked up a nail. She pinched the iron between her thumb and fingers then, with all her strength, she swung the hammerhead down.

Boone gripped her fist an instant before impact.

"You were about to smash your thumb."

"I was about to show you how—" She glanced up and behind. He was looking at her hand, cradling it in his fingers and rubbing the spot she had been about to hit as though she had actually done it.

She dropped the hammer, mesmerized by the expression in his eyes—tender and angry all at the same time.

Her heart started to thump harder. The oddest sensation fluttered in her belly.

This man was not like any she had ever been acquainted with. He was not one that her mother would approve of. Not a gentleman with smooth hands and a bank account full of money. Gentlemanly sons-in-law were all-important to Mama. After the scandal of Papa's death, she had devoted her life to seeing her girls married to pillars of society.

Clearly, Boone was not Mama's vision of a good match.

Nor was he the hero she had pinned her childish dreams upon; that distant, misty man who was strong, adoring and admirable in every way.

Although, Boone did look like him; strikingly so.

No, this man was an outlaw, hard of expression with a dangerous glint in his eye, but not, it must be said, when he looked at her.

Still, this supposed dastardly criminal was her legally wed husband and his expression had just turned soft, perplexed-looking. His lips pressed together in puzzlement.

And…and yes, completely and without reservation, she wanted to kiss them.

He turned her slowly around, keeping hold of her nearly injured hand. She moistened her lips, ready and wanting his kiss most desperately in spite of the fact that it was not prudent. She rose up on her toes.

"You've seen an amputation?" he asked.

He might have dumped water on her, her confusion was that great. How could she possibly have misread the moment so miserably?

"Naturally." She snatched up the nail then the hammer.

Once again she tried to pin the nail to the wood, but she hit wide. On her next try she managed to get the blamed thing into the lumber a full quarter of an inch.

She heard Boone chuckle.

With her next fell of the hammerhead she knocked the nail sideways. It came out of the wood and skittered across the table.

"Apparently," she said with as much pride as she could fake, "this is more difficult than it seems."

"But you witnessed an amputation? With or without fainting?"

"I could hardly faint when I was assisting the doctor—your brother."

Boone leaned against the table, his thigh pressing the wood. My word, he was uncommonly tall. Even when she hoisted up to sit on the table she had to lift her gaze.

"You don't look like—" He shook his head. "I would never have guessed."

Really? "What do I look like?"

Fluff and feathers? Sugar and spice? A helpless, swoon-prone female?

He didn't answer. He simply looked her over long, slow, and with that same speculation in his eyes that he'd had before.

This time she did not want to kiss him—well, of course she did, but she would not do it. No persuasion on his part would make her feel like a fool again.

A pesky strand of hair had escaped her bun. He twisted it about his thumb, drawing her face up, lowering his.

"There was a lot of blood—at the amputation."

He let go of her hair, lifted her chin with his finger. "Arm or leg?"

"Both."

The corner of his mouth twitched. She wished it hadn't because it was ever so appealing.

He dropped his hand. She scooted down the table, putting a respectable space between them.

"Tell me about yourself," he said.

"I'm not half as interesting as you are," she had to admit. "I'm just a common girl raised by my widowed mother along with my two sisters and my dear cousin Rebecca—your sister-in-law."

"I want to know more. It seems that you and Rebecca are especially close."

"Oh, yes, to be sure." Even having been parted for only a short time, she missed her cousin dreadfully. "You could say we are partners in crime but, really, is it a crime to not want to be restricted by another, even if she is your mother? And when you think about it, no one wants to be married off to the butcher and become his third wife."

A heavy downpour of rain suddenly pelted the roof. One of the horses whinnied.

"You? A third wife? Can't see it. You are my first, by the way."

"That's a relief. But it was Rebecca destined for the butcher. Mama figured that after she shoved Randall Pile belly-first across the dance floor of the Kansas City Ladies Cultural Club, the butcher was her last hope."

Her mother's thinking where Rebecca was concerned had always been flawed. Her cousin was a tall beauty and could have had her pick of any man had life and Mama not belittled her confidence.

Rebecca had never known the lively woman Mama had been once upon a time, only the bitter one she had become.

But in the end it had all worked out for Becca. She

had married a wonderful man who was even taller than she was.

"I have the feeling that you, my sweet, little wife, were never without a suitor. I reckon you could have had your pick of men."

"Sadly so." She frowned, shook her head. "It's tedious when every male you meet falls immediately in love with you, and you—or me—knows that the emotion is shallow because they only love the way I look and not me at all."

As Papa had loved her. She still remembered the way he'd snuggled his pretty little girl close, vowed he'd love her forever. But he had not.

Every day growing up, she'd missed her young mother.

"Hard to blame the fellows. You are uncommonly pretty."

"It's inconvenient always being fawned over," she said, forcing her thoughts away from the past. "How will I ever know if someone really loves me or just the blue eyes and lacey frippery? If you want to know, Boone, I was thrilled when you refused to marry me."

"I'd have refused to marry anyone. It had nothing to do with you." Boone looked at her from under lowered brows. "I don't think I've thanked you for saving me from Scarlet Cherry, though. Thank you, Melinda. You are a brave woman for taking me, and all this, on."

"I could hardly have allowed that woman to become baby Caroline's aunt." The very thought set her teeth on edge.

"And yet you've gone to lengths to make sure that I, a convicted felon, get introduced as her uncle."

"In spite of appearances, I believe you have an honorable heart."

"You're confusing me with my brother. I've done ugly things in my life, not so much as I've been accused of, but you're mistaken to think I have any honor in me."

No, she was not mistaken. She would stake her finely honed women's intuition on it.

"Have you robbed widows?"

"Not unless it was their money I took from a saloon."

"Have you orphaned children?"

"That I have not."

"Have you whipped little dogs in the street?"

"Only once and that because the small beast was biting my ankle."

"Drowned a kitten, then?"

Boone crossed his arms over his chest, frowning deeply.

"Quit trying to make me into some sort of a hero. I'm not. I've brawled and thieved. I've cheated and only bedded women of low morals. And now, judging by the look on your face, I've disappointed you."

"I was fine until the women of low morals. Really, Boone, even a temporary wife does not want to hear about former loves."

Why that should bother her, she could not imagine. But it did, even though they were not devoted newlyweds in the typical sense.

"I never loved a single one of them."

Oh?

Her heart tapped a happy, smile-filled dance. Against common sense, her insides felt dizzy.

He lifted his hand, clearly inviting her to come closer. Every unwise emotion within her urged her to claim that elusive kiss. She could… This time he would fold her up in those great strong arms and give her a never-to-be forgotten moment.

Tender feelings for Boone were rushing upon her too fast.

"Time for soup," she announced then hopped off the table and bolted for the barn door.

The dog followed her quicker than Boone did. He did not emerge from the barn until she was halfway across the yard.

Chapter Six

At the outskirts of Jasper Springs, Boone questioned the wisdom of bringing Melinda along. But, had he left her at the homestead, possible prey to a wandering King, worry would have distracted him from the task at hand.

And he was distracted as it was. His pretty little wife had him turned inside out and upside down. It had been a near thing yesterday.

Only soup saved him from giving her a kiss in the barn. He'd never touched an innocent before and didn't intend to do it now, especially not when the innocent was his wife.

Hell's curses, that made as much sense as a bee in a hat. In the normal way of things a man taught his innocent bride a whole lot more than kissing.

"At least folks are out and about today," Melinda observed, saving him from confounding thoughts.

He'd told her to ride close beside him because he couldn't imagine getting out of town without some sort of trouble. It was a relief to see that she hadn't chafed at his instruction.

Their mounts consisted of the wagon's team and Stanley's mule. Not the quickest form of escape if the need arose, but better than being slowed down by a buckboard.

All that remained of that clumsy contraption were the wheels and frame. The lumber had been put to better use as protection for the house; shutters for the windows and reinforcement for the door.

With folks going about their business, he reckoned the Kings were not in town. Didn't mean they wouldn't come, though. He'd better be quick about his business.

"People sure do look skittish," Melinda said. "Even without those nasty brothers in sight."

On the boardwalk to Boone's right, a young mother spotted him. She gathered her children into the folds of her skirt. The poor woman looked like a worried hen as she hustled her brood into the nearest open shop. Lucky thing for the children that it happened to be the bakery.

A man smoking a cigar studied him from the safety of his porch. The barber came out of his shop, swiping a razor across a strop.

He felt their stares burning between his shoulder blades long after he rode past.

"It's not the Kings who've got them on edge, Melinda." He sat taller, straightened his spine and his Stetson. "It's me."

"You?" She glanced at the barber, a pretty frown creasing her brow. "But you've come to save them."

"They don't know that," said Stanley, who rode on the other side of her. "To them he's just another outlaw. For all they know, worse than the King boys."

"I'm sorry, Boone. Here you are risking so much and they—"

"Are reacting like any sane person would. Like I hope you would if a killer came to town."

"You aren't a killer—well, not in a murderous sense. That one time hardly counts since it was a child against a man and a clear case of self-defense."

"All you know about me is what I've told you. What if I'm a liar?"

"What if I'm my mother's obedient child?"

"Don't think better of me than I deserve, Melinda."

A pair of old men whispered behind their hands, glancing at him then quickly away and back again.

"Old coots," he heard her mutter under her breath only a second before she shot them a bewitching smile.

The old coots appeared flummoxed, but only for an instant. Somehow Melinda had turned them into blushing, smiling, hat-tippers.

He nearly fell backward off his horse when he realized what she had done—used her beauty as a weapon. And so sweetly that he doubted anyone but Stanley would have noticed.

As charming a weapon as her smile was, hell if he was going to let her use it against the Kings.

"There's the doctor's office." Stanley pointed to a small white building on the north end of the town square. "I say if he won't see reason and come to the homestead, we tie him to the mule and take him."

"Stanley Smythe!" Melinda's eyes grew round, teasing. "Are you suggesting we kidnap him—break the law?"

"I'm suggesting that we get out of here before someone gets trigger-happy." He glanced around. "These people are scared. Who can say how they might react to having Boone in town?"

Boone had always figured he'd end up getting shot. If not by a lawman or a bounty hunter, then by someone he'd robbed.

Even if he did survive capturing the Kings, he might not ever have the freedom that Mathers promised. The only reprieve he might get was when he met his Merciful Maker. If he could take care of some of the Kings first, judgment day might go easier on him.

"We'll go around the back," he said. "It'll be best if no one sees the doc leave with us."

If the Kings thought the doctor just hightailed it out of town, so much the better.

"I'll go in first." Melinda slid off her saddle, lightly hitting the ground before he could have a say about it.

She was right, though. Better for the doc to be charmed by a lovely woman before they hauled him off to the homestead. Might make him more receptive to things if he were bedazzled.

Melinda slipped quietly through the back door.

"Dr. Brown?" they heard her call from inside.

For a moment the only sound was the crisp wind howling between the buildings and the sparsely leafed branches of the trees scratching together.

Then Boone heard a woman scream.

He was off his horse and inside the back room of the office with his gun drawn before the wailing died. Billbro ran a step ahead of him.

"Get that filthy beast out of here!" The doctor bellowed, stethoscope in hand. He stood at the head of a bed with a woman lying on it. He pointed the instrument at him. The doc's finger was long, as narrow as the rest of him.

If he cared a fig for Boone's drawn weapon, it didn't show.

All of a sudden an image flashed in his mind. There and gone in an instant, but one he would not forget. He and his brother facing each other; Boone pointing a gun, Lantree an instrument of healing.

Stanley rushed in then hauled Billbro outside. The dog placed his huge bulk in front of the door, ignoring Smythe's efforts to yank him down the steps.

Doc Brown glared at Boone, at the gun still gripped in his fist.

"If you're going to shoot me, I ask that you wait until Mrs. Coulter has delivered her baby. I reckon the Kings can wait a few hours for their revenge."

A distressed whimper came from the woman in the bed.

"Don't worry, Mrs. Coulter." Melinda sat in the chair beside the bed and picked up her hand, patting it with reassurance. "Mr. Walker hasn't come to shoot your doctor."

"In that case, put away your gun and go wait in the other room until I have time for you." The doc turned his back, clearly expecting his orders to be obeyed. "All of you. I've got enough trouble without the three of you hovering."

"Is something wrong?" moaned the soon-to-be mother, her face dampened by sweat.

"Naturally not." Melinda stroked the woman's brow, her voice calm and soothing. "Men have no business in the birthing room, that's all he meant. Isn't that right, Dr. Brown?"

"Of course." The slight hesitation in his answer told Boone that something actually was wrong. "There's nothing to fear, Mrs. Coulter."

"But—" A sudden contraction cut off the woman's words.

"I guess you and the doctor wonder why my husband

came charging in here like a madman with his gun flailing about."

Flailing about? He had been in complete control of his weapon.

"He heard your cry and figured it was me, is all. In spite of how things look, we mean you no harm."

"What is it you do want?" the doc asked, impatience edging his voice more than alarm now that Boone had holstered his gun.

"You," Boone stated.

"Like I said, go wait in the outer room and I'll be with you when I can." He nodded his head in the direction of the front room. "I've heard about you, Walker. If it's money you want it is in the desk, top drawer. Help yourself to all I've got and be on your way."

The comment stung, even though it was deserved.

"Sir." Stanley peeked his head around the door frame and nudged Billbro over. "It's imperative that you come away with us—and immediately. We can protect you from the Kings."

"Why?" The doc looked from Boone to Smythe to Melinda and then shook his head. "As you can see, I'm busy."

"Your life depends on this," Stanley urged.

The doc pinned Stanley with a stare and shook his head. "My life isn't worth much at the moment, but there're two lives here that are."

"I reckon you've heard that we've taken over the Ramsey spread," Boone said by way of explanation. Who could blame the doctor for guessing they might be up to no good? "We've fortified it. You'll be safer there than anyplace else."

"Again, why?"

"I'll explain it all on the way, but every minute we delay is another minute that the Kings might show up at your doorstep."

"We can't leave now, Boone," Melinda said, her expression serious, her gaze pleading. "Mrs. Coulter needs help."

"Look, I don't know why you all are set on saving my hide—I reckon I'll be grateful when I find out. But I won't leave now. Besides, there's still time. There are lookouts who will sound the alarm when the Kings are getting near town. Even then there'll be some time since those boys will go straight for the saloon." He brushed the damp hair from Mrs. Coulter's face. "I won't leave you, little mother."

"I won't, either." Melinda squeezed the woman's hand.

"I'd like a word, Mrs. Walker," Boone stated, slashing her a frown.

Melinda did follow him to the back porch. That was something.

"I'm not leaving that room, Boone." She touched his arm. For as delicate as her fingers were, they conveyed strength, both of body and of character. "You heard the doctor, something's wrong. He'll need my help and he'll get it."

"You aren't who you look like." Who was this woman he had married?

Sweet and feminine, yes. A practiced flirt, absolutely. But that in no way lessened her intelligence. Now here he stood, looking into her compassionate blue eyes, seeing the courageous spirit behind them.

"Nor are you. Although I expect you don't know it."

"I'm going to the saloon." If the Kings showed up, he wanted to get the measure of them. "See if you can work your magic on the doc. Get him to come along peacefully so we don't have to hog-tie him."

She crooked her finger at him, indicating that he should bend down. There must be something she had to say that she didn't want anyone to overhear.

Going up on her toes she kissed his cheek. "Take care, Boone."

He stepped back, nodded. No one had ever done that—kissed his cheek and wished him well.

His heart was in free fall and he didn't know what to do about it.

Keep his attention to what he had come to do, is all.

"Smythe, come along with me."

He pointed to the deputy. "You stay here." As though the dog had intentions of doing anything else. He had become completely bonded to Melinda.

If Boone was not careful, the same thing could happen to him.

Only trouble lay that way.

Even in midafternoon, with the sun high outside, the interior of the saloon was dim. Deep shadows engulfed the far corners, perfect for Boone to sit and watch without being seen.

Folks kept to themselves, leaving him and Stanley to observe from their shaded cove. If anyone else realized Boone Walker was among them, they didn't make it known. Mostly, they went about their business of playing cards, drinking and flirting with a pair of comfortable women. An older man went upstairs with one of them. The poor gent had to lean on the lady's arm just to make it to the top step.

Now and again he heard the doc's name mentioned in low, somber tones.

Boone swirled the whiskey in his glass but didn't drink it. Stanley did the same with his water.

"You going to drink that, Smythe?"

"Not with a fly drowned at the bottom."

Boone slid his whiskey across the table, nodded for the lawyer to take it. Stanley slid it back with one shake of his head.

All at once a boy rushed inside. "They're comin'! At a trot—five minutes!"

The kid rushed outside followed by every soul in the saloon. Except for the barkeep.

Even the old man hurried down the stairs, tugging his pants over his hips, his hired lady supporting his elbow.

"Here we go," murmured Stanley.

"You don't have to stay. You shouldn't. This isn't your fight."

"Your brother paid good money for me to see to your freedom. I haven't quite finished the job."

"Doubt if he intended for you to risk your life."

"He did, indeed, when it came to Melinda that's exactly what he said—what I agreed to. 'Protect her with your life' I believe were his exact words."

That's what Boone intended to do, as well. Couldn't say he didn't mind the help, though.

"Barkeep," Boone called, "you going to lock the door?"

The bartender took a rifle from under the counter, set it on the bar and emptied the bullets from it.

"Not unless I want to replace the windows again. If you're carrying, you'd better put the weapon here." He walked to the end of the bar where the whore who had been with the old man stood. He gripped her slender shoulders in his hands. "You ready, sweetie?"

"As much as I can be."

She wasn't ready. An illiterate would be able to read the fear in her eyes.

Boots pounded on the boardwalk.

The first man to come in, heavy-footed and lust glistening on his fat mouth, was Lump.

The whore grinned and opened her arms to her customer. Boone wondered if Lump even noticed that the lady's hands were trembling.

If he did he was probably glad for it. While Lump undressed her going up the stairs, another King appeared in the doorway.

"Good afternoon, King Efrin." The bartender smiled, but Boone recognized the insincerity behind it. Boone was familiar with the false gesture since it had been directed at him many times. "How may I serve you?"

Efrin King lifted his crooked beak of a nose an inch, pranced in with his steps long and regal, a statement of his perceived superiority.

His clothing was finer than Lump's was. By choice or Kingly decree, Boone didn't yet know.

The question was not answered when the next brother filled the doorway. This one wore a long coat with a patch on the sleeve. His Stetson looked frayed at the brim. He didn't look haggard, quite, but he lacked his brother's polish. He also lacked his trim figure. Buck had an indulgent swell to his belly.

"Good day, Master Buck," the bartender said. "And welcome."

Next through the doorway came a youth, the first sprouting of hair over his lip thin and blond.

"Howdy, Merle!" Bird King launched his lanky body over the counter, digging a pair of shiny spurs into the wood, gouging it.

He grabbed two bottles from a shelf, heaved back over the bar then sat at a table. The young fool opened them both, guzzled from one then the other.

"Much obliged." The kid lifted a bottle in salute to Merle.

So far the outlaws had not noticed him and Stanley watching from the corner table.

"I want your best." Efrin King stared hard at the barkeep. His eyes narrowed, snakelike. His voice had a cold, hissing quality to it. "I'm disappointed that you did not anticipate that."

Boone had seen a lot of evil men in his time, but none looked worse than this one.

"Next time, I'll do better, sir—that is, Your Highness." Merle set a bottle and a glass on the counter.

"Buck." Efrin shot a glance over his shoulder at his brother. "Polish the goblet."

"Shine your own damn glass," Buck growled.

"Please, allow me," the bartender said quickly, clearly wanting to prevent an altercation between them.

The woman upstairs moaned loud and low. Dime to a dollar it was not from pleasure.

After a long indulgent sip of alcohol from his extra-clean glass, Efrin smacked is lips.

"Buck, take the money box."

Merle looked submissive, giving the box over, but under that, Boone saw a few other emotions. Fear, anger—and worry. For the first time, he truly saw the other side of the crime; wondered how Merle was going to get by with his livelihood missing.

Boone remembered the faces of other barkeeps looking at him from the wrong end of his gun. Some of them angry, many frightened; all of them worried. They couldn't know that he would never pull the trigger. Somehow that didn't make him feel any better about himself.

Not surprisingly, the second in command didn't object to being ordered to do this task. Boone guessed he had taken the money many times.

Leland King was missing from the group. Boone prayed that he was sick at home and not in Jasper Springs causing trouble—not serving twisted justice to the doctor.

It took a good deal of self-control not to go racing back to the doc's office. He wanted to, but there were some things he needed to make clear right here while he had most of the family in one place.

Might as well start now.

He nodded to Stanley then stood, purposefully scraping his chair across the floor.

Boone Walker, destroyer of innocents, stepped into the light.

For an instant Efrin's composure slipped. For once, it was good to see someone fear his reputation.

His majesty gathered himself quickly, though. He indicated with noble-looking tilt of his head that Boone should sit at a table.

Bird King whooped. "Boone Walker! Lump said it was you but I figured he was off his mind again. I thought you was tried and convicted. Saw in the *Gazette* you was put away."

"Things change."

"You may sit and regale me of your crimes." Efrin

lowered his fancy-garbed body into a chair. He crossed one polished boot across his knee then flicked his fingers at an empty chair.

No doubt, the tyrant had made someone lick those boots clean.

Buck sat next to Bird who finished off his first bottle with a belch.

Boone continued to stand. He felt Stanley beside him. As small as he was, it was a comfort knowing the lawyer was there.

"You really kill all those men?" Bird asked, his eyes alight in anticipation.

"Them." He shot the kid a cool glance. "And more."

"We've heard the stories. Join us," Efrin said. "We've run Jasper Springs for a few years now. We could use a man of your talent. You must have noticed that our word is law."

Hooking his boot toe around King's chair leg, Boone swiped it out from under the man. Efrin sprawled backward, his head slamming the floor. He reached for his gun. Boone stomped on his wrist. He didn't let up on the pressure even when two of the outlaw's fingers began to spasm.

"Was law." Boone drew his gun. He heard the whisper of metal against leather when Stanley drew his. "This is my town now. You and your brothers can get out—or die. Choice is yours."

He knew damn well they wouldn't get out of town, but the threat needed to be issued, the viper's nest stirred.

Merle ducked under the bar.

Boone leveled his gun at Buck's face. "Place your piece on the table, barrel toward you. Same for you, kid."

Buck cast his older brother a glance as he slid the gun

toward Boone. It was there for half a second then gone, a smirk of contempt for his regal sibling.

Bird stood, dropped the bottles from his fists and then did as ordered.

"I'll take that money box."

Buck shoved the cash box toward him.

"You, kid. Trot upstairs and bring down your brother. Smythe, keep your aim on the stairs in case the fool comes down with more than one of his weapons hanging out."

A defiant expression moved across Efrin's eyes. His free hand jerked across his body. Boone bent and snatched the weapon from the outlaw's holster.

He felt the meanness of the expression he shot at King, the narrow tilt of his eyes, the grim, angry set of his mouth and the slight baring of his teeth. This spectacle of brutality was necessary to show his dominance over them.

It was a damn lucky thing that Lantree could not see him in this moment. His brother would be ashamed of who he had become. Lantree treated others with care and concern.

Boone did not. The more afraid of him these outlaws were, the more likely he was to survive. And not only him but Melinda and his lawyer, as well.

"You can't ride in and take over our town." Efrin glared up at him, not looking at all like royalty in the moment. Only an ugly, fading outlaw.

"Just did it."

Boone lifted his boot from Efrin's wrist. The joint would smart, but he didn't believe it was broken.

Lump stumbled down the stairs, his brother propelling him.

"It's Boone Walker in the flesh," Bird said as though that would impress his single-minded sibling.

"You're mad if you think you can take Jasper Springs. It's ours," Efrin hissed, but he was scooting on his backside toward the door when he said it. "Come on boys."

With a curse, Buck helped his brother off the floor then propelled him toward the door.

Lump turned in the doorway after his brothers had exited, cast him a sloppy glare. "Or our women."

Remembering the whore's moan, he aimed his gun at Lump's boot. He meant to hit leather, but if the man's toes were long, hell's curses, he didn't mind if one of them got bloodied.

A kingly voice, wrought with agitation, carried in from the boardwalk. "The three of you against him and I ended up on the floor. You imbeciles!"

Buck shoved his brother down the steps, turned and gave Boone a quick nod.

Hell's curses, what did that mean? Was it some odd outlaw respect or a promise of retribution?

In the end it didn't really matter. He'd thrown down the challenge.

He ought to have bound the four of them and delivered them to the law, but his gut was uneasy. Had been since he'd left Melinda alone.

With one of the four missing, there was no time for making arrests now. Every passing second ate at his nerves. He wouldn't take an easy breath until he saw that his wife and the doctor were safe.

He had to get back. That meant turning the Kings over to the law another time. But so be it.

Stanley stood watch at the window.

Merle emerged from his hidey-hole behind the bar.

"They've gone," Stanley announced.

Boone tossed the money box to Merle. The look of relief that passed over his face when he grasped it in his hands made Boone feel ashamed. He'd survived by robbing saloons. All of a sudden he regretted every time he'd done it.

Boone had a feeling that living life on the straight and narrow just might be the only way for him in the future. He wondered if, following that path, he might become a man that his brother would respect.

That Melinda would. She liked him, he knew. He saw it in her smile, in the flash of caring in her pretty blue eyes. He felt it in the gentle pressure of her fingers when he was the lucky recipient of her touch.

Not that he deserved her caring or his brother's forgiveness, but he did hope.

He heard a small voice in his mind, heard it so clearly that it startled him. His soul had begun the narrow path to redemption, the voice suggested.

God grant him the wisdom and the honorable nature to follow that voice.

Was it really suggesting he follow a certain career path? He wasn't sure it was possible to go from an outlaw to—to that.

In this moment all he knew was that Melinda might be in danger. There wasn't time to consider life spinning on a dime and shooting him off in an unbelievable direction.

Not only unbelievable but impossible.

He ran for his horse, Smythe only a step behind him.

If he managed to keep the doctor alive, maybe he'd be able to face his brother again.

* * *

Dr. Brown inclined his head toward the door of the waiting room.

Melinda followed him into an area with three chairs and a divan. Cold sunshine spilled through the front window but didn't do much to warm the room.

She expected to see an anxious father pacing, but did not.

"Have you ever seen a baby delivered, Mrs. Walker?"

"Many times. My husband's brother is a physician in Montana. I was his assistant for a time."

Dr. Brown looked surprised but not disbelieving.

"So you recognize that we have a problem with this birth?"

"The baby ought to have come by now," she said. "Perhaps it is turned wrong."

"That's what I fear. She—"

A fist pounded on the door.

"Kings!" a boy's voice shouted. "Four minutes out!"

"Not enough time." Dr. Brown scraped his fingers through straight black hair, glanced out the window, his frown deep and worried. "If they kill me right off, it'll be up to you to deliver the baby. Can you do it?"

Could she? She'd seen it done, helped Lantree with two such births, but on her own she would not know what to do.

A distressed cry came from the other room.

"We have to leave." She gripped the doctor's hands in hers to press her point. "Take her home where her husband can protect her."

"Mrs. Coulter is a widow. Her husband was shot in the back by Efrin when he refused to kneel down and lick the manure off his boots."

Dr. Brown's brain must be spinning, trying to save his patient while fearing for his own life.

Boone. She needed Boone. He would know what to do.

But Boone was not here and they couldn't wait on him.

"Do you have a buggy and a horse?" she asked.

"A buckboard and a team."

"A gun?"

He shook his head.

The buckboard would have to do, although a buggy would move faster.

"Go hitch it up. We're going to the homestead. I'll wait with Mrs. Coulter."

First thing going back into the labor room Melinda opened the back door and called the dog in. The doctor might not like having him indoors, but Billbro was their best protection at the moment.

The clock in the waiting room tick-tocked in the silence, marking the time slipping away. Each swing of the pendulum brought the Kings closer to town.

Mrs. Coulter moaned, hissed out a breath.

"They're coming, aren't they?"

"They are. But we are leaving. Can you find the strength for that?"

She gritted her teeth and nodded through a contraction.

"You're married to that outlaw?" she said, the cramping apparently subsiding.

"I am."

"Aren't you scared every minute?"

"I'm scared now—but if Boone were here I'd be less scared."

It was true. She trusted her outlaw husband completely. Logic would suggest she ought not to trust any man she had known so briefly, especially one accused of so many things. But Melinda trusted her intuition, knew it to be true that a good heart beat inside the outlaw's chest.

Although most people, like Mrs. Coulter, would think her a fool for believing so.

"Well, I reckon your husband wouldn't have allowed Efrin King to shoot him in the back, left you a widow and expecting. Prideful nonsense—"

"I hear something," Melinda whispered.

Yes, and so did Billbro. His hackles rose but he did not growl.

Melinda rose from the bedside and walked to the window. She peered out. A man was tying his horse to a tree nearby. He looked pleasant enough with a half smile on his face even though no one was around to see it—except her, and that was because she was spying through a curtain.

His gait was unhurried. She didn't see a weapon strapped to his thigh. As he walked toward the office, he glanced at trees and twittering birds.

What concerned her was that he chose to come to the back door when there was a perfectly good front door that any respectable person would use.

She bit her lip, listening for a sound to indicate the wagon was ready to go.

Nothing—only the footfalls of the man's boots crossing the dirt.

Perhaps he would turn aside, go into another establishment.

Billbro growled, he, too, not anticipating that easy of an outcome.

She heard the jangle of a harness over the loud thumping of her heart. Please let it be already attached to the horse.

"Stay here, deputy." She stroked his head, his long ears. She had no doubt that he understood her. "Don't let anyone but the doctor touch Mrs. Coulter."

Billbro's long, soft tongue flipped out and licked her wrist. She kissed his snout in return.

If it was true that the Kings would go to the saloon first, Boone would be busy there and not be able to get back here in time to take control of this emergency.

It was up to her and the dog to get everyone to safety.

She stepped outside, a smile on her lips, a practiced sparkle in her eye. With any luck, this congenial-looking fellow was not "royalty."

"Good day to you, sir," she said. "I couldn't help but notice you looking about on this lovely fall day. I suppose you are a lover of nature, as am I."

"Nothing sweeter than the twitter of a little bird, unless it's the smile of a lovely woman."

He didn't seem a threat, which made the hair on her arms rise. One of the Kings, maybe the worst of them, was said to put on a charming facade.

And, yes, just there in the breast pocket of his elegant coat was a bulge—a Derringer, possibly.

How long could she keep an evil man charmed?

She blinked her eyes, fanned her face with her fingers. "You're making me blush."

"And a sweet pink color it is."

Had he realized it was caused by pure terror, he

would pounce upon her immediately, of that she had little doubt.

"If you're here to see the doctor, he isn't here. There was an emergency at some homestead or another—I'm not sure quite where, exactly. It was exceptionally urgent, though, judging by the way he left me waiting."

"You must be new in town." He mounted one step of the porch while he spoke. "I'd have noticed you."

"Yes, indeed." She took a step down but, oh, how she longed to turn and run. "Jasper Springs seems a charming place. Have you lived here long?"

"Long enough to know that you are, by far, the loveliest woman to ever walk our streets."

His smile was serene; his brown eyes expressed nothing but congeniality. But his fists clenched; one then the other. Oddly, in rhythm with the clock, not that she could actually hear it ticking at the moment.

"Mercy." She pressed her hands to her cheeks, as though his compliment had been her undoing. "And I'm so pleased to have met such a fine gentleman. Among those I associate with, there are so few."

"Ah, then I'm correct in guessing that you are the outlaw's wife." He moved closer to her than respectable distance called for.

"Sadly, I am."

She held to her spot, listening for the sound of the doctor entering the office. Please, please, please, let it be soon—her palms were beginning to sweat.

"I imagine he's rather coarse—rude to a fault."

"You wouldn't believe the things I must put up with! Crude language, ill-gotten gains and even—" she lowered her voice and her lashes "—other women."

He reached for a curl at her temple, twisted it around his thumb. Suddenly his eyes lost the happy-puppy look and took on the sly, cool stare of the copperhead he claimed as his nickname. The hold on her hair tightened, pinched. "Not a man who pleases you under those skirts, either, I reckon?"

His brow lifted. He gathered a hank of her skirt in one fist and tried to tug her down another step.

This went beyond her experience in flirtation. She shoved him but he grabbed her wrists in a bruising hold.

His grin flashed. In her mind she saw a serpent's mouth open, dripping venom from sharp fangs.

"Billbro!" she shouted, her heart nearly beating out of her throat.

Behind her, glass shattered. The dog leaped through the window. Midflight he took Leland King down, his jaws clamped around the outlaw's shoulder.

Instinct told her to run for the door and lock it behind her, but she hurried down the stairs instead to where King's horse was tethered. She freed it then slapped its rump. It circled nervously but didn't go far away.

The back door opened.

"Let's go!" Doc shouted, carrying Mrs. Coulter in his arms.

Melinda dashed after him, through both rooms then out the front door. Climbing onto the buckboard, she gathered the horses' reins in her fists. She'd never driven anything this unwieldy, but she'd seen it done.

As soon as Dr. Brown laid his charge on the wagon bed she jiggled the reins and shouted. The wagon jolted forward but trudged along slowly. Leland would be able to catch them by running alongside.

A gunshot split the afternoon silence, immediately

followed by another. The sharp reports made the horses bolt and her heart constrict.

Billbro! That ugly-hearted criminal must have shot him.

Chapter Seven

Only a mile outside of town the horses calmed down. No matter how she slapped the reins—shouted even, the animals refused to quicken their trot.

From behind, she heard Mrs. Coulter cry out, the doctor curse.

The road was too rough. Bouncing over ruts, heaving up, slamming down. How would the poor woman survive this?

"Hold up!" shouted Dr. Brown.

"We can't, not yet."

"I need you back here. Now!"

Melinda hauled hard on the reins. Before the team had come to a stop, she scrambled over the bench.

"They've heard the shots. We don't have time—"

"She doesn't have time," he whispered. "This baby's got to be turned."

"What do you want me to do?"

"For now, soothe Mama as much as you can. Hold her hand while I try to maneuver the child into a better position."

Stroking Mrs. Coulter's brow and squeezing her hand

did little good. What the doctor was attempting would be beyond painful.

"It won't be long now," she crooned. "Before you know it you'll be holding your beautiful baby."

Melinda prayed that would be so; that even if the little one survived its birth, no harm would come to it from the men pursuing them.

But even before she uttered "amen," she heard hoofbeats pounding the road, coming fast and hard.

"Doctor!"

"I can't deal with it now."

Melinda lay Mrs. Coulter's hand down, across her breast. Scanning the wagon, she looked for a weapon. The bed was empty except for the doctor's bag sitting open beside his knee.

There would probably be a scalpel inside. She would not touch it, though, just in case— No! That was unthinkable—it would not happen.

Figures appeared on the road behind them. She couldn't distinguish who, or even how many there were with all the dust being stirred.

Perhaps there was something stored under the wagon. She scrambled down. Crawling underneath, she spotted cobwebs, dried weeds—and just there, tied to the bottom of the wagon bed was a broom.

Willing her fingers not to tremble, willing her belly not to empty itself, she untied the broom then crawled back out.

Standing in the road at the rear of the wagon, she held her splintered weapon, pole end toward the approaching riders.

A movement, a blur is all it was, caught her attention. It didn't travel the road, but cut across open land.

Barking, the blur raced toward her.

"You good dog!"

She thought the deputy was going to bowl her down but he whirled hard in front of her. Teeth bared, he waited for the riders.

There were two.

Since staring at the road would not slow them, she glanced down at her canine protector.

She was certain the dog had been killed. Leland'd had a gun. She'd heard two shots. Her heart had shattered thinking she had lost her wolfish friend. That perhaps he had given his life for her.

"Good, wonderful dog." She ruffled his fur.

The blood covering his muzzle was not fresh. It had to be Leland King's. That thought did not shatter her.

A mule brayed. A mule!

"Thank you, thank you, thank you," she murmured.

Keeping hold of her weapon because she did not know if Boone and Stanley were being followed and a broom might be required, she scrambled back into the wagon.

Kneeling beside the doctor, she took Mrs. Coulter's hand again. Her grip through the next contraction did not feel as strong.

"It's all right, Mrs. Coulter. My husband is here now. Stanley, too.

Stanley tied his mount to the rear of the wagon, then in a single leap, probably unheard of among lawyers, hit the bench and snatched up the reins.

He yee-hawed the team into motion while Boone was still tethering his horse beside the mule.

On the run, Boone snatched a rifle from his horse's saddle then made a leap for the side of the wagon. He pulled himself up and over the edge one-handed.

Even with her attention riveted on surviving the next half hour, she couldn't help but feel a thrill at seeing how strong the man she had married was.

If only—oh, never mind. That was a thought she would consider another time.

Crouched on one knee at the back of the wagon, Boone raised the rifle to his shoulder. Melinda's hip bumped against his solid thigh as she knelt beside Dr. Brown.

She scooted sideways so that she would not disturb his aim when he needed to fire the weapon.

But that brief touch gave her courage. Just knowing he was there, strong and in charge, gave her the gumption to breathe.

She took one more glance at his broad-shouldered, powerfully muscled back before she gave her full attention to helping the doctor deliver the baby.

Boone could have taken shelter behind the buckboard gate and left them exposed, but he had not.

No, this horrible, wicked outlaw presented his body as a living shield.

If she lived to see tomorrow, there was every chance that that she would wake up half in love with her husband.

Even the road was an adversary. Its cursed unevenness knocked Boone's aim every which way. Worse, every time the wagon wheel crashed into a gouge in the earth, the poor woman in labor cried out.

"Riders getting closer!" he shouted to Stanley. "Get those horses moving!"

It was a damn foolish thing to say. The animals weren't racehorses and they were pulling a wagon with five people plus a large, blood-smeared hound.

As far as he could tell from this distance, there were four riders coming hell-bent for leather.

A short time ago, when he and Stanley had heard the gunshots and raced for the doc's office, they hadn't found anyone.

Sure had found a mess of blood, though, and wagon tracks.

For every second of that hellish ride out of town, panic had bitten his nerves, made him want to shout out in rage because it might be Melinda's blood. His beautiful wife, whom he had sworn to protect, might be wounded, or worse. He'd prayed; lifted his heart to God and begged.

Then, suddenly, there she had been, standing in the road as though she meant to protect the doctor and his patient with a damned broom.

His heart had shifted in that moment in a way he didn't understand. All he knew was that he had never felt this emotion for another person—not even his brother.

That was something he would have to consider later. Right now his attention was consumed with trying to peer through a dust cloud.

The four riders emerged from the haze. He figured it was Leland who was missing and that the blood on the ground had been his.

King Copperhead must have skipped the social outing and gone straight to deliver twisted justice to the doc.

Judging by the blood crusting the dog's muzzle, it had to have been Billbro who'd delivered justice.

Boone heard Melinda and the doc speaking, but with the wagon creaking, hooves pounding the earth and Stanley cursing the horses to greater speed, he couldn't tell what they were saying.

Still, he did sense the mood of the words. Anxiety but not panic.

"You can do this!" The doc's voice was urgent, loud enough to be heard now. He wondered if it was Melinda or the young mother he was encouraging.

Then he heard Melinda say something like, "Butt presenting."

Lord, don't let that be the case. He'd lost a baby sister that way.

Not being able to help with what was going on behind him, he focused his attention on the swiftly approaching outlaws.

He drew a bead the one in front. Lump, unless he missed his guess. A damned, blasted, accurate shot was impossible with the wagon heaving.

Luckily their shots weren't any more precise.

But they soon would be because unless something changed, they would be overtaken. As easy to shoot as ducks napping on a pond.

Behind him, the woman cried out, her scream so raw that it cut his heart to the quick. But then another cry filled the air, high-pitched, urgent—and being used for the first time.

He'd find out later if the newborn was a girl or a boy—if its mama had survived.

For now, if any of them was going to survive, he had to do something. Popping off misaimed shots was not slowing the villains down.

Hell's curses.

With the newborn's cries ringing in his ears, he tucked the rifle between his arm and his ribs. One-handed, he loosened his horse's reins where they were tethered at the back of the wagon. With a tight grip on the leather, he maneuvered the animal closer to the buckboard. When it was nearly alongside, he made a leap onto its wide back.

Circling the horse around, he galloped toward the Kings.

The dog-wolf leaped from the wagon and raced ahead of him, teeth barred and looking like a hound from hell—or an avenging angel.

Boone thought he heard Melinda scream his name.

Pulling into the yard of the homestead, the animals winded and everyone shaken to the core, Melinda glanced back at the road.

With the rolling terrain, she couldn't tell if they were still being pursued. If they were, that meant that Boone was— No he was not. She refused to think it.

She stood in the wagon bed, looking for dust out on the road and listening for gunshots.

Nothing. Just the cold wind howling across the ground.

Tearing her thoughts away from Boone, she focused her attention on the baby. They needed to get the infant warm.

With some effort she banished the panic gripping her belly and concentrated on something that she had some control over.

Climbing down from the wagon she turned toward the doctor then reached up. "I'll take the baby."

Mrs. Coulter was unconscious. It would take both of the men to get her inside.

Melinda hugged the child close to her heart. The doctor had taken off his shirt and wrapped her in it, but her tiny head was still wet, cold and exposed. She covered it with her hand while she hurried inside the house.

Luckily, the coals in the hearth of the main room were still warm. She stirred them then added a log.

Dr. Brown and Stanley carried Mrs. Coulter into the bedroom.

The doctor would be busy for some time. The care of the little girl was in her hands.

If only they had bothered to cook breakfast this morning, the stove would still be warm.

She'd give a hundred dollars for a pot of warm water to bathe the baby in.

Placing the infant against the warmth of her own skin was the best way to warm her, she had learned from Lantree. It was the first thing he did after a birth; place the newborn against its mother's chest.

Melinda unbuttoned her shirt then loosened her underclothes. She unwrapped the tiny girl, tucked her inside her camisole and hugged her close to her heart.

"There now, sweeting," she crooned. "Let's get you warm. We'll make you clean and pretty for your mama."

While she set about building the fire in the stove one-handed, Melinda felt the baby's skin begin to warm. Thank the Good Lord.

Stanley came into the kitchen. Upon seeing more of Melinda than he must have thought proper, he spun around.

"Baby all right?"

"I believe she will be once she's warmed through." Little Miss Coulter turned her cheek toward Melinda's chest. "How is her mother?"

"Coming around. Doc expects her to be fine."

"Just in time." Melinda glanced at Stanley's straight, slim back. "This baby girl is getting hungry. There's a shawl in my trunk. A white one, very soft. Can you fetch it for me? Then get me something to use as a washcloth and a towel. Also, if you wouldn't mind carrying the pot of water to the table?"

Stanley returned with the items she had asked for at the same time as the water finished heating.

With the room and the water warmed, Melinda removed the baby from inside her camisole. She placed her on the table and began to wash the small limbs with the warmed cloth.

"She's lovely," she said to Stanley who did not approach the table until Melinda had properly buttoned up. "So pink and pretty."

"I wonder what her name will be."

"Something to do with courage, I would think, considering everything she went through to be born."

"I'd suggest Melinda," he said.

At Dr. Brown's call, Stanley went back into the bedroom.

While she washed the baby, she kept one ear open, listening for something that shouldn't be. Half an hour had passed since they'd ridden into the yard and still there was no indication that they had been followed.

By anyone.

Boone.

An image of his handsome face flashed through her mind. But, no—she couldn't think of him yet.

There were still things that needed to be done. Plans to be set in place in case—no, never mind that. Plans were needed in any case.

"Boone and I will move into the barn," she called over her shoulder to Stanley who had come back into the room to heat some water for tea. She dried the little girl's head, admiring the fine brown hair tipped with blond. "The rest of you will need the house."

"That won't do and you know it. It's not proper."

"I don't know it, Stanley." She would not charm him to her way of thinking. She didn't have the heart for anything at the moment but getting this lovely little one clean and in her mother's arms. "Boone is my husband and it's the most proper thing in the world for us to sleep in the barn."

"Melinda…don't go thinking that the two of you have any kind of future. You'll only get your heart broken. He's lived a criminal's life. He's not the kind of husband you need."

"The kind who would place his body between me and a bullet, do you mean?" She swaddled the baby in the shawl, hugged her close.

Maybe Stanley, having been so involved in driving the wagon, had not glanced back and seen what Boone had done. But there would never be a time when Melinda did not see it. Boone had told her he would protect her, but seeing him do it at the risk of his own life? Well, it changed everything. He was, beyond a doubt, the man she had believed him to be. She was, beyond a doubt—

"I promised that—"

"I promised some things, too. To Lantree, to Boone, and I recited wedding vows before God."

"You recited them before Judge Mathers. We all knew the marriage was a farce."

"Just because there was no courtship, no wooing, does not mean that those promises were meaningless."

"Not meaningless, then," Stanley said softly, touching the child's curled fist where it poked out from under the shawl. "Just not promises made forever."

Melinda turned, carried the baby toward the bedroom.

What Stanley said was true. In the beginning neither she nor Boone had intended to be married forever.

At the doorway, she pivoted. Stanley had been gazing at her back, his eyes reflecting an emotion that seemed equal parts resolution and apprehension.

"I'm not saying that anything has changed, only that—"

That there were some things she wouldn't say out loud, not until she had them settled in her own mind.

For now, all she wanted was for Boone to come back.

They would bed down in the loft.

Glancing around the barn, Melinda decided that it made the most sense.

For one thing, the heat from the stove below would rise and help to keep them warm. For another, the big hay door had a window in it and would give them a better view of the road.

While preparing the space, she repeatedly closed her mind to the thought that Boone might not come back.

She would not believe that he was dead, that the last thing she had done in her new husband's presence was to desperately, helplessly, scream his name.

No. Boone was coming back. He was not dead. There had to be another reason that the sun had set and he hadn't returned.

This was not like when Papa died. Just because it was cold and dark like that other night so many years ago, it did not mean the same thing. With great effort, she put Papa out of her mind.

She glanced at the cozy space she was creating and sighed. It wasn't a palace, or even actually indoors, but the cracks between the wallboards weren't so wide. All in all, the nest did seem inviting, far better than sleeping in a too-crowded house where Stanley would keep everyone awake with his snoring.

She had hauled up a wood crate then covered it with a checkered cloth that she found in the tack shed behind the barn. She had also found a canvas bag into which she had stuffed a candlestick, candles, matches, a pitcher for water and a tin mug.

The small covered table set with the candle and the pitcher looked cozy. All it lacked was a vase of flowers. But being October, she was not likely to find any, especially in the dark with villains ready to leap out from behind the bushes. But she had found a small pumpkin so she set that beside the candlestick.

As it turned out, the tack room was a treasure chest. It seemed that the previous owners had left in such a hurry they had been forced to leave most everything behind.

All that needed doing now was for her to haul more straw up the ladder, form it into a bed and then cover it with the blankets she had discovered among the abandoned things.

Stanley had visited during his turn at watch. Luckily, he did not try to force her to return to the house.

There wasn't room for a bird to move in, not with the doctor and Stanley sleeping in the small front room and Mrs. Coulter, who was doing splendidly by now, and her infant daughter having the even smaller bedroom.

Perhaps the reason Stanley did not try to make her come inside was that he didn't believe Boone was coming back.

Stanley was wrong. She would not consider that he was not.

Boone was not Papa. She knew that.

Melinda shook her head, took a breath and then gathered up a skirt full of straw. She climbed the ladder with it, reciting the reasons that Boone would have been delayed hours past sundown.

When the straw bed was the right shape and size, covered with three blankets, she glanced around the loft.

This, she realized with no little bit of pride, was the first home she had made for herself. Clearly, one did not need lavish surrounds to feel fulfilled. All one needed was—Boone.

She had the oddest feeling in the pit of her stomach that any place she spread a bed with him would be home. And any place that she did not, would not be.

This thought made her slightly uncomfortable, but not in a horrible way. It's just that she had known him for such a short time to be thinking such things.

Also, she wondered if he really saw her or just some delicate and sought-after vision of womanhood, which she happened to resemble, curse it. Perhaps.

But then again, intuition could not be denied. Sometimes a woman knew things, or at least suspected them.

But where was Boone?

Logic and Stanley hinted that he was not coming back. One good man against four—maybe even five evil ones—the odds were not in Boone's favor.

She had been fighting this devastating thought with every breath, every heartbeat. But now, with the work done, and nothing left to occupy her mind, the obvious conclusion shouted at her.

She actually felt sick, her skin damp and her throat swelling.

Boone was dead.

Just like Papa. But that night she had not been worried, just a child slumbering happily under warm blankets. She had not known that Papa was not in bed, safely
curled next to Mama.

Then Mama had screamed. On small shaking feet she
had dashed to the head of the stairs. Mama was on the
floor, the preacher's arms around her and the sheriff a
looming shadow in the doorway.

"Stop!" she gasped out loud.

Boone was not Papa. He was a more honorable man
than her father had been.

It had taken years to understand that his death had
been his own fault. That no matter what a good and
charming child she strived to be, Papa would have still
gone out that night.

With effort, she put her father back in the misty past.

Taking a breath, she noticed that there was one more
thing to do, after all. Odor lifted from her body in a
wave. Coming back down the ladder she could smell
herself quite clearly.

When Boone did come, she did not want him to mistake her for livestock.

She set a pot of water on the stove to warm, took a
cracked old wall mirror from the tack room and secured
it to the wall behind the stove. She removed her ripe-
smelling dress.

Gazing into the mirror, she decided that she looked
as bad as she smelled. She shoved her undergarments
down to her waist then unpinned her hair.

It fell across her shoulders in a dirty blond tangle.

Running from outlaws did wreak havoc on a lady's
appearance.

Unbidden, an image of Boone's broken body lying

on the ground flashed in her mind. What she ought to do is get Stanley and go look for him because what if he were wounded and in need of help?

Going to search for Boone seemed logical on the surface, but in truth was far more complicated.

Stanley was standing watch. He would never leave the people inside the house unprotected; she would not want him to.

If she tried to go to Boone alone, Stanley would notice and hog-tie her to a stall door. She would do no one any good tied up. She needed to remain here in case the Kings did come. While she was not a queen with a firearm like Annie Oakley, she would be able to help.

During her time in Montana, Grandfather Moreland had at least taught her the difference between the stock and the barrel of a rifle.

For now, she was stuck here with nothing to do but fret over the unknown and clean her smelly self up.

If only Rebecca were here. Her cousin would play her violin and everything would seem easier to face. Since Becca was not here, Melinda imagined a lively tune coming from her instrument. Sadly, try as she might for lighthearted, the melody turned morose.

She dipped a cloth in the warm water, watched in the mirror as water dripped down her nose, chin and throat. Rinsing, wringing and dipping the cloth, she felt the tears behind her eyes swell.

Willing them not to spill, she washed under her arms. Dipped, wrung the cloth and squeezed her eyes closed trapping the moisture that, when it escaped, would mean that she believed Boone to be dead.

Unseeing, she washed her breasts, over, under and across.

"Melinda," murmured a deep voice from behind her.
"Boone?"

She spun around. With a short leap she flung herself against him, wrapped her arms around his middle and squeezed.

"Boone!" Now the tears that she had been fighting slid freely down her face. She hugged him tight, rejoicing in the solid warmth of him. She listened to his heartbeat, to the rise and fall of his breathing. "I thought—no, I didn't, I knew you'd come back."

He touched her, his arms coming around her back, pulling her tighter against him. Even though his hands were cool against her skin she made no attempt to move away or to cover her nakedness.

She didn't understand why, but this intimacy with Boone seemed right.

Chapter Eight

He hadn't expected to come back. Charging toward outlaws worse than he was on an old wagon nag, with little ammunition, his survival hadn't seemed likely. Hell, he still couldn't figure out why he was still breathing.

He'd expected to die, but instead here he stood with the woman he had married clinging to him as though she cared.

Heaven in an embrace, that's what it was. Holding an angel wouldn't feel as healing.

"Melinda, I need to look at you."

He wouldn't press her when she said no. But he knew of no other way to cleanse his mind of the past few hours. He needed to look upon beauty in the same way a drowning man needed a breath of air.

Would she even understand that there was nothing sexual in the asking? That he would not defile her?

She glanced up at him, not shyly but not with seduction, either. Those blue eyes held his gaze with understanding.

He couldn't quite figure out how this lovely innocent would understand anything about him, though. Her gentle world was as far from his as the earth was to the moon.

Beauty and the beast—it was all he could think of to compare it to.

She stepped away from him, her soft palms gliding down his arms until she captured his hands.

She let him look.

Just as he had suspected, the Creator had formed her perfectly. The slope of her shoulders, the delicate hollow at her throat, the shape of her breasts, the ivory hue of them, tipped by the darker flush of her nipples, not like any woman he had ever bedded. Melinda was sweet perfection.

A gift for any man.

Especially, in this moment, for him.

The memory of blood, of cracking bone and gunshots, the crackle of flames and screams of terror—all of this faded in the presence of his wife's purity. Light penetrated his darkness for the first time in hours. Or maybe, when he thought about it, years.

He lifted her hands, kissed one then the other.

He touched the straps of her camisole where they hung in the crook of her elbows. The fabric felt smooth under his callused fingers. Lifting them, his hand brushed her inner arm, grazed the outer edges of her breasts.

Despite the purity of his intentions, he was a man, and things within him that were not so pure began to stir.

The very last thing he intended to do is to defile her perfection with his worldliness.

It's true that he was a thief, had robbed and terrified folks. But he would not steal Melinda's innocence.

"You look done in," she said, adjusting her camisole, taking her beauty back. "I've made us a bed in the loft."

"I can't sleep with you."

"There's nowhere else you can, unless it's in the tack room."

Couldn't sleep there, either. "Bird King's in the tack room."

"Oh, well, that's good news, I suppose. Now, up you go. I'll bring you some tea. We need to talk about everything that happened."

"I reckon we do." But he wasn't going to do it in the damned bed. He wasn't made of stone. "Thank you, Melinda. You are—"

What? How could he find the words to tell her what she had become to him—even more, what she could not be?

"Full of wifely concern. Now get up there before you fall over."

She kissed his cheek. Again, it stunned him that a simple gesture could mean so much.

"Shall I send the doc to the tack shed?"

"To heal a man who wants to kill him?"

She shrugged and the lacy strap of her camisole slipped off her shoulder. "I'll ask."

She started to step into her gown but, judging by the sniff she gave it, she didn't want to.

He removed his coat and put it over her shoulders. It hung off her, but gave proof that there was nothing that Melinda would not look fetching in. "Let's go. I'll bring your trunk on the way back. Besides, I want to get a look at that baby. Anyway, if it comes down to who gets seen by the doc first, I want to make sure it's Billbro."

"He's hurt?"

Boone nodded. "Poor dog is pretty banged up."

Returning to the homestead, he had carried Billbro on the saddle in front of him and made Bird King walk on a lead tied to the horse. He hadn't found it in him to give a damn that the Vulture's arm was broken, not after he'd taken a knife to the dog.

Outside, cold wind blew every which way. It snatched the smoke coming out of the chimney, streaking it east.

"The baby's a girl," Melinda said, clasping the coat closed.

"That's good. Did her mother survive?" He'd feared she would not.

"Amazingly enough, she's doing well."

Stanley stood watch on the porch, his coat hiked up around his ears and his rifle braced across his chest.

Coming up the steps, they exchanged nods. He had a lot to tell the lawyer, but not tonight.

Tonight, if the new mother was willing, he would hold her baby. New life was to be cherished, be it a human child just starting out or a sinful one given a new path. Gazing at the little one's perfect innocence might finish the cleansing that Melinda had begun; help him see more clearly the new path he was taking.

If he was going to go on with this business, act as ruthless as those he was bringing down, he would need a few hours to not feel so dirtied by it.

There was no denying that he was a hypocrite. His soul might not carry the guilt that the souls of the Kings did, but it was far from sinless.

Not that it mattered. The Kings had caused a lot of misery to a lot of folks and he meant to put an end to it.

The doc had asked why he cared. That was easy.

Doc and Lantree were of a kind. He owed his brother

a great deal. Given that his life was worth about a nickel, he might never have the chance to make it up to him. But he could through the doc.

Boone sat with his back against the hay door, looking out the small window set into it. The loft offered a good view of the acreage surrounding the homestead.

At this elevation he would be able to spot invaders from some distance away, as long as they were coming from the north or the west.

The loft also had the advantage of having the stove directly under it. The chill wasn't as sharp as it was in the rest of the barn.

Melinda had chosen the space well.

He closed his eyes for the first time in what seemed forever.

His bride sat on the straw bed that she had built for them, her frilly underclothes peeping out from beneath his coat.

She watched him. Clearly she wanted to know every detail of what had happened since he'd ridden away from the wagon this afternoon.

Her silence must be due the fact that he looked as bone-weary as he felt. For all that she would be curious, it appeared that she was not going to press him.

"You look like an angel sitting on a cloud instead of a pile of hay," he said because he wanted to think about anything but what had happened tonight.

Funny, the sincere compliment made her eyes narrow and her brows dip in a frown. He had a strong feeling that she wanted to utter a sharp retort, but she bit the words back.

"They burned down the store—tried to burn Edward Spears inside it," he said because he needed to.

"I thought I'd never see you again, Boone."

Moisture stood in her eyes.

For him? That couldn't be.

He shook his head. "If it wasn't for the dog, I reckon those fools would be dancing over my grave."

"Poor Billbro." She scooted to the edge of the loft and looked down to where the stitched and battered animal lay on a bed beside the stove. "Good wolf," she called down.

He couldn't see the dog from where he sat, but he heard the big tail thumping on the straw.

"Are they fools? Could we be that lucky? What happened?"

She needed to hear about it and, as much as he didn't want to remember it, hell, he needed to talk to someone.

It was an odd thing, being on this side of the law. Felt as if he had worms in his gut, knowing that in the past he had made folks feel what he had felt today.

"I rode out, figuring to buy time, maybe take a couple of them down before I—" He'd ridden away, not expecting to return. He'd run headlong at the outlaws, but held off on shooting until he was close enough to do more than scare them. He'd kept Melinda's face in his mind to remind himself that this was worth doing. "Luckily, I wasn't alone like I thought I was. The deputy charged ahead. He got to Lump King, ripped him off his horse. Took him down by the shoulder."

"By the shoulder? That's what he did to Leland, too." Again, she leaned over the edge of the loft. "Good, good, Wolfie."

This time the deputy whined.

Boone stared at her in silence for a moment, remembering how grateful he had been when he'd discovered that it had not been Melinda's blood on the ground. From seeing that blood and until he'd seen Melinda alive and safe, it was as though the world had grown gray and sluggish then suddenly burst alive with color and action.

"After he got Lump, Billbro went after Bird. Bird saw him coming and drew his knife. That's how he got the cut across his belly, the blow to his flank.

"I saw red. I swear I haven't been so angry since Martha Mantry."

In his mind it was all too fresh. Lump rolling around in the dirt, crying and screeching. No one seemed of a mind to help him. Boone figured they were too scared of the wolf to do anything but run. Bird had lost his seat, fallen backward off his horse's rump. Billbro had set upon him fast as a flash. When Boone noticed the glint of the knife, the spurt of blood coming from the dog's side—

"It was you who broke his arm?"

Hated to admit it had been him, but he could be a brutal man when the need arose. Someone like Melinda would never understand that.

Surprisingly she looked at him with approval. As much as he liked it, he didn't want her thinking that he was some sort of hero. While he wanted to make a better life, he was the bad twin, always had been.

Ever since he could remember, he'd been the one riding the neighbors' sheep, pulling the girls' braids and chasing the hens until they were too agitated to lay. Lantree had been the one to soothe the neighbors and their sheep, comfort the girls and round up the hens. Later on, Boone had been the first to get rolling-on-the-ground drunk while Lantree was the one to carry him home.

When Mama said her prayers, Boone always heard his name mentioned more than anyone else's.

"I don't know if I could have gotten the knife away without doing it but, like I said, I was seeing red."

"And a lucky thing for our deputy that you were." She scooted closer to him. The ruffle of her flirty-looking petticoat slid out from under the coat and grazed his dirty boot. "So what happened to Efrin and Buck? Did Lump just roll around on the ground like a stuck pig?"

"While I was scuffling with Bird, Lump managed to get back on his horse. Took off after his brothers. They were all in a panic, shouting about being chased by a wolf. I reckon they're scared of dogs."

"I reckon, but probably scared of Boone Walker's reputation more."

"That's not something I'm proud of." No matter what he did in his life, a wicked reputation was bound to follow him. "You asked if they were fools. No, not all of them. But all of them are cunning and ruthless."

He'd seen the anguish on the faces of the people when the merchant had been trapped in the burning store, the outlaws whooping and cheering.

It shamed him to the core that he had ever intimidated innocent folks—that the name Boone Walker had become a thing to fear.

"You're wrong, Boone. You aren't like them in any way."

"You a mind reader?" He would never have admitted his shame out loud, but evidently he didn't need to.

"No, you can relax about that. But I'm fairly good at reading expressions."

"No one's ever been able to do that." Only Lantree when they were young and he'd been a more open soul.

She flashed him a pretty smile. "Well, no one's ever been your wife before."

"Don't put too much store in that, Melinda." He plucked up a length of straw, chewed on it for distraction because he suddenly wanted to put some store in it. "I can never be the husband you need. You and I, we're from different worlds."

Her answer to his obvious point was to laugh. "Are you telling me you are not from our lovely planet Earth?"

"This is serious. We would never suit."

"I hope you haven't set me on some insipid pedestal, Boone Walker. Nearly every male I have ever met has done it. I had hoped that you would be different."

Nope, he wasn't different. He was guilty of that crime, so he remained silent.

She huffed out a breath, sounding exasperated.

"You have! Let me tell you something, Mr. Terror of the Plains." She narrowed her eyes at him. "You are judging me the same as folks judge you. They take one look at you and, without you even making a move in their direction, assume you are the beast on the Wanted poster. That you are going to eat them alive. It's the same for me. They see my face and assume they need to fall in love with sweet and perfect me."

She crossed her arms over her sweet and perfect bosom. "It's a trial. I don't need to tell you that."

"All right, I admit it. I have thought you sweet and lovely, but short of perfection in that you have some trouble with accepting authority."

Her mouth opened but she snapped it closed. He'd

caught her there. She couldn't rightly defend a short-coming.

"Thank you. I appreciate that. It's a relief to know that you see how we do suit, being that neither one of us bends meekly to authority."

Hell's curses! She'd maneuvered him into supporting her way of thinking. Not only was his wife independent but clever as a whip.

"If in the future, you treat me like I'm too pretty to have a brain, too sweet and perfect to have a backbone… If you insinuate that I am somehow too pure for my un-soiled feet to touch the ground, well—you don't want to know what depth I will sink to in order to prove you wrong.

"I'm a flesh-and-blood woman no better or worse than any other."

She took a breath, long and slow, in and out, appear-ing to gather her patience to calmly deal with her dim-witted outlaw.

"Now, then," she said with a sweet and—curse him for thinking it—lovely smile. "What happened to the storekeeper?"

As much as he would like to show her how wrong she was about them suiting, he was weary to his soul. Right now she would be able to spin him around at every turn.

All he wanted was to rest his head against the wall and doze. The sooner he told her what had gone on, the sooner he could sleep. Maybe. If he could only forget what he had seen.

"I'll start at the beginning, since you won't settle for anything less, I reckon."

"See how well you know me already?"

A vision of her, half naked, a washcloth dropping from her fingers, seared his mind.

"While I was breaking Bird's arm—" The memory of cracking bone made him want to vomit. Still, he feared he'd be called upon to do worse than that before this thing was over. "The others rode back to town like their pants were filled with ants."

He told her how Bird had shrieked and cursed when Boone had hauled him up to standing.

"You broke my arm."

"You cut an officer of the law."

The sun had begun to set, casting shadows long on the ground, while he'd tethered the young outlaw around the waist then tied the rope to the saddle horn.

"Hey, boy,' Boone had whispered as he'd knelt beside the wounded deputy. Blood oozed from the slice on his ribs, seeped from the one on his flank. He'd had to resist the urge to break Bird's other arm. "You all right?"

With great care, he'd hoisted Billbro onto the saddle, secured him and then climbed up after.

"Well, I was glad to have captured one of them at least. Took him to the marshal's office. Got turned away. It seems that the lawman's too much of a coward to keep Bird locked up. Figures the others will only break him out."

"He's right about that, don't you think?"

"Doesn't mean he's not obliged to do it."

"Then what happened?"

"Hell, Melinda, in town it was a scene out of Hades."

He broke out in the cold sweats just recalling it. He'd heard gunshots, screaming coming from the area of the store.

"Efrin had corralled about twenty folks, forcing them

to watch the burning building while he made proclamations about the Kings still ruling Jasper Springs."

After leaving the sheriff's office with Bird still tethered, Boone had stayed to the outskirts of what was going on. There was only one reason Efrin was terrorizing folks—to get Boone to show himself.

And folks were terrified. Their faces reflected the flames. Staring at the burning store, their expressions were tortured. Women were screaming, men, too. The fire burned so fierce, so hot, it shot up out of the roof. Even from his distance the heat had been blistering hot.

Bird started to say something; probably yell for help. Billbro had snarled. Boone had drawn his gun and shoved it under the armpit of the Vulture's broken arm. The kid had seen the wisdom of keeping silent.

"Buck held the crowd at gunpoint to make sure they didn't run, or try to help. When I got there, they'd already tied up Edward Spears and put him inside his store."

Melinda looked pale, surely shaken by what he was telling her even though he wasn't giving her every ugly detail.

Efrin had tied Spears's hands behind his back. From where Boone hid, he had a clear view of what was going on. Wished he hadn't, though. The storekeeper appeared at the front of the store but as soon as he tried to run out the door, Buck popped a shot at him.

Not to kill quickly, in twisted mercy. Clearly they wanted him to burn. Efrin had lifted his arms in the air. The evening breeze ruffled his coat behind him. Hell if it didn't look like he was a demon commanding a sinister symphony, his orchestra the screams of the horror-stricken crowd.

"So, Spears has got his arms tied behind him, running from the front door to the back. He can't come out the front because every time he tries, Buck shoots at him."

Of the brothers, the only one not accounted for was Leland. He wished Lump was also unaccounted for. The monster's full attention was on terrorizing Miss Trudy Spears. It made him sick to see the poor girl crying for her father while trying to dodge Lump's grasping hands.

"I heard gunfire coming from the back of the store so I figured it had to be Leland keeping Spears from going out the back way."

It was full dark and he was done with hiding in the shadows.

"Utter one little croak and I'll break your neck," he had said to Bird, leading the horse and his hostage down a dark ally.

Peeking around a building, he'd spotted Leland pointing his pistol at the back door of the burning store.

Boone tied his prisoner to a post with a rope, the tether to the horse bound around Bird's chest. "You make a sound, I whistle for the horse. He'll come and leave you split down the middle."

He didn't know if the horse was trained for that, but Bird seemed to believe it.

A stand of brush grew behind the store. Boone hid in back of it.

Leland cackled when Spears wove an unsteady path toward the back door. The building was full of smoke. Spears began to cough. Breathable air would be running out.

As Leland raised his arm to fire, Boone leaped on him from behind. Falling to the ground, he snatched the weapon from King's fist. He knocked him out with a blow to the temple.

He'd rushed inside the store but was blinded by smoke.

"Spears!" he'd bellowed. A cough came from the right so he'd shuffled that way.

Boone had bumped against him before he'd seen him. It was luck more than anything that he'd found the back door and was able to drag the storekeeper through it. He'd led him into the brush and leaned him back against a small trunk.

"You all right, Mr. Spears?"

He'd gasped in some air, coughed a bit more, then nodded.

Boone had pressed Leland's gun into Spears's fist, then taken off at a run toward the saloon.

Melinda reached for his hand, squeezed it. "I'm afraid to ask what happened to Mr. Spears and Trudy."

"I knocked out Leland then brought Spears out. It was close. His clothes have burn holes where the sparks got them. His eyebrows are singed but he'll be all right for now."

"And Trudy?"

"Lump was making his way toward her, last I saw. I couldn't do anything for her in the moment. Had to get the rest of the Kings away from the people."

Melinda's jaw dropped. "How could you possibly do that, and you just one man?"

"Only one way. Go after someplace that meant something to them. The saloon. When I set fire to his shed, the barkeep put up a fuss, but I reckon he saw reason when I— Anyway, he saw the wisdom of setting his shed ablaze to draw the Kings away from the store.

"I believe Miss Trudy made it safe away since Lump was with them when they came hell-bent for the saloon."

"It's a wonder folks just don't up and leave this place. Maybe now they will, with the store gone and nowhere to buy goods."

"They won't leave, not any more than they'll try to save a man from burning. I heard Efrin promise to kill any of 'his subjects' if they try. He'll do it, too—has done it."

Melinda was silent, her blue gaze resting on him, clearly troubled.

Finished with all that he could tell her, he fell silent, exhaustion and revulsion weighing his body.

He'd told her only what he had to, to satisfy her need to know. The rest would remain inside his head. He didn't want it there, no more than the other folks who had lived it did. But spreading the story around would only serve to give perverted glory to the outlaws.

He would not give them that.

Tales of perverted glory had been told about him. He wasn't sure why, except that when he robbed a saloon many of the patrons were drunk. No doubt they'd spun half-remembered stories into things that had never happened. After a time, one story built upon another until the simplest robbery became the crime of the decade.

Like the time a whore had followed him out of the saloon berating him even though he had not taken her money. She'd pounded him on the back, cursing while he'd mounted his horse. He'd galloped away and never seen her again.

But the story reported far and wide was that he had robbed then kidnapped a lovely young virgin, how he'd carried her away on his horse never to be seen again.

No wonder his name held such fear.

Hell, he reckoned, no matter what good he ever did with his sorry life, it would never make up for the past. Even if he answered the small voice that had come to him in the dark and confusion of the burning store, if he tried to take the path that it urged him to, his past might make it impossible to follow.

Melinda lay back on the bed of straw, reaching her arms toward him.

"Come rest your head, Boone."

He ought to refuse, knew he should.

But settling beside her, he did rest his head, on her bosom, just as she invited him to.

His eyes closed. He felt light, drifting as his muscles gave up the tension of the day. The only sounds were the wind rattling the doors and the steady thrum of his wife's heartbeat.

"Sleep now. You were quite a hero today," she murmured.

He didn't feel like a hero but it mattered that she thought it of him.

She stroked his hair. He smelled flowers.

Falling, drifting down into sleep, he felt at peace.

When Boone's breathing became shallow with deep sleep, Melinda lifted his head and wriggled out from beneath him. But she didn't go far.

She lay on her side face-to-face with him, close enough that she felt the warm beat of his breath on her nose.

Inhaling his scent, she took his essence into her lungs, into her heart, relieved beyond belief to feel life pulsing through him.

Today she had nearly become a widow. Tomorrow or the next day she—no, no—she would not.

But she might. The thought would not stop constricting her heart no matter how she willed it to.

One could not deny the possibility simply because one didn't like it.

Papa had taught her that.

A hank of blond hair crossed Boone's cheek. Just there, at the tips, was a smattering of dried blood.

Not his, not this time.

She scraped it off with her fingernail.

Stroking his cheek with the backs of her fingers, she felt the coarse scrape of his beard stubble. He was rough where she was smooth.

His eyes moved under his lids. Perhaps his sleep was troubled with all the ugliness he had experienced today.

The things he told her about were sickening. She was certain that there were other horrors that he hadn't burdened her with. But it was easy to see he was reliving them while he slept.

"Hush now, husband," she murmured, smoothing his brow.

To her relief, the dream appeared to stop. Oh, and his lips curved in a slight smile.

Her heart ached for him. He seemed to think he was not worthy of redemption. But she saw a man who stood for the innocent even at the risk of his own safety.

She had seen this quality in him more than once. It troubled her that he did not see it in himself.

He had been right when he'd said they were from different worlds, but not in the way he thought.

Bold and capable, that was Boone's way, while all she

knew to do was smile and bat her eyes until her adversaries were charmed.

Hers was a silly talent, one that she had spent some time developing. As a child she'd studied grown women, how they smiled to get their way, how they laughed and blinked their eyes just so. And all because in her childish heart she felt that she hadn't the power to keep Papa at home where he belonged.

She remembered the day Mama had cried, the day and the hour that she changed from a happy woman to a bitter one. Melinda had been forsaken. In that hour of grief, she'd vowed to never feel that helpless again.

However, all the charm in the world had been no match for Leland King.

Had Boone been there, he would have knocked the fellow flat and tied him up. Because Melinda's only weapon was looking pretty, Leland had been able to flee and then join his brothers in terrifying the people of Jasper Springs.

Even Billbro had better defensive skills than Melinda did. The dog had saved her life today and Boone's, as well.

Surely she ought to be as able to defend those she loved as well as a dog-wolf could.

"I think," she whispered to Boone because he was asleep and he would never know what she was saying to him. "That I would like to remain married to you."

She touched her fingertips with a kiss then lightly transferred the kiss to his mouth.

"But you need someone who is not an ornament. A woman of substance. I picture her as taller than I am and not frightened of sleeping out of doors. A lady who can shoot a tin can off a tree stump at a hundred yards then turn the gun on an attacker hidden in the brush, and all without her knees quaking.

"If you knew who Annie Oakley was, you would admire her greatly. Someday she'll be so famous everyone will know her name."

She sighed. Her breath must have tickled his face because one side of his mouth lifted.

Oh, how she wanted to really kiss him, but with him awake to kiss her back.

To her misery, as things were now, she was no more than a liability to Boone. Someone he had no wish to be responsible for but, for the sake of his future, was.

If she was going to do something about that, she needed to learn actual skills. She needed to be useful if she was going to be a woman who was a match to Boone. A wife he could be proud of and depend upon.

There were people, like Mrs. Coulter, who would call her a fool for choosing to be an outlaw's bride, who would tell her he could not be trusted. Once a killer and a thief, always a killer and a thief.

But they were wrong. Despite his reputation, regardless of who the public judged him to be, she knew better.

She had not been the only one naked a short time ago.

Boone's soul had been bared to her. What she'd seen was a man who regretted his past, who feared he would never be free of it.

One who wanted redemption, needed absolution.

In capturing the outlaw gang, it wasn't only freedom he was trying to earn.

"I think—yes, I'm quite certain," she murmured, "that I love you."

Chapter Nine

Just because Melinda decided to become a protectoress, a woman of derring-do, did not mean that she no longer appreciated the rustle of fine petticoats around her ankles or a touch of lace at her wrists.

There was no reason that a woman could not look her best while shooting a gun.

Climbing down the loft ladder, she spotted the deputy sitting beside the stove.

He thumped his tail. She knelt beside him then kissed him between the ears. He tasted dusty but it didn't matter, he was a brave, loyal friend.

"How are you feeling?" In answer, he licked her hand. "Rest as long as you want to. I'll bring you something to eat."

When she stood, Billbro stood with her, revealing an empty can of meat.

"I see that you've already been fed."

Earlier this morning, before daylight, she had turned over on the bed to find Boone gone, the hollow in the straw where he had lain cool to the touch.

Looking out the loft window, she had seen him carrying a lantern into the tack shed.

Walking past the barn mirror, she gave it a passing glance, spotted a strand of hair that had come loose from the bun at her nape. She tucked it behind her ear then stepped outside.

The sky was beginning to lighten. Clouds on the eastern horizon streaked in pink and orange.

Given the early hour she doubted that Boone had taken the time to eat.

Walking slowly across the yard to keep to the dog's pace, she wondered if the afternoon would bring rain. She hoped not, she had skills to acquire.

Deputy Billbro lowered his big body gingerly down onto the front porch. She was relieved to see that he was alert, his nose twitching, sifting the scents of the early morning.

Inside the house the fireplace was snapping warm and the kitchen stove already lit.

Stanley sat at the table with a mug cupped in his hands, his head drooping over it. He must have kept watch all night long.

He glanced up when he heard the scrape of the iron skillet that she set on the stove.

"That coffee smells like heaven."

"Just this side of," he answered, blinking the sleepiness away. "There's more."

She poured a cup and set it on the small table beside the stove to sip while she prepared pancakes for everyone. One could only guess that Mrs. Coulter must be ravenous after what she had been through.

And not just the new mother, she realized. All of them had been through a great deal and would need energy to face what was still to come.

She'd better fry some potatoes, as well.

"I didn't realize you could cook."

"Mama could be a hard woman, appearance was everything to her. But she did make sure that we were not mere ornaments. We all learned the womanly skills," she explained as she poured dollops of pancake batter onto the skillet. "But, Stanley, I've come to a revelation having to do with what is womanly."

"If something happened in private last night, no one need know about it. The marriage can still be annulled with no one the wiser."

"Stanley Smythe! Kindly keep your mind out of my straw bed. I'm a married woman and will make my own decisions in that area of my life. But you can put your mind at ease. I'm as unsullied as the day I was born."

"I'm relieved to hear it."

"What I have concluded, though, is that I am going to grow proficient at shooting a gun, and you should, as well."

"There is no need for you to even hold one, since you will be out of harm's way at all times."

"If you believed that, you would not have spent the night sitting on the porch with a rifle across your lap." She scooped up a stack of pancakes, added a mound of potatoes then set it in front of him. "It would be good if you knew how to use it."

He arched a brow then stuffed his mouth with food.

It had to be said that there was some satisfaction in silencing a lawyer.

"Good morning. Breakfast smells wonderful." The doctor entered the kitchen, rubbing a hand through his mass of thick hair while carrying the baby. "Thank you, Mrs. Walker. I can't recall the last time I've had something to eat."

"Can you shoot a gun, Dr. Brown?" Melinda prepared him a plate, set it in front of him then took the baby.

"Until lately I've never felt the need. I meant to get one when the Kings began threatening me. I never had time to make that purchase let alone learn how to use it."

"I'm going to ask Boone to teach me to shoot. You should join us."

In her opinion, anyone depending upon Boone for safety ought to be willing to help.

"Maybe not your mother, little Diana. What a pretty baby you are." Melinda nuzzled Diana's soft hair, breathed deep of the newborn scent.

"Have you tended Bird King? Under the circumstances, no one would blame you for ignoring him," she said. "If you don't want to set his arm, I'll see if I can manage it."

"Sure did want to ignore him. Couldn't, though. I splinted the arm earlier this morning." He chewed a mouthful of potatoes, closing his eyes as though the common food was a treat.

That must have been why Boone went to the tack room so early, to make sure the doctor was safe.

"Boone's brother would have done the same."

"I'm confused about a lot of things." Dr. Brown set down his fork. "Boone Walker. He's a killer and yet here he is, the only one standing between me and murder. I don't understand."

"How could you possibly, without knowing that my husband is not at all who he is portrayed to be, nearly not, at any rate." Melinda swayed back and forth, rocking the baby even though the child was not fussing. "The truth is that he has been deputized to bring down the King gang."

The doctor arched his brows, looking stunned for a moment. "It makes a certain sense. A killer after killers. Do you trust him to do this, Mr. Smythe? What if he turns on us? Hightails and runs?"

"I do trust him." Stanley lifted his arms, indicating that he would like to hold the baby. She was quite a popular lady. "So much so that I had his case reviewed by Judge Harlan Mathers. Mr. Walker's first trial was a farce. Mathers should have overturned the verdict upon first review. The one and only killing my client committed was in self-defense. The others were made up by folks who love sensationalism."

"I hardly know what to think about that. On the one hand, I reckon I can relax, but on the other I suppose I'd feel better if we were being defended by a man of experience."

"That's exactly why we all need to learn to defend ourselves. Boone is only one man against that gang," Melinda pointed out.

"He never should have been put in this situation." Stanley shook his head. "I argued against it, but here we are. What time are we attending those shooting lessons, Melinda?"

Boone wished the sun would set.

At the first sign of twilight, he was calling this shooting lesson off.

He'd thought Melinda's idea of turning law-loving folks into marksmen, and in a single afternoon, was unachievable. Couldn't hardly turn her down, though, not when she pleaded with him with sincere blue eyes.

It might have been possible had she been applying

her feminine wiles, trying to sway his decision with a charm that no woman he had ever seen could match.

But, no, she had won him over by sheathing that weapon and presenting her request in all sincerity.

Since he was helpless against that sort of persuasion, here he was explaining to Stanley for the tenth time the correct way to align the sight on his rifle to the target.

"Yes," Stanley said. "I've got it now. I see."

The bullet missed the can setting on top of the corral post and exploded in the dirt.

He clapped the lawyer on the shoulder. "You've nearly got it!"

It wasn't that the lawyer wasn't willing. Hell, he was putting all his effort into learning, but chances were that whatever caused him to need glasses also prevented him from having an accurate aim.

Given time, the doc might make a decent shot. Not now, though. Boone sensed that every time Brown aimed for the can he saw a beating heart, one that he had taken an oath to protect. Even if his mind told him to shoot to prevent a greater harm, everything he had ever stood for would slow him down, maybe get him killed.

When things came to a head, Boone would make sure the doc was not in the line of fire.

"Boone!" Melinda lifted her rifle to her shoulder. Her back was straight, her gaze focused. The ruffles of her sleeves fluttered in the breeze. "Come position my arms. I don't think I've got things quite right."

Hell's curses! She might not have things right this time, but once he showed her she would. He would instruct her and she would learn, first try.

Melinda was smart. Her eye was sharp. Even more

distressing, her nerves were steady. Of them all, she was the best.

The hell of it was, in spite of the fact that he would need her dependable shot, when the pot began to boil, he would make sure she was far from the danger.

"Are you woolgathering?" She glanced at him with a frown. "I doubt we have time for that."

She was right. They might have hours, they might have days. Distractions of any kind could not be afforded.

Coming to her, placing one hand at the nip of her waist and the other under her arm, he faced the biggest distraction of them all.

The scent of flowers rose from her hair. The heat of her skin seeped from under her blouse and warmed his fingers. His wife was properly covered, from the lace branding her fair-skinned throat to the ruffles dusting her boots.

Melinda could be wrapped head to toe in a burlap bag and all he'd see was the way she had looked in the dusky light of the barn this morning. He had eased out of the bed in the predawn to meet Doc in the tack room, but halfway to standing he'd stopped and simply stared at her.

The strap of her camisole had slipped off her shoulder. Sweet cream is what her skin looked like. Silky blond hair had fanned her face and across her throat. He knew it was silky because he had touched it. Her fingers, too, where they were twined in the strands.

Giving his mind a mental shake, he adjusted her aim, slightly over and up.

Stepping back, he watched with pride as the can flew off the post. Why he should be the one to take pride in her accomplishment, he couldn't quite figure.

He reckoned it had to be because she was his wife. Without warning, his gut twisted.

A temporary marriage was what they had both agreed upon. That's how it began and how it would end. Melinda was much too fine a woman for the likes of him.

Melinda shot the can off the post a dozen times in a row. Stanley's shots came closer to the target by a few inches while the doc continued to look green every time he pulled the trigger.

"Time to call it a day," Boone announced.

Even though it wasn't quite twilight, it soon would be. With shadows growing long, it would only make it harder to teach the impossible.

"I'll do better tomorrow, once I've slept on the matter," Stanley declared. Boone was pretty sure he also uttered a curse under his breath. Slump-shouldered, the lawyer walked toward the house.

"I reckon I'd better see to Mrs. Coulter and the baby." The doc caught up with Stanley in four long strides.

"Now teach me how to shoot the pistol," Melinda declared.

"It's getting dark and it smells like rain's on the way."

"What if I need to know how to use this?" She cradled the weapon in her hands. "Before daylight or in a rainstorm?"

"Use the rifle."

"What if the rifle isn't at hand and the pistol is?"

He sure wished the rain would slide in quicker. Being alone with his wife was beginning to give him ideas that were not appropriate.

In the past he'd never appreciated the value of a chaperone. He did now, if only for the distraction. If Stanley were here Boone might not be staring at his wife's lips, wondering if they tasted as sweet as they looked.

Hell.

"We'll do our best with what we have."

"Fine, go back. Get warm by the fire. With what I've learned so far, I'll figure it out on my own."

"Or shoot your fool foot off."

He stood behind her and lifted the weapon, her hands cupped in his. He breathed in her scent, felt the silky texture of her skin under his callused fingers. "Bend your elbows just a bit."

"Why two hands? In the dime novels it's only one."

She turned her head to glance up at him, her eyes wide, her gaze full of curiosity. Why did her lips have to be so peachy-looking, so moist? And what was that half smile—an invitation?

Maybe, but only in his imagination.

"Two hands are steadier. Now, part your legs." Hell's curses! "Slowly squeeze—"

The shot exploded. The can flew off the post then tumbled across the dirt.

"I like this, Boone."

She glanced at him again. This time her eyes had a simmer to them. Her breath came quicker. He knew because her back was against his chest.

He could only wonder if she felt the runaway gallop of his heart.

"Try it again," he said. This time he let go of her hands. Didn't step away, though.

"Are my legs spread correctly?"

He nodded because his voice was trapped in his throat, nearly strangling him.

Looked as if he'd be taking the night watch and the midnight watch. Predawn watch, too.

An hour into the midnight watch Boone shrugged the large oilcloth higher around his shoulders, tugged his Stetson lower.

Sitting on the bench, covered by the roof of the house's front porch, he wasn't exposed to the full force of the rain, but it blew in at him when the wind gusted just so.

By rights, it was the doc's watch, but the doc wasn't fighting the battle that Boone was. Not the battle against the Kings, he didn't mean that. It was a battle against himself. The man he used to be against the man he wanted to be.

Before he'd been arrested, he'd spot a woman, feel a pull to bed her, then ask if she was willing or pay her fee. After an hour his itch would be scratched for a while.

Seemed as though lately that itch was getting worse. Whenever he was near Melinda, sometimes when he wasn't but only thinking about her, it felt as though he had hives.

Earlier tonight he'd found himself scratching his arm even though the itch was lower down. Sure wasn't going to use his wife to sooth that yearning, though.

The trouble was that he feared Melinda was the only one who would be able to take away this bodily craving.

He stared across the yard at the barn where Melinda was sleeping, tapped his boot on the porch.

Hell's curses, even if he did indulge, the itch wouldn't go away. He knew that as well as he knew that the wind blowing at him was cold and wet.

He could not have a taste of Melinda then expect to just ride off.

The old Boone would have done it. Kiss a woman goodbye then scarcely remember her name, if he ever knew it to begin with.

That's the Boone he stood face-to-face with now, as if the two parts of him were duelists in the street at high noon.

The old Boone lying with Melinda in a tangle of straw and hot limbs. The new Boone sitting on this cursed porch in the rain, respecting the hell out of her.

Right now he didn't know which man he was. If Melinda came to him, hot and reckless, he didn't know what he would—

Hell's damn curses! She was coming to him, trudging through the rain from the barn, a steaming mug of something in each of her small hands.

Might as well have stayed in the barn for all the good his self-imposed isolation was doing.

He'd better outdraw the old Boone if the new one was to have a chance.

From halfway across the yard all Melinda could see of Boone were his eyes peeking out from between the oilcloth and his dipped hat.

Rain obscured her vision, but even through it she could tell that he was troubled. And who would not be, sitting for hours on the front porch bench with only the biting rain for company?

Hot coffee ought to help, especially if he intended to sit out here all night.

"Boone." She came up the steps under the shelter of an umbrella gripped awkwardly between her arm and ribs. Steam curled comfortingly out of the mugs she held. Hopefully the sight would help warm him. "I think you're turning blue."

"What are you doing out here? It's the middle of the blamed night." He didn't seem as pleased to see her as she had hoped he would. "You shivering, gal?"

Gal? Was that an endearment? She thought not, unless it was an endearment laced with annoyance. Although, how someone could be annoyed with another person who was delivering hot coffee in the wee hours of a watch was hard to imagine.

"I couldn't sleep. It didn't seem right, you alone out here watching over us all while we snuggle under our blankets. I thought something hot would help."

He lifted one side of the oilcloth in invitation, but he seemed reluctant about doing it.

Maybe he was simply chilled and grumpy, because who would not be? Surely once the coffee heated him, he'd be glad she'd come out.

Letting the umbrella fall, she ducked under the oilcloth. She scooted close to Boone while he tucked the covering under her hip and behind her shoulders.

Under the waterproof covering, she passed him one of the mugs then cradled the other close to her chest.

Boone was right, she had been shivering. Not so much now, not with the warmth of the coffee building, not with the heat of their bodies filling the space.

Truthfully, here under the oilcloth, she felt warmer than she had felt alone in the straw bed.

"Thank you," Boone said.

Good, then, it had been the cold making him ill tempered. She would happily sit here with him until dawn to see the smile that just transformed his face.

"I've been thinking about you." He sipped his coffee then tucked the mug back under the oilcloth.

In what way? She hardly knew what to feel about that. Was he thinking about the fact that they had nearly kissed? Was he happy about it? Was he unhappy about it? Did he want to try it again or did he regret it? If he did regret it was it because he saw her as fluff and no substance? Did he feel—?

"What is it that makes you strain at rules?"

"What makes you strain at them?"

"I asked you first—but I reckon in my case I was born with a bit of a hellion in me. I doubt if that's the case with you."

He wanted to know things about her that only Rebecca knew. Not even Mama understood why she chafed at unreasonable limitations. And Mama was at the core of them.

"No, Boone, I wasn't born this way. I was born Papa's 'pretty little doll baby'. All I wanted was to toddle about after him and make him happy like Mama did."

She leaned against Boone's arm, rested her head against his shoulder and stared out at the rain.

Most of the time she didn't think about the night that everything had changed. She certainly didn't dwell on it. But her husband wanted to know and she supposed he had a right to.

"Mama used to laugh. When I was tiny, she liked to kick up her heels, sing and dance even when folks thought it was inappropriate. One time she even visited an unwed pregnant mother who was shunned by everyone. Mama felt sorry for the young woman and invited her home. She shared tea with her on the front porch where everyone could see. They laughed out loud and spent the afternoon stitching baby clothes. As young as I was, I do remember the neighbors walking by scowling at Mama and, for the world, I did not know why."

In those days Mama had been like a songbird. So bright and happy, making other mamas look dull by comparison.

"You take after your ma?"

"I did, once upon a time. There was nothing I wanted more than to be bright and shining like Mama."

She couldn't speak for a moment. The sound of rain pattered all around and she thought of how much this night was like that other one.

"Then one night Mama quit being bright and shining.

"Papa went out after midnight, it was raining—freezing cold like it is now. I didn't know until later that he was leaving us for another woman, another family. The woman he went off with was the one Mama had befriended. Her child was Papa's."

"Well, hell. I'm sorry, honey."

"The thing is, they died that night. The bridge was icy and the buggy went over."

The memory of that long-ago night still had the power to constrict her throat with emotion. She washed down the lump in her throat with a gulp of coffee.

"My handsome, wonderful Papa was gone just like that. He said he would love me forever, but I was only four and he was gone because he loved his unborn child more than he loved me.

"I was so sick. I couldn't eat or sleep. My grieving made Mama angry. She wasn't the mother I remembered anymore. She was sullen, angry and judgmental. One day I shouted that I wanted my old mama back. Well, she—" Melinda needed more coffee because that blamed lump would not go away. How could it be so hard to talk about something that had happened so very long ago? "She sat the three of us girls down and made it clear that it was Papa's own fault that he had died and she did not want one more tear shed over him. As young as we were, Mama made sure we understood. My little sister didn't—how could she really?—but my older sister and I, we took it hard. Papa was our hero."

"That's a hard thing for anyone, especially a small girl."

"Yes, but harder for Mama. She became the subject of gossip—of jokes, even, for a long time. She became a woman none of us knew. She was stern and overly strict in an attempt to regain respectability. The smallest broken rule was a threat to that in her eyes."

She took a silent moment, gathering the past, putting it back where it belonged.

"You asked why I strain at rules. It was never about rebellion. It's because I wanted my mother back. I was looking for the one who laughed out loud and sang even louder. I hoped that she would miss the way we used to be and join me again. I was looking for my mother."

"You never found her again?"

"No, but in time Rebecca came and took her place. We became closer than sisters. Eventually we became allies in resistance to Mama's husband hunt."

"Seems it shouldn't have been a challenge for a woman like you to get one of your own choosing. Big town like that, men must have been after you like fish after a floundering fly."

"I wonder if you can understand how tiresome it was."

She closed her eyes. A crush of men's faces flashed through her mind. Not one of them stood out from another. "For my two sisters, the husband hunt was more than enough. But for me and Rebecca? Well, we wanted something else."

"Adventure?"

"That's part of it. We always did have a knack for finding that, but Mama called it mischief. Then, when Melinda went to Montana to find her grandfather, I missed her dreadfully. So, naturally, I left home to find her. And then I left Montana because—"

She nearly blurted out that she had been looking for the kind of man that Rebecca had found.

That is not the sort of thing one said to one's husband unless she was prepared to say that she had found it in him. And even though she had found it in him, she was not prepared to tell him so. Not until she felt he knew her, the woman, not the ideal.

"Because adventure is an alluring thing," she finished with a half-made-up response.

"I thought you left Montana to tell me about my family."

"That's absolutely true, and one cannot deny that it has been an adventure."

"Not sure that's what I'd call it. Adventure tends to be fun. Sitting in the rain, staring out at movements that you hope are nothing? That's just misery."

Said like that, so true. However, sitting close to Boone, feeling his warmth and sharing the dark, with the only sounds his voice and the drumming rain, she was content.

"It is beyond the everyday," she agreed with a smile.

"I will give you that." He smiled back and it gave her

heart a tickle. She could honestly say that no man had ever tickled her heart.

"I've learned to shoot a gun. That would never have happened in Kansas City. In fact, Mama might faint when she discovers I know how."

"If being the next Annie Oakley would make her faint, I wonder what would happen if she knew you'd married an outlaw."

She laughed because what else was there to do? "I am a good shot. Cans all over Jasper Springs are shivering in fear of me."

As suddenly as it had appeared, his smile fell away.

"It's easy to shoot a can." He groped for her hand, found it then squeezed and didn't let go. "Hope—no, pray—that you never have to shoot a man."

"I've thought about that possibility. Given our situation, how could I not?" She wondered if… "If it came down to one of us or one of them? Boone, I think I could do it."

"That's not a thing a person can know for sure." He squeezed her hand again, tighter, but not painfully. "The doc would freeze up. He doesn't have it in him to take a life. Smythe might do it, if he could aim worth a penny. And you? For all that you think you could take a life, reality is a whole lot different than what goes on in your mind."

"That may be true, but the Kings won't hesitate to kill one of us. I can't stand by and let them."

"No. I reckon you can't. Just pray it doesn't come to that. The man I shot, he was no good, but that one act marked me. Believe me, Melinda, you don't want to have the blank stare of someone you've killed looking up at you. It cuts your soul, brands you a killer. No matter the necessity, you've still done it."

Maybe so, but how could she watch someone she loved be cut down?

Boone didn't speak, neither did she. They watched the rain drip from the roof overhang. She supposed he was lost in private thoughts as much as she was.

"I'd kill for you, Boone."

She would not stand helplessly by while some evil soul did him harm. That's what would cut her soul.

Boone dropped the oilcloth from his shoulders, lifted his hand to cup her face. He stroked his thumb along her cheek while he looked into her eyes, seeming to judge; to weigh.

"I'd kill for you, too."

With two fingers under her chin, he lifted her face. Still searching her eyes, he must be seeing her soul.

He lowered his mouth, claiming a kiss. A penetrating kiss. His hand crept from her chin to the back of her neck. The earthy allure of him, the scent of his maleness, ricocheted from her lips to her belly to her toes.

She dropped her coffee mug, heard his hit the porch.

Wrapping her up in those big Viking-like arms, he pulled her to him. Chest to chest, heart to heart, he kissed her until she couldn't breathe, didn't care if she ever did again as long as he went on holding her.

But he didn't go on holding her. He broke the kiss and, setting her away from him, stared into the curtain of rain.

"Forgive me." Even from profile, his expression looked grim. "I shouldn't have done that. In the morning you will move back into the house, share a room with Mrs.—"

Without warning he stood and snatched up his rifle. He whipped her behind him.

"Riders coming. Stay behind me."

Chapter Ten

Two horses halted at the edge of the yard. Judging by their heaving sides and the white mist huffing from their noses, they had been ridden hard.

"Hello the house!" one of the riders called.

"That's a woman," Rebecca said. Boone felt her step forward and shot out his arm to stop her.

"Stay put."

"But—"

"Don't argue." He felt impatience begin to simmer but stuffed the emotion down. There was only so much a man could deal with at one time.

"But it's—"

"Later."

"Please lower your gun, Mr. Walker. It's Trudy and Edward Spears."

"Have you been followed?" He kept his rifle at the ready in case things were not what they seemed.

"I doubt it." Edward Spears spoke up. "It's why we've come at this time of night, to reduce the odds."

Boone lowered the weapon but slashed a backward glance, reminding Melinda to remain behind him. Surprisingly, she did. She didn't like it. He could feel her resentment clean through his coat.

With his short temper and Melinda's pique ignited, it ought to be an interesting night in the loft. Clearly his prudent plan of having her sleep in the house had just been ruined by the arrival of newcomers.

Boone came out from under the shelter of the porch, crossing the yard in long, mud-sucking strides. He opened the big barn door to let the horses and riders enter.

"May I come out from behind you now?"

His wife sounded overly compliant. Yep, this was going to be a very long night.

"Thank you for opening to us," said Trudy. Poor woman looked like a rat that had got dumped in a river. "We had no place else to go."

They wouldn't, of course. He had wondered what they would do now that they had lost everything in the fire that had taken not only their store but their home, too.

"Welcome!" Melinda wrapped Trudy in a hug, not seeming to be bothered that her own clean clothes were getting wet and muddy. "Come along, Miss Spears. I'll find something dry for you to put on."

Miss Trudy climbed the ladder, shoulders bent and looking weary, defeated to the bone.

Melinda rummaged through her trunk, which she kept stored at the foot of the ladder.

"This should do nicely," she murmured, tucking the dress under her arm. She climbed up after Miss Spears.

Moments later the women came down.

The gown Melinda had selected was a pretty cream-hued thing that was five inches too short on Trudy. The sleeves didn't reach her wrists and the bodice was not filled out.

But dry was dry and the young woman was smiling. In fact, she twirled around, laughing as the lace and ruffles fluttered at her shins.

"I've never worn anything so sweet!"

Melinda grinned and clapped her hands. "It looks lovely on you, Trudy. You must keep it."

"Oh, I couldn't." She wanted to. A blind man would be able to see how much she did.

"It would be a crime if you didn't. Really, it was made for you."

Would Trudy believe that? How could she when the dress was too small?

He didn't understand women. The pair of them were hugging and laughing as though the fit of the gown didn't mean a thing.

When he turned to Edward Spears with a shrug, he saw that the man was looking at his daughter with moisture standing in his eyes.

Oh. The fit of the gown didn't mean a thing. He saw that now.

Melinda had not given Trudy a cast-off dress, but a fine one, maybe her best. But what she had really given her was the first step toward a new start.

Who was his lovely wife, really? She was kind; he'd never met a better person. She had an intuition that allowed her to see another's need and to meet it with a generous heart. And yet she had just vowed she would kill to protect him. Would she be able to cross that line? He couldn't imagine it.

Hell, his plan for the newcomers had been to meet

their basic needs. To question them and then see them dry and secure.

But Melinda had given so much more.

If he meant to be a better man, it wouldn't hurt him to learn a lesson from his generous wife.

Boone had an extra shirt and pants that Mathers had sent along. They'd be miles too big for Spears, but he offered, anyway.

When the refugees were dry, sitting on hay bales in ill-fitting clothing and holding hot coffee, with the deputy resting his head on Melinda's feet and his tail on Boone's boots, Spears was ready to tell his story.

"After you saved my life, and I have no way of ever thanking you for that, I knew the Kings wouldn't be well pleased. So Trudy and I hid in the brush beside the gully near the bank.

"Efrin King was yelling orders about how no one better give us shelter. Made an edict that anyone trying to leave town would be shot on the spot and left for the birds to feed off of. Buck was so mad at being out in the rain that he was ready to shoot anyone. Didn't matter if they were trying to leave or shaking in their parlors.

"Then there was the issue of Bird King having gone missing. Leland went from house to house, thinking someone must have him. Every place he went into, he shot off his gun. Sounded like he broke something each time. Windows, chairs, probably wedding china, too. From the way the women cried out, so dismayed-sounding, that's what I'm guessing. They never did find Bird."

"They won't," Boone said. "He's on the other side of that wall, in the tack shed."

"Dead?" It was hard to mistake the hope in Edward's expression.

With Boone's reputation, it was understandable that Spears would think that he'd killed him—probably in cold blood.

Boone shook his head. "Arm's broken, though."

"I reckon that will have to do for now."

Apparently, Spears expected him to murder Bird at some point.

All of a sudden Melinda slipped her hand into his. It felt as if his heart stopped dead in his chest. How could it be that he had married the only person in the world who understood what was inside him, that he didn't have it in him to kill again?

She knew he had committed that crime and others, yet here she sat, squeezing his hand, supporting him.

How could a man do anything but love her? No, not just "a man." How could he, her husband, do anything but love her?

"I was so terrified hiding behind the saloon," Trudy said. The conversation had gone on without him being aware. "Every time Lump called my name I was nearly sick. He was hunting me. I couldn't look but his voice kept getting closer. It felt like he had nothing on his mind but finding me."

No doubt, assaulting Trudy Spears had been his single intention.

"You're safe here, Miss Spears," he said. "There's not much space in the house, but you and your father are welcome to stay. For tonight there's a bed in the loft, the two of you can sleep up there."

"With all I already owe you, I wouldn't put you out

of your bed," Edward said. "But my Trudy, she's nearly dead on her feet."

In spite of the fact that she had recently twirled around in her new dress, Boone figured it had to be true. Just yesterday the poor girl had nearly seen her father burned to death and been pursued by a monster through it all.

"My wife and I will be comfortable down here," he said.

Even though they all knew it wasn't the exact truth, they nodded and smiled as though it were.

After the Spearses climbed the ladder, Melinda leaned her head on his shoulder, crossed one slender arm over is chest and hugged him.

"I'm proud of you," she murmured.

"Can't think of why you should be," he answered, barely above a whisper. "Here, lay your head on my lap. Sleep if you can."

She kissed his cheek. This gesture never failed to disarm him. Then she curled up on the straw bale and lay her head on his lap. Nuzzling her cheek against him, she settled in.

It couldn't have been more than a few seconds before her breathing changed and he knew she was asleep.

One by one he loosened the pins from her hair. He spread the sunshine mass over her shoulders, down her back, to help keep her warm.

Rain drummed hard on the barn roof.

He touched her back, stroking his fingers through the tresses, feeling at peace.

But not completely.

With his free hand, he picked up the rifle and listened for sounds beyond the rain.

* * *

Seven adults, one infant and a huge canine gathered for dinner in the parlor because the kitchen was too small.

Dr. Brown was not happy about Billbro sharing the space, but as far as Melinda was concerned, he deserved the comforts of home and family as much as the rest of them did.

Stanley sat on the floor near the fireplace, his plate balanced on his lap. Trudy sat on the couch casting side-long glances at him.

That was interesting given that they had spent two hours this afternoon in close company, carrying bucket after bucket of water from the creek to fill the two large barrels on the back porch.

Stanley peered up at Trudy then quickly away. Boone, sitting on the floor near Stanley, didn't appear to notice. No, and neither did Edward Spears who was focused on his meal.

But Melinda knew a budding romance when she saw one. Sitting on the couch beside Mrs. Coulter, Melinda nudged the woman with her elbow. The new mother glanced up with a smile, but really, the only love she recognized was the one she shared with her infant.

All of a sudden Melinda missed Becca dreadfully. Her cousin would have recognized the nudge immediately. They would have shared a glance, acknowledged the unspoken secret, then set about further matchmaking.

She could only admit, glancing around the congested room, she felt a bit lonely. There was not a person here who truly knew her, had shared her past, beyond the past several days, that is.

There was a bond growing between her and Boone, but it was still new, so fragile that she didn't know what would become of it.

If only Becca were here, Melinda would feel more confident. Hard times were coming, trials that she prayed she would find the pluck and the cleverness to overcome.

Food would soon be scarce, for one thing. In the beginning they had planned for only the three of them. With all those they were sheltering, their supplies would soon run out.

Then what? A trip to the mercantile was out of the question. The Kings had burned it down.

One could only wonder what the folks in town would do for food.

"I wonder," she murmured, tapping her finger on her chin to concentrate.

"Wonder what?" Boone asked, glancing away from Edward in the middle of a conversation.

"Well, I wonder how much food the Kings have set aside. When they destroyed the store, did they think of that?"

"Indeed they did." Edward nodded, his expression grim. "While Buck was tying me up, the others were carrying out cans and dry goods. They laughed about bringing the town to its knees. In case we haven't been there for two years already. From what they were saying they were going to take what the butcher had. The baker, too."

There was silence for the space of sixty seconds. No doubt everyone was as perplexed as she was about what was to be done.

"Here on the ranch, we'll get by," Boone said. "There's game on the property. The dog and I will hunt."

"We're more fortunate than the folks in town." Stanley shook his head. "If they go beyond town limits, they'll be killed."

"Thank you for taking all of us in, Mr. Walker, Mrs. Walker," Mrs. Coulter said. "I realize we are a drain on the resources you have."

What was her given name? Melinda wondered. After helping deliver Diana, she figured she ought to know.

"Of course you are welcome here. Little Diana is a delight to us all. And, please, do call me Melinda?"

"I—yes... Won't you call me Giselle?" she asked after a hesitation.

But that silent space of time said more than words. Clearly, she wasn't comfortable being on a first-name basis with an outlaw's wife.

Melinda glanced at Boone, hoping that he hadn't read the same thing into the gap. Whenever someone showed contempt for him, it broke her heart. Then it made her bristle.

His gaze back at her was clouded, troubled-looking. He might as well have told her out loud that, even if he did care for her, he would not remain married to her. In that regretful gaze he communicated that he would never saddle her with a lifetime of that sort of rejection.

Well, by sugar, one had to actually mount a saddle before it could take her anywhere.

"There's something that you all need to know," she said. "None of you ought to feel that you are putting Boone and me out of our house because this isn't our house. It belongs to the town of Buffalo Bend. We are only here until my husband captures the King family and hands them over to the law." Really there was no need for them to know what Stanley already did, that she and Boone had agreed to a temporary marriage.

"He's doing it because Judge Mathers offered him his freedom in exchange."

"As Mr. Walker's lawyer, I argued against the bargain," Stanley stated. "Boone ought to have been a free man on the merit of his wrong conviction. But here we are."

"Yes, here we are." She glanced again at Boone. He didn't seem happy to have everyone in on his secret, but Giselle's attitude had been undeserved and she meant to make things clear to them all. "You might think that rounding up these criminals will be an easy thing, given my husband's past as you understand it, but you are wrong. Boone is not the killer that he has been portrayed to be."

She had to stand up because she was suddenly feeling too hot for her clothes. "He only killed one man. A man who, I might say, had it coming. Imagine challenging a child to a gunfight! You can't, naturally. It's beyond imagining. That villain might have been the slower shot, but in the end he took Boone's innocence and his future. I, for one, intend to help my husband get it back."

Stanley stood beside her but didn't speak. From the beginning, the lawyer had been the first to take Boone's side.

Shoulder to shoulder with Stanley, sharing this bond, all of a sudden she didn't feel nearly as alone.

Trudy cleared her throat. "Thank you, Mr. Walker. My father and I owe you even more than we thought we did."

"As do I." The doctor nodded his head, his thick dark hair catching the firelight.

"I've wrongly judged you." Giselle hugged her baby close. "May I call you Boone?"

He nodded, but given the expression on his face, he ought to be called Mr. Curmudgeon.

No doubt he thought she'd overstepped, but it seemed the wifely thing to do, and it felt rather nice.

Coming out of the house, Boone had no choice but to tuck Melinda inside his oversize coat with him.

He shouldn't be that close to her since he wanted to shake her, but the wind was whipping cold and she had given her own coat to Giselle.

There couldn't be much left in her trunk, having given some of her clothes to Trudy and some to the destitute young mother.

"I can't help but notice that you are cranky," she muttered.

"Cranky as hell." All with good reason.

"They needed to know the truth."

"Not from you." Only steps away from the barn, he kept his gaze trained on the light that spilled into the night from under the door.

"Yes from me! I'm your wife and they were thinking things about you that—"

He gripped her shoulders, pinned her against the barn wall. "You are not my wife!"

She arched a delicately shaped brow. "I am the woman who has a signed certificate of marriage. I'm also addressed as Mrs. Walker. I am the woman who has shared the loft with you, whose bosom you have slept upon."

She curled up her fists and pressed them against his chest. "That makes you my husband."

"Not the one you deserve. I'm—"

"Mine."

"No."

But he was hers. Whether he ought to be or not didn't change the reality.

Oh, hell. He cupped her cheeks in his hands then came down upon her lips, kissing them hard. Then he gripped the collar of her blouse, pulled the buttons until they popped open.

His hands were chilly. He knew it but he shoved them under her camisole anyway. He petted, squeezed. He nibbled the flower-scented skin of her throat and then kissed her mouth again, tasting her deeply, intimately.

His mind roared, silently begging her to stop him, to push his cold hands, his ruined soul, away.

All she did was thump her head back against the wall, close her eyes and sigh.

This was wrong, he was wrong—his anger, his passion, he knew it was all wrong. But somehow in spite of what he knew, delving into her seemed right. It went to show how bad his judgment had always been, would always be.

His exploding feelings for this woman couldn't possibly be honorable.

He ripped away from the kiss. Breathing hard, he dropped his hands from her chest, felt bereft.

"Melinda, I cannot be the man you need."

She stepped out from under his arms where his hands fisted on the barn wall.

Wind caught her dress and blew it. She tugged the bodice together then opened the barn door.

He followed her inside, feeling miserable to his core.

She dashed for the ladder. Halfway up, she turned.

"I fear that you already are."

Her voice carried to him, a whisper among the shuffling of horse's hooves.

Hell, if he didn't fear the same thing. But it didn't change the fact that he could not continue forever as her husband.

Boone was right, of course. Just because she wanted the others to know the truth about him, and he was not going to tell it, did not mean that it was her right to expose it.

Perhaps if she were the wife of his heart, she would have that right. But she was not and, given what he had said an hour ago, she would not be.

Had she not pointed out that he had slept upon her bosom, perhaps he would be up here in the loft and not on the barn floor where it was hard and cold.

Of them all, he was the one who most needed rest. He was also the one getting the least of it.

She felt miserably guilty about that. What would happen if she tried to charm him into coming up here?

One never knew until one tried.

Rolling off the straw bed, she crept on hands and knees to the edge of the loft then peered down.

Boone, his head reclining on Billbro as though the animal were a hairy pillow, stared up at her through the dim light.

"Boone Walker," she said in her sweetest inflection

with her most winning smile. "You've simply got to come up to bed. You'll catch a chill down there."

Drat! Without as much as a blink did he show any indication that she had swayed him. Gentle persuasion was her gift, as Rebecca's was the violin and Lantree's was healing.

Just now, when she needed her skill the most, she realized what a silly one it really was.

Still… "It's ever so cold and lonely down there." She offered a sweet pout and when that didn't work she added a winking dimple. She had yet to see the man who could hold his own against a feminine dimple.

"What are you doing, Melinda?"

"It's what I'm not doing that concerns me." And fascinated her. Even from the beginning she had not been able to charm him.

The fact that he looked past all that trickery made the butterflies in her belly awaken and flutter madly.

She let her smile fade, to be replaced with the frown she was really feeling.

"That's more like it," he said. "Now, what is it that can't keep until a decent hour?"

"Why do you think the Kings took all the food?" she asked, settling onto her belly and gazing down at him with her chin cupped in her palms. Truly, that puzzle was one of the things keeping her awake.

"I reckon they'll use it for bargaining. As a way to keep folks under their control."

"They will make demands." She ought to have thought of that. "Yes, and one of them will be Bird. They'll want him released."

"I reckon so."

"We'll need our wits about us. More than ever."

"Not 'we.' I want you as far away from the danger as possible, Melinda. I said I would deliver you safely home to Montana. My word hasn't meant much in the past, but I mean this."

"I trust that you will. I have from the beginning." She steepled her fingers under her chin, gazing down. "The thing is…you didn't sleep last night. You'll be better prepared to meet our enemies if you get some rest."

Boone sat up, ruffled Billbro's fur and got a lick on the hand in thanks.

He stood, stretched then climbed the ladder. Within seconds of lying on the hay bed, with hands clasped behind his head, his eyes dipped closed. But they blinked open a second later. Fatigue shadowed his expression.

This worried her because if he wasn't alert, their enemies might seize the advantage.

"I'll sit over here by the window." She really did want him to sleep and thought he might not if he was worried about—well, clearly things could easily get out of hand between them.

He shook his head, reached one arm toward her and crooked his finger in invitation.

Now she was confused. What did he want of her?

Probably the same thing she wanted of him, or perhaps only warmth and comfort.

But since it was cold and his big, bold body would be warm, she lay down. When he tugged her in with his arm, she scooted back against him.

"I'm glad I failed to charm you," she murmured but doubted that he was awake. His breathing felt slow and even against her back. "Maybe you see me."

"I see you, and you do charm me."

A second later she heard a quiet snore.

Chapter Eleven

Startled, Boone woke from a deep sleep. At first he thought it was due to a sudden noise. But, no, it was because he had reached for Melinda and embraced cold, empty space.

Sunlight streamed through the loft window. He'd overslept. He never overslept.

Probably because he never slept deeply to begin with. That's what came of living life on the run.

While he was no longer on the run, he faced more danger than he ever had. At least in the past the danger had only been to him. Now he carried the safety of several folks on his shoulders.

He sat up, rubbed his hand over his beard stubble, trying to wrap his mind around it. One day he had been paying his debt to society, responsible for nothing, then the next he had the care of a wife and a tenderfoot lawyer. And now five others, one of them an infant.

Coming down the ladder he stopped at the mirror, splashed icy water on his face from the bowl Melinda had placed under it.

The slap of water braced him, made him appear

alert—or maybe that look came from a sound night's sleep.

A night's sleep that he suspected he owed to his wife. What was it about her that, as delicate as she was, put him at ease?

That was a question he could puzzle over forever.

Closing the barn door behind him, he jogged across the yard. For now it was enough of a puzzle to figure out what to do about the folks in town running out of food.

Coming in through the kitchen door, Boone found Trudy grilling a slab of ham. It smelled good enough to make his mouth water.

Melinda, standing in profile, stirred up something in a bowl. Watching the slender curve of her back, the circular action of her arm and the way it made the swell of her breast jiggle—well, it made his mouth water all the more. Even his stomach growled.

The rumble made Melinda look up. A blush spreading across her cheeks made him think that while she spooned around whatever was in the bowl, she'd been thinking about what had happened against the barn wall last night.

Hot blazes, he couldn't get that moment out of his mind, either. There was no way he was going to forget the sound she had made when he'd touched her.

Lucky thing he wasn't prone to blushing since Trudy was looking at him. If he and Melinda had both been blushing she would have figured something intimate was going on between them.

And why not assume it, since in the natural way of things it would be true.

But they did not have a marriage in the natural way. He had a dirty past. He was not half good enough for his lovely, high-spirited bride. Even if he was twice as good a man as he was, he would fall short of deserving her.

"Smells good in here, ladies," Smythe announced, entering the kitchen with a wide grin on his face.

Even though the lawyer greeted them both, he was gazing at Trudy alone.

Boone squinted to make sure he was seeing right.

Yep, the lawyer looked smitten.

Now, that was something to smile about.

Melinda must have noticed his grin. She winked at him then nodded toward Stanley.

When Trudy and Stanley seemed caught up in private conversation, Boone sidled over to Melinda, bent his head to hers.

"Looks like we've got a secret to keep," he murmured.

For some reason Melinda lit up, her eyes all atwinkle.

"Thank you, Boone."

"For what?"

"It's just that this sort of thing is something I share with Rebecca. Being so close, we know each other's minds. We can look at each other and know things. I've missed it. I'd like to think I have that bond with you."

He sucked in a breath, hit by the intimacy of the sort of sharing that went beyond a physical touch. He'd never had it with anyone. All of a sudden he wanted this spiritual connection, the bond that time and distance would not diminish.

Reckoned he'd had it at one time with his brother, but this, with his wife—he guessed that was why it was called the holy bond of matrimony.

If things were different, he'd kiss Melinda, now in front of Edward and the doc who were just now following their noses to breakfast. He'd proclaim that bond.

But he wasn't worthy, and everyone would know it. If, somehow, he managed to capture the King gang, and do it without undue bloodshed, maybe then—but that was a big maybe.

Better if he kissed her forehead, just friendly-like.

That was a link they could share. Friends.

Still, just now, looking at how Smythe and Trudy were gazing at each other as if the world and its troubles were far from them...hell, he wanted that.

"Anyone dream up a way of getting food to the folks in Jasper Springs?" The doc pulled out a chair and sat at the table. Edward followed him.

Melinda poured what Boone thought to be corn-bread fixings into a pan then slid it into the stove.

"It ought to be a raid," Edward said, seeming oblivious to the goings on between his daughter and her beau. "They raided me and I want my goods back. My customers, they're suffering."

Sounded fair enough, but Melinda was the only dependable shot among them. She was also the last person he was going to allow near the King ranch.

"As right as that sounds," he said. "I can't see how it would be successful."

"You must know a way," the doc said. "Meaning no disrespect, but of us all, you've the most experience at... at expropriation."

"Thievery, you mean." No disrespect, but a kick to the gut none the less.

A kick that didn't hurt him as much as it appeared to hurt Melinda. She curled one closed fist against her belly as though she had been struck.

Right there was the reason he could not remain married to her. Suspicion would follow him all of his life, assuming he lived through the process of gaining his freedom. No matter where he went tabloid stories would make up lies about him.

"Given my experience, I say it won't work." It was the truth. "The Kings, every last one of them, would need to be away. And even then there would be others at the ranch who would fight us."

"All I know is that we can't let—" Edward was interrupted by an urgent knock on the door.

Boone opened up. A boy bolted across the yard toward a horse whose reins had been left dangling in the dirt.

Something blew across the porch. Boone stomped on it then picked it up. He held an envelope made of the finest paper he'd ever touched. Fit for royalty no doubt.

"Hell's curses," he muttered when he opened the damned thing up.

Melinda plucked it from his hand and read out loud. "'You are hereby summoned to meet with King Cobra at the Jasper Springs saloon at high noon this day, October twenty-seventh, to discuss a matter of great benefit to you.'"

There was a postscript. If Boone failed to show, the butcher would lose his right hand.

"I'm worried about those Kings. What's to say they haven't set us up in a trap?" Trudy dried a pot with a dishcloth then set it on a shelf. "And lured Boone away in order to leave us defenseless?"

A valid fear; one that had been discussed up and down, left, right and in circles. In the end, the butcher's hand was deemed worth the risk.

"We aren't exactly helpless. The men are on guard."

Melinda would feel a good bit more comfortable if any of them could shoot. She stooped to tuck a shawl blanket around Diana who slept sweetly in her little crate bed. "We'll be safe."

Somewhat safe, at any rate.

"I'm taking Bird his lunch." She stood, lifted the plate from the table that Trudy had prepared.

"Be careful," she advised, her pretty freckled face looking downcast. "You have a weapon?"

Melinda nodded. She had the pistol that Boone insisted she carry in her skirt pocket.

In her opinion, it might not be wise to go into the small shed with it drawn. It wouldn't do to have Bird wrest it from her.

Melinda carried the plate of food down the porch steps.

She glanced at the sky, judging the time. Noon sun hit the earth without warmth.

Boone ought to be walking into the saloon about now. She could see him in her mind. He would open the door, walk inside, his hand within easy reach of his weapon. She saw the grim set of his mouth, how his eyes would be narrowed and his expression razor-edged. As clearly as if she were there, she heard the slap of his boot heels walking across the floor.

After that she refused to see anything because Boone was alone, facing murderers whose lives would be simpler if he were dead.

She took a breath and pulled her shoulders back to better focus on the job at hand. Acting weak and fearful would do no one any good.

Delivering the young criminal's meal without a chaperone made her feel uneasy. It didn't matter that he was somewhat weakened by his broken arm and that his ankle was bound to the wall by a short tether, the Vulture was a threat. She would treat him as such.

She would open the door and shove the plate toward him with the toe of her boot, that way she would never even have to step inside the shed.

"Maybe I'll shoot you between the eyes—or...or maybe in the gut. Let you suffer like my husband, like he—"

Giselle! Her voice, catching on a sob, had come from inside the shed.

On the run, Melinda heard Giselle scream then Bird laugh.

Her first thought was to dump the food and grab the gun. But there was already one too many weapons in the small space. Besides, Bird was young. Many a boy was ruled by his stomach. Lunch might be her best weapon.

On the other hand, the thing to remember about this boy was that he was not an unsullied innocent. Handling him as she would other men would not suit, no more than the weapon hidden in her skirt would.

Shouting for the men's help would be the worst thing she could do. As soon as Bird heard the commotion, he would shoot Giselle.

She and Rebecca had acted their way out of many unfortunate predicaments. But this? This was life-threatening. There was every chance that her skills were not equal to this situation. But what else was she to do?

With her hand trembling on the door latch, she reminded herself that she was Mrs. Boone Walker. Wife of the most violent of them all, the worst of the worst.

Even though he was not here, his reputation was.

She opened the door, a frown of censure on her face.

"Young man, I suggest you set that gun down beside you." She indicated a spot beside him with a jerk of the lunch plate.

He had shoved the pistol against Giselle's temple, his free leg wrapped around her middle.

"Can't rightly blow her brains out if I do."

Melinda shrugged her shoulders then sat beside him. She fluffed her skirt as though his murderous intentions did not concern her in the least.

Setting the lunch plate on her lap, she made a show of smelling the delicious aroma while her heart raced and her stomach heaved.

"A boy like you must be hungry all the time. Wouldn't you like to eat?"

"Soon as I'm finished with this." He traced the barrel of the gun along Giselle's jaw, flicked away the tear hanging from her chin.

"Oh, my." Melinda tilted her head, frowned severely. "Perhaps you haven't seen what happens when a head explodes. I have. Many times in fact. Although I've never seen blood and brains on top of anyone's dinner before. I imagine it's quite a gory gravy."

Bird's mouth sagged open.

Giselle cried out but there was nothing to be done about her distress at the moment.

"I recall a time when Mr. Walker wanted to shoot someone at the dinner table but I wouldn't allow it. In the end, he dragged the fellow out back of the house and then shot his head off.

"Of course, Boone's shirt was smattered with all sorts of ugliness so I made him change it before we ate. Oh, I just realized that you don't have a change of clothing."

By the looks of him, he took pride in his appearance.

His garments must have been of the best quality. Well cared for until Boone had ripped his shirt in the process of breaking his arm.

"I imagine if it means so much to you to shoot Giselle, you ought to strip down first. But don't expect me to look away in maidenly modesty. Nor Giselle, since she has been without the male form ever since you Kings murdered her husband. But, all things considered, you aren't much to look at yet, not like Mr. Coulson was.

"Now, now, no need to look so cross. It's the truth. Really, what you ought to be thinking of is what you will eat. If you ruin this meal, there won't be another until afternoon three days from now since we will all be grieving for Giselle and trying to deal with her hungry infant. No one will have the heart to feed you. Surely you understand."

"What I understand is I'm going to shoot her then you, just so you'll quit your yapping."

He would; she had no doubt of it. Sweet-talking a coiled rattler would be less terrifying.

"Boone did that once. A boy about your age was bedeviling him with his bleating. It was understandable considering that my husband was about to shoot his dog. Of course I felt bad about the dog, but I never said anything because he would have shot the cat, too. In the end he didn't shoot the cat. We brought it with us but I was nearly sorry we did. It was a job, I will tell you, washing the boy's blood off its fur."

"You're full of stories, lady. All of them lies."

"Not all of them. I've seen quite a lot in my time with Boone. Last night over dessert he told everyone the story of the time he drowned a man in the river just to use him as fish bait. Poor Giselle looked as white as the dead man."

"I never puked so hard in my life," Giselle said, apparently gathering the presence of mind to go along with the grisly tale.

The gun sagged. "The two of you are making that up."

"I half wish I was making this one up, young man. But the truth is I was there. I stripped off my clothes and waded naked into the water to gather the fish feeding off the body."

"You lie," Bird said, but his eyes had grown round.

It was a relief to see the blood returning to Giselle's face. Perhaps she had hope that Melinda would be able to spin their way out of this.

"What about the time he robbed a bank and killed the seven customers inside?" Bird asked. "That one true? I read it in a dime novel."

"Now, that's just an insult. There were ten people. It was reported as seven because there were already three other robbers in the bank when my Boone came in. I suppose they didn't deserve counting, being worthless drifters.

"I'm half sick of speaking with you, Bird King. Giselle, are you prepared to die right now?"

"I reckon so, if there's no other way about it."

"So am I. Honestly, as Boone's wife, I've been expecting it for some time. But you, young man? Are you ready?"

"You should know that her husband is mad for her."

Melinda felt her respect for Giselle grow. Here she was only a trigger itch from being shot in the head and yet she managed to control her panic enough to build depth to the tall tale.

"He will be disconsolate," Melinda affirmed with a sigh. If her voice quavered he would merely think it was from sorrow. "Even I don't like Boone when he's disconsolate. My guess is that he won't kill you at once. Oh, and count on me and Giselle watching in ghostly form, cheering while he takes his time dispatching you. Surely you believe in ghosts? The stories I could tell about that! Boone has quite the menagerie following him.

"Well, anyway, he'll start with your fingers is my guess, snipping them off from pinky to thumb. That's what he did when someone accidentally ran over the cat with his wagon. As I recall those shears still have dried blood on them, but I reckon that will be a small worry to you. After that he'll likely snip off your not-even-fully-mature member. Have you even put it to proper use yet?" She glanced at his crotch and shook her head. "He'll probably send it home to your brothers tied up with a pink bow."

Finally the fool was beginning to turn pale. His hand shook. This would not do since he still had the gun directed at Giselle's temple.

"Of course, you still have a choice. Eat this delicious meal in somewhat clean clothing, or kill us then sit here hungry and wondering what my husband will do to avenge us. The choice is completely yours."

Indecision clouded his expression.

Lightly, Giselle touched the barrel of the pistol, curled her fingers around it and moved it away from her face.

Bird yanked it back. Cussing, he stared into Giselle's face. Without a doubt, he was half a second away from pulling the trigger.

But he was distracted. Boone had warned her about hesitation and she saw it in Bird.

In the second he took to gloat about his power over Giselle, enjoy his kill, Melinda snatched the gun from her skirt pocket.

She shoved it hard at Bird's temple. The thought of pulling the trigger flipped her stomach. Even so, she forced her hand not to tremble.

Startled, the kid's attention pivoted to her. In an instant of confusion, he loosened his grip on the gun.

Melinda snatched it away.

With both guns pointed at his chest, she tried to scramble beyond his reach but Bird was fast. He grabbed her skirt.

Luckily, Giselle was just as fast. She kicked Bird's arm, then hurried behind Melinda and the safety of the two weapons.

"If you're gonna tell him about this, might as well go ahead and shoot me quick, do me a favor."

She took a step backward, then another, her knees locked so they would not give out under her. Giselle grabbed her at the waist with both arms, her weight sagging against Melinda's back.

"Of course I'll tell him," she answered while pulling the door closed. "You can count on the same kindness that you and your family showed Mr. Coulter."

Outside, with the door bolted, Giselle slid down in a faint.

Melinda's knees gave way. Kneeling on the ground she bent over Giselle and vomited onto the dirt.

Jasper Springs looked as it had the first time Boone had seen it, except that the general store was an ash heap with a few blackened beams sticking out of the mess.

With the exception of the cheerful gurgle of the spring, town was silent. Everyone was holed up inside, probably too scared to stick their noses out the door.

A dog ran back and forth along a front yard fence, barking a greeting—or warning. A curtain from the window moved aside then fell instantly back into place.

When he approached the saloon, Boone decided it would be best to circle around it a time or two to determine whether the Kings were even inside.

If they were, he wouldn't risk walking into a trap. While the outlaws had demanded the meeting, he would determine the location.

Three passes in front of the open door and there was still no movement within the dim interior.

On the fourth pass, he reined the horse to a stop and waited. A chill skittered across his scalp. Could be a trap, after all—but for the folks back at the ranch.

He whirled the horse around, ready for a hell-bent race toward home.

Boot steps slammed the boardwalk. Buck King stepped out of the saloon.

"His Fartin' Majesty says you can approach his exalted presence now." Buck spewed a glob of spit over his shoulder, back through the door he had just come out of. "Says to dust off your boots first."

"If your brother wants a get-together, he can meet me at the spring. Not alone. I want you all there. Bring the butcher."

"You've got yourself some balls, I'll say that for you."

"My town, my rules."

Dismounting the horse, Boone led it toward the spring. He made sure not to look behind him even though it felt as though half a dozen stares were crawling on his back.

Wasn't sure whose they were. Outlaws after his blood or folks hiding behind curtains wondering what unholy mess was coming upon them next.

Sitting on a boulder at the spring, he dipped his Stetson in the cold water then let the horse drink from it. He was in the middle of his own refreshment when he heard footsteps crossing the dirt, coming from the direction of the saloon. Finishing his drink leisurely—deliberately—he guessed there were at least three men.

It wasn't until the boot falls stopped that he glanced up, water dribbling from his fingers and chin. He wiped his sleeve across his face.

"Where's Lump?"

Efrin led the procession. If the man had tail feathers they'd be splayed like a strutting peacock's. To the left of His Highness stood Buck. Boone wondered if a scowl was his singular expression. Flanking Efrin on the right was a man who could only be Leland.

"You'll kneel in the presence of your king," announced his royal idiocy.

"You always been crazy?" Boone asked, settling more comfortably on the rock.

"Just since puberty," Buck explained. "Before that he was just a mean cuss."

"Shut your disrespecting face!" Efrin roared, his royal dignity slipping.

What the sovereign didn't seem to notice was Buck's gun hand inching toward his holster then clenching in a tight fist.

"Please, Mr. Walker, ignore my brothers." Leland

strode forward, his hand extended in greeting. "They've always been a contentious lot."

Deliberately, Boone folded his arms across his chest. "You accosted my wife."

"Just a bit of friendly banter."

"Left a bruise."

"Such fair skin." Leland shrugged, withdrew his hand. "I beg the pardon of you both."

He didn't. Even though he spoke the words, the snicker in his eyes was unmistakable.

"Where's the butcher? If his hand isn't on the end of his arm I'll shoot you all where you stand."

"Fetch him, Buck," ordered Efrin.

Buck, his face flushing vivid red, spun on his older brother. "I'm done with you ordering me around!"

"Better fetch him." Boone arched a brow. "I reckon you've heard I'm a man of little patience."

Damned if Buck didn't growl like a cornered cougar while he stomped across the road to the saloon.

"I reckon there's a good reason you dragged me from my lunch?"

"I don't like your insolent tone. I insist that you stand while I speak."

Boone wondered how a lunatic could be the leader of this group, unless, as he suspected, they were all lunatics.

"That so?" He stood, paced off the distance between them. Efrin had to look up to make eye contact—way up. "Here's what I insist. Give back the food you took from my store."

"Who made it yours?"

Boone grabbed King by the shirtfront, lifted him to the toes of his glimmering boots.

"I did." He held the criminal, glowering gaze to glowering gaze.

The standoff ended only when the villain glanced away.

Boone set King back on his feet and yanked the lapels of the fancy coat back into place.

"Brought the butcher," Buck announced, shoving the man forward.

Any fool could see that his hands were bound too tight. His face was chalk white. No wonder he was trembling.

"Cut his bonds." Boone ground his teeth, felt the tick in his jaw. Boone Walker, the legend, surged within him. "Then bring the lecher."

"Maybe you got the balls to disturb him while he's—"

Boone drew his gun. It slid from his holster, a deadly hiss of metal across leather. He was every bit the fast draw that his reputation painted him to be.

"Go get him. When we're all together, tight and cozy, you'll tell me why you brought me here."

Power was the only law the Kings respected. If his wasn't more threatening than theirs, he might not ride out of here.

"Go home, sir," he said to the butcher in a kinder tone. "You'll keep your hand."

A moment later, after a long, tense silence, Buck came out of the saloon dragging his brother by the ear.

"We'll talk now," Boone said, his voice cold, in command. "I've already wasted the day on the four of you."

He assumed it was Bird's release that they wanted to discuss. It would be springtime in hell when that happened. He had one outlaw in custody and there he would stay.

"We'd like to allow you to join us," Efrin said. "Last time, you refused. This time you will not. You may sit while we discuss it."

Hell's curses.

Boone returned to his boulder because it was close to his horse. He jammed his gun back into the holster but kept his hand at the ready.

"We respect you, Mr. Walker," Leland said with a single nod of his head. "We're as alike as snakes twined in a pit."

He knew he ought to say something. There must be an intelligent thought still in his mind. Couldn't quite summon it, though.

"There's no need for us to be at odds." This from Efrin. "Rule this town with us."

"Already do." He picked up the horse's dangling reins, pretended to casually stroke the leather. Things here were not going to end well. He needed to be quick away. "Why would I share it with you?"

"For protection—why else?" This from Leland. "We offer safety—freedom of a sort."

"We'd be allies. With your talents, you'd have our backs, the same as we'd have yours. Safety in numbers," said Leland. "No more life on the run. We've got a fine, high life here."

Leland's smile looked as genuine as fool's gold.

Unless he missed his guess, Fancy Pants was counting on Boone's bounty to give him that high life.

But the reality was they hadn't said anything that wasn't the truth.

In many ways, he was like them. By hitching up, he would know what they were doing at all times. And he would gain a sort of freedom without having to risk his life or anyone else's.

Looked at in a certain way, the offer made sense because he would live a life he was accustomed to, a life of corruption.

No standards to live up to. No more struggle trying to be good enough, fearing that he didn't have it in him.

What the hell did he know about being respectable? About as much as the dung beetle crawling across his boot.

Mathers had given him a tweaked and tarnished badge. Went to show how much confidence he actually had in him doing the right thing.

A damaged symbol for a damaged soul.

Respect for law and order would not keep him from hitching up with the Kings. But there was something that would—or rather *someone*.

In this moment of temptation her lovely smile flashed in his mind. He would take a bullet in the brain before he would betray Melinda's trust.

Never once had she wavered in her belief of him.

If she was so dang certain that he had a future obeying the law, maybe he did. He'd never met a more clever person in his life, nor one more spirited.

The truth was he'd rather die on this very spot than see disappointment in her eyes. Disappointment that he put there.

Boone kicked the insect off his boot.

"You all haven't asked about your brother. I find it odd, being that alliances mean so all-fired much to you."

"Figured you had him," Buck said, finally letting go of Lump, who stared blankly around before lumbering single-mindedly toward the saloon and his interrupted pleasure.

"That being the case, we figured you'd already killed him." Leland folded his arms over his fancy coat. "Decided we'd forgive you for it when you become one of us. A life for a death, so to speak."

Boone calmly mounted his horse. In the guise of a casual attitude, he didn't draw his gun even though he figured he was going to need it.

He nodded in what would appear to be a friendly parting gesture. As though he meant to agree to the unholy merger.

A hundred feet down the road, he turned, rifle drawn from the saddle pack, cocked and ready to fire.

He settled his aim on Efrin's chest. It gave him pause to think of actually pulling the trigger, but folks lived with regrets. They were a part of life.

"Last I saw your brother he was alive," he called. "What you boys need to know is that I'm going to clear you out of Jasper Springs, hand you over to the law. This is my town. Surrender now or I'm taking you down, one by one or all together."

With that, he spun the horse around then doubletimed it down Main Street. The buzz of a bullet zinged past his ear.

What got his attention more than that was seeing the butcher standing in the doorway of his shop, a hesitant grin on his face, his hand raised in salute.

Chapter Twelve

The fact that he hadn't been followed didn't make Boone feel any easier.

Figuring that the Kings were doing the same thing that he was—planning an attack—made him feel twitchy in his gut.

When he galloped into the yard, Stanley was standing watch at the homestead door. He'd passed by Doc Brown and Edward doing the same a hundred yards back.

The lawyer waived, sauntered down the steps.

"There was trouble while you were gone. The women are upset—all of us are, but your wife was—"

Melinda and trouble? Boone didn't take the time to hear about it from Smythe, but took off running across the yard toward home—the barn, that is.

The lawyer had called Melinda Boone's wife. What the blazes?

Bursting through the door, he found her staring blankly at her reflection in the small square mirror.

She was pale, distress haunted her gaze.

"Melinda?" he called softly.

At the sound of his voice she suddenly turned.

"Boone!"

In a flurry of ruffles and lace, she flew into his arms.

Wrapping her up, he breathed in the scent of her hair, felt the silkiness of the strands fondle his cheek.

She clung to him, but no more than he did to her.

Somehow his sweet, spunky wife had become his sanctuary. When the ground was shifting at his feet, she was constant.

In the moment of his greatest weakness, of nearly irresistible temptation, she had called him back from a decision that would have damned his soul forever.

And all because she trusted him.

For a fact, his days of walking the outlaw road were over. He wouldn't take the easy way. Her confidence in him had made him a new man.

Didn't understand it, but it was real nonetheless.

Boone Walker, the depraved one, had surrendered— to a woman. A virtuous woman, no less.

He owed her everything—more than his life. That's why, when this ordeal was over, he would deliver her to Lantree and then go his way. It didn't matter how deeply he had come to care for her, that with his dying breath, whether it be tomorrow or when he was an old man, he would think of her. It only mattered that she lived a happy life.

To his shame, that is something he could not offer. Hell, he couldn't even offer financial support. The only way he knew of to make a living he'd just sworn off.

But all that was a problem for another time.

"Honey, you look shaken to the core."

When she nodded, her hair tickled his nose.

"Why?"

She glanced up, her blue eyes wide, shining with unshed tears.

"Well… I…" He'd never known her to be at a loss for words. Something about that broke his heart.

"Hold on." He swept her off her feet, carried her up the loft ladder.

It seemed right to go there because that is the spot where he had been comforted, his strength renewed. That small space was the closest thing he'd had to a home since he was a kid.

Didn't take much to know why. Melinda made it so.

Lowering her to her feet, he stepped away from the floral scent of her.

He sat against the wall where he had a view of the surrounding land.

Even though his wife needed him now, retribution was on the way and he needed to be on the watch for it.

He opened his arms. She came to him, sitting on his lap and nuzzling her head against his shoulder.

"What happened, honey? It's really got you on edge."

"Bird almost killed Giselle." She gripped his jacket with her small hands. They trembled.

"Is she injured?"

Bird would answer for the wicked thing he'd done, whatever it turned out to be.

Covering her hand with his, he stroked his thumb across her knuckles. Her fingers relaxed.

"Poor Giselle," Melinda said quietly. "All she wanted was justice for her husband, but she didn't take into account that Bird would be quicker and stronger than she was, even though she had a gun and he was tethered. I was on my way to feed him. If I hadn't been—"

She glanced up at him then quickly away, but not so

quickly that he didn't see the moisture welling in her eyes or feel the tremor that passed through her shoulders.

"Well, in the end I was going, wasn't I? Alone, though, since the men were on watch."

"You ought to have let him go hungry."

"Yes, but I hadn't planned on going inside the shed, not until I heard Giselle scream."

"I'm not trying to reprimand you."

"Good because—" She gave him half a smile and shrugged.

That smile was reassuring. It was a relief to see the color rising in her cheeks, the twinkle of blue mischief returning her eyes.

Anyone who dimmed Melinda Walker's fire deserved to be hanged by the toes and he reckoned Bird King had been the one to do it.

"You will be glad to know that I did have a gun in my pocket, just like you said I should. Of course, it was useless."

And, just like that, his sparkling, courageous wife was fully back. She sat straight but remained squarely on his lap. It seemed so natural to have her there; as though that's the place she was meant to be.

"Why was the gun useless?"

"Since Bird had already taken the one from Giselle, and the space was so small, I thought it would be best if he didn't know I had one. I didn't think I'd come out the winner if we started shooting at each other."

"I'm afraid to ask. What weapon did you use?"

"Oh, well… I suppose you'll find out, anyway." She shrugged. The sweet gesture made her look so damned appealing. If he didn't need to know what had happened he might—no, he wouldn't. Couldn't. "I made up lies about you. You might be happy to know that it was your reputation that scared Bird into letting us go."

"I'm beginning to think it has its uses. What did you tell him?"

"Just that you killed a boy and his dog, blew a man's head off before dinner one night…oh, and there was the bit about the time you drowned a man and used him for fishing bait."

He stared at her, stunned.

"No need to look so stricken, Boone. The cad deserved it for accidentally killing our cat. I believe that the mental picture of me wading into the water naked to retrieve the feeding fish unnerved Bird enough that when Giselle told him that you were devoted to me and would have revenge, he believed it. And I told him you were going to cut off his fingers."

"Well done."

"But, Boone, I did have to draw the gun. He was so enjoying the anticipation of killing Giselle that there was the moment of hesitation you told me about. I used it to surprise him."

"Is he dead?"

"He wishes he was since I told him that you were also going to cut off his tender part and send it to his brothers wrapped in a pink bow."

"Tender part?"

She glanced at his crotch, arched a brow and nodded.

"Lord have mercy. Honey, you have a rare talent."

"I do?"

"How many people could face a killer armed mainly with her brain and come out unharmed? Melinda, I am in awe of you."

"Oh—you are?" She blinked at him, her cheeks

flushed with what could only be pleasure. "There's Rebecca, she could do it. The two of us were as skilled at getting out of trouble as we were getting into it."

"I'd like to see the idiot madman who might try to hold his own against the pair of you."

To see her smiling again made him feel warm inside, gooey even. It felt as though he had lost something precious and suddenly found it again.

"Well, there was the time that Rebecca and I rousted a whole gang of villains who were about to kill Grandfather Moreland. Of course, I was wearing snakes on my head and Becca was playing funeral music."

"They must have been terrified."

"Oh, they were and it was satisfying to see, but in the end it was your brother who saved the day. But if it hadn't been for—"

"I love you, Melinda." He cupped her face between his palms and kissed her quickly. He shouldn't have, but a declaration of love deserved a kiss. "I reckon I shouldn't say it when we haven't got much more time together—I just want you to know that you have captured me, completely, and I won't forget you."

Melinda twisted around, repositioning herself so that she straddled his thighs. She placed her hands on his shoulders, gripping with her fingers, gazing at him hard.

No—not quite hard, there was humor lurking in those clever blues.

"Do you imagine I will let you?" she asked. "Boone Walker, you may have escaped prison, but you will not escape me."

"I'm not the kind of man to get married. I wish I was, but I'm not."

"You already did."

With that she lifted up on her knees and kissed him. Not a maidenly peck, either. Far from it. She tangled her fingers in his hair then, pressing her lush little body against his chest, ground him against the wall, where he could do nothing but answer her kiss.

Hell, that was a lie. He could have refused it if he'd wanted to. But right now there was nothing he wanted more than to strip the clothes from her, feel her heated skin against his and eat up her soft moans when he took her.

Hell again. Hell's curses! There actually was something he wanted more.

He wanted to honor her. Giving in to his bodily urges without intending to spend the rest of his life with her—he wouldn't shame her that way.

What made this decision so impossible was that it wasn't simply bodily urges drawing him to her. It was the heart and soul of the woman.

Melinda sighed, pulled back. "You left me, Boone. Right in the middle of that kiss, you left me."

"What if we created a child and I was gone?"

"Gone where? You said you loved me. What is it that's—" she waived her hand in the general direction of west "—out there, that you want more than you want me?"

"Not a single thing." It was true; there wasn't anything he wanted more than Melinda. The day that he signed the legal papers annulling their marriage would be the worst of his life. "But there is for you."

"No, Boone. You are wrong about that." Melinda pushed away from him and stood. "For me, out there, there's nothing. Only men who never see past my smile.

Until I married you, I thought I was doomed to be adored."

She marched the few steps across the loft then started down the ladder. When all he could see was the top of her head, she popped up again with only her face in view.

"Just so you know, I've put my own personal bounty on you. I'm in hot pursuit even though it looks like I'm going down the ladder."

"What's the price on my head this time?"

She smiled, arched a pretty brow. "Oh, it's high. You'll find out what it is as soon as you admit that I will always be your wife."

Her face dipped out of sight one more time, but not for long.

"And there will be babies—lots of them."

At midnight a gunshot disturbed the silence. At a quarter past the hour, another rang out, this one coming from a different direction.

Before going out to sit his watch, Boone had told her that this was a tactic meant to keep them on edge, to make sure they didn't get any sleep.

Lying alone in the straw bed, she could say with certainty the tactic was working. She was restless. Looking out the window, she saw the lamps in the house burning.

Apparently everyone was restless.

Although it had to be said that lying in bed awake or huddled in front of the fireplace in the house had to be more restful than riding around in the dark shooting off guns.

Below, she saw Boone sitting on the paddock fence, his rifle across his lap. The frigid light of a full moon shone on him.

He needed coffee and she needed company. Putting on her heavy coat and only that—very well, she also put on boots but not stockings—she went outside. Crossing the yard toward the house, frost crunched under her feet.

"Evening, Melinda," Doc Brown said when she came up the porch steps. He sat in the rocker bundled in a blanket, taking his turn at watch.

"Evening, Doctor," she replied then hurried inside, grateful for the warmth that enveloped her.

Everyone sat in the parlor, just as she had imagined they would be doing. The only one sleeping was Diana.

As soon as she closed the door behind her, Giselle leaped up to embrace her. They had been through something horrendous together. It formed a bond.

"Can I get you anything?" she asked.

"I've just come to get coffee for Boone."

"Here, hold Diana for a moment while I fetch it."

"If only the shooting would stop," Trudy said, but she openly snuggled close to Stanley on the couch, sheltering under his arm. That cozy happening would not be going on without the gunfire.

Stanley looked—different.

He'd changed over the weeks that she'd known him. He still wore his glasses at the bridge of his nose, his boots hadn't yet lost all of their shine, but he no longer had the timid look of a tenderfoot.

And why not? He was in love. Somehow that alone made him seem taller. Perhaps it was his affection for Trudy that made him stop scowling at her and Boone the way he had in the beginning.

Giselle returned with the coffee. Melinda bid the people and the warmth good night.

Crossing the yard she saw frost on the brim of Boone's

Stetson and the shoulders of his coat. Bright moonlight made it glitter.

Poor man must be shivering. He still had two hours of his watch to go before Edward relieved him.

Another gunshot cut the silence. She misstepped, dribbling hot coffee on her fingers.

The burn was worth it because Boone smiled when he saw her.

She raised a cup to him.

"It smells like heaven. I could kiss you."

"Here, hold mine and I'll climb up."

He took the mug. When she scrambled up, cold air rushed up her coat nipping at her nether cheeks. Maybe she ought to have taken the time to dress properly.

Or not. There was something delicious about the secret—about sitting beside Boone with only a layer of loose cloth between his hands and her imagination.

"Now you may kiss me," she said, settling close to him on the rail.

He handed her mug back to her. While he did not kiss her, he did put his arm around her shoulder to pull her tighter to him.

"You don't want to kiss me, after I braved the cold to be with you? To think I could be warm and toasty in—"

"I want to."

"Well, then, please help yourself to my lips." A husband who declared his love had every right to a kiss and more.

"What's my bounty?"

"I told you when you would find that out."

He peered at her from under lowered lids. "I reckon an innocent kiss wouldn't hurt anything."

"It could only help warm us up."

Her husband kissed her forehead, chaste and sweet. Truly, it was the same way he kissed Diana.

Two shots shattered the night at the same time.

"Are they coming any closer?" she asked, deciding to forget the offense of the kissed forehead for the moment.

"I don't think so." Boone took a long swallow of coffee. "Those fools are wearing themselves out."

"They still have the food."

"How's ours holding out? We've got to be running low."

"There's enough for two days, three, if everyone but Giselle rations it."

They sat in silence, she gazing up at the stars and he staring at the darkness beyond the corral. She assumed he was gnawing at worry the same as she was.

"I could have freed up the food." Boone's voice sounded grim, guilty even.

"And what did they want in return? Our souls?"

He shook his head. "Only mine."

She leaned her head against his shoulder. He cupped her face with his big palm.

"Some things aren't ours to give away," she said. "I'm glad you came home."

"It was because of you."

"Was it?" She turned her face, kissed a callus on his hand.

"I thought I might do it, join them—that's what they wanted. In that second, it seemed an easier way to get my freedom. But then I saw you, there in my mind, smiling, believing in the man I could be. It was you who kept me from making the biggest mistake of my life."

"No, Boone. That was all you. You are a stronger person than you know."

"I think I need to kiss you now." He set his coffee on the rail, wrapped both of his arms around her.

"I'm naked under the coat."

"I noticed."

Melinda stared at her breakfast oatmeal waiting for it to look appealing.

Across the table Giselle was speaking to Trudy, but Melinda found it difficult to focus enough to join in or even pay attention.

Last night, Boone had noticed she was naked under the coat, given her a rousing kiss that she was certain held a heart full of emotion.

In the very moment that she thought he was about to slip his hand under the soft wool, caress her until she couldn't see, couldn't breathe—truly, his fingers had been plucking at the button over her heart—all of a sudden he'd patted her on the head and sent her off to bed. Alone.

Alone more or less. An hour after she'd stomped up the loft ladder, he came in.

She'd heard the creak of the rungs as he'd climbed, felt the shift of the straw when he lay beside her. Was well aware of the strip of cold air between their bodies.

Before he'd declared his love they had slept her back to his belly. For the warmth, is what he'd claimed.

She knew better of course; it was for the comfort of human contact.

As of last night, he apparently no longer wanted that. Not if it offended his newly found sense of honor.

Blast the man! At least her troubled outlaw chased away the night chill.

Absently she slid her oatmeal toward Giselle. A

mother with a suckling child needed food more than a heartsick bride did.

"I imagine your papa will be relieved to hear the news," Giselle said.

News? Melinda chastised herself for being so caught up in her own self-pity that she missed something critical.

Perhaps even wonderful.

There could only be one reason Edward Spears would be relieved about anything these days. Trudy and Stanley becoming engaged!

Given the intimacy the pair displayed in front of others, what, she could only wonder, happened in private? Well, such privacy as there was in a home with so many people staying in it.

No doubt Trudy was the recipient of more romance than Melinda. She, a married woman, in the seclusion of the loft, was all but a stranger to it.

Oddly, seeing Trudy's joy made her feel lonely. When she ought to feel giddy happiness for her friend, she was sullen, sulking and feeling sorry for herself.

That would not do. If tonight her husband shared the bed, and she was not convinced he would, she would not be naked under her coat. No, indeed. She would be naked on top of the blanket.

"Congratulations, Trudy. Stanley will be a wonderful husband."

Melinda knew it beyond a doubt. Over the past weeks, she had become fond of the little lawyer. He had become her big brother, in heart if not reality.

Suddenly someone shouted and cursed vigorously from the area of the barn.

"Stanley?" Trudy bolted up. "I didn't think he knew those words."

Melinda also stood. "All men know them—some just don't use them unless—"

She forgot what she was going to say when Edward began to curse and swear.

"I'll take the baby into the bedroom," Giselle said. She closed the bedroom door behind her and didn't come back out.

"I wonder if Papa refused to let Stanley court me."

That was unlikely since the courting had already begun in earnest. Trudy's father would hardly object at this point.

"We'd best go see." Melinda took Trudy by the arm, urging her toward the door.

Something was going on and she was not about to be left in the dark about it.

Boone, Dr. Brown, Stanley and Edward huddled in a tight circle.

Dr. Brown gripped a boy by the arm. The adolescent struggled, trying to bite and kick. Unless she was mistaken, this was the King's messenger boy, the same one who had come before.

"Stanley! Papa!" All four of the men spun around when they heard Trudy's cry.

Stanley crushed something in his fist.

Trudy hurried across the yard toward him. Melinda ran a step behind.

"What is it?" Trudy snatched a piece of paper, fine-looking paper, from Stanley. Before she could unfurl it, he snatched it back and ripped it apart.

"What is it?" Melinda whispered, turning to Boone.

Stanley put his arm around Trudy's waist. Edward placed his hand on her shoulder.

"A demand," Boone answered gruffly.

She hardly recognized the man she had married. Anger boiled hot and furious within him—it fired his eyes, stiffened his posture. His hands flexed as if he were crushing stones.

It could hardly be denied that each of the men looked like erupting volcanoes.

Boone took a breath then let it out in a slow hiss. "Lump is demanding Trudy. If she doesn't come, they're burning the food."

Chapter Thirteen

Melinda jumped, startled when Boone suddenly snatched the youngster from Dr. Brown.

He gripped the front of the child's shirt, bent over and stared him down. He looked as violent as his reputation portrayed. At least that is what the messenger would see.

Melinda saw something else. This show of bluster was for a purpose.

"You scared of me, boy?"

Defiantly he shook his head.

Melinda decided that the spot of urine blossoming on his pants said otherwise.

"You ain't nobody." The adolescent kicked Boone's shin. Her husband did not acknowledge the blow.

"Who are you?"

"That ain't no never mind to you, but I'll be riding with the Kings, just as soon as I prove myself."

"Hell's curses, I feel like I'm looking at myself at your age. Don't go that way, kid."

For his wise advice, Boone received another kick in the shin spiced with a string of profanity.

"I'm going to let you go with a message of my own. You tell Lump and the others, they want Trudy, come and get her. I'll be waiting."

That said, he released the aspiring outlaw. When the boy turned, Boone booted him in the rear and sent him sprawling.

"Better get used to it down there. That'll be your life and no mistake about it."

He looked up with dirt crusting his tears, but in Melinda's opinion, the boy did not take Boone's message to heart. She only hoped that something would get through to him before he lost his soul.

No one moved, no one spoke, until the boy rode off, vanishing behind the crest of a hill.

"How long do I have, Boone?" Trudy asked, her shoulders straight but her chin wobbling.

Everyone looked to him. Somehow, in spite of his past, he was the one with answers, the one in charge.

Boone placed his big, capable hands on Trudy's shoulders, smiling while he looked down at her.

"You have your whole life, Miss Trudy. We're all going to do whatever it takes to keep you safe."

"Load the guns," Stanley snapped. "We need to practice."

Boone dropped his hands. He stared at Stanley then at each one of them.

Except Melinda. He avoided looking at her and she knew it was deliberate.

"Load the guns in the wagon. Come midnight, all of you are hightailing it for Buffalo Bend."

No!

Surely he didn't mean to stay here and meet the Kings by himself?

Even now he wouldn't meet her eye, but turned rather and strode quickly toward the barn.

"Boone!" she called.

She might as well have been a bug on the ground for all the attention he paid to her.

This would not do. She hurried after him.

"Boone, stop!" She pounded his back with her fist.

When he spun around, his expression was hard.

"You can't make me go." Frustrated, tears pricked her eyes. "I'm staying with you."

"No, you aren't."

"You'll have to tie me on the wagon, then. I'll fight you."

"You won't fight me because you know as well as I do that if they get by me here, they'll come after the wagon. And you're the only one who can shoot worth a damn."

"But—"

"Everyone over there?" He inclined his head toward the group walking into the house. "They have nothing to do with this. I agreed to it, they didn't."

"When I said 'I do'—" she touched his face because it was so dear to her and if he sent her away she might never see it again "—I agreed, Boone. I'm staying."

"Even if you're their best hope? They need you. It would be different if you couldn't shoot a cow at ten feet. But, you—you'd make your Annie Oakley sit up and take a look. It's up to you to see them safe away, just like it's up to me to get rid of what Kings I can. You see that, don't you?"

The misery of it was that she did see it. She also saw that Boone would probably be killed if he faced the gang alone.

How could he force her to make an impossible choice?

Hard truth kicked her in the heart, reminding her that he was not forcing a choice. Just pointing to the only choice there was.

He touched her chin with one big finger, lifted her face.

"I'm counting on you, honey."

Then he kissed her, sweetly, tenderly, while hot tears streamed down her cheeks.

Bread and butter sat on the dinner table, sliced and ready to eat. But even with the enticement of strawberry jam, all anyone did was stare at it.

Taut nerves twisted Melinda's stomach, making her feel half nauseous. She went to the window, gazed out at the night.

A storm was gathering, which seemed fitting.

"Do you think we ought to wait so long to leave?" Trudy asked. "Maybe we should go now?"

"No. I want to be sure the Kings aren't on the road already," Boone said. "For now it's safer here. But if they haven't shown by midnight, we can assume that they don't want to leave their beds. At least the storm's in our favor."

In the window's reflection, she saw Giselle finish feeding Diana then button the front of her shirt. She stood, carried the baby to Boone.

"I owe the folks in this room so much," she said, setting Diana in his arms. "Doc, for bringing my baby safely into the world, of course, but I never expected to be beholden to an outlaw and his wife. When I first saw the pair of you, I was frightened; quite distrustful. I just want you to know that when Diana's old enough to be told what happened here she will know that Boone Walker, a hero, saved her life."

Giselle's footsteps crossed the wood floor, becoming quiet for the time that she walked over the rug.

"I still can't figure out how you talked Bird out of killing us." She touched Melinda's arm where it was folded around her middle. "I'll puzzle over it the rest of my days."

"Well, the gun spoke rather loudly. But, still, it's not so hard to convince men of things." Melinda glanced over at Giselle, tried to smile. "You understand."

Giselle shook her head. "I wish I did. If I could do what you do, my husband would be here today. You, my friend, could have talked Efrin into licking his own boots clean."

When Diana began to fuss, Giselle kissed Melinda's cheek then went back to her infant.

Melinda focused her gaze past the window's reflection. Lightning skittered across the horizon, but closer to the house the sky still glittered with stars.

"You going back to Jasper Springs, Doc Brown?" she heard Edward say.

"It used to be a good place to live. For the sake of those who didn't make it, I'd like to go back. Make their deaths count for something. For now, I reckon I'll wait and see."

Wait and see if Boone—if he killed enough of them to free the town before he was murdered?

If he did survive it would be because others died. Not that they hadn't freely invited their fates. But given Boone's feelings about killing, would he be able to live with the regret?

This and similar questions had lashed at her all afternoon. It was hard to remember when she'd been so sick at heart.

No doubt she couldn't remember because she never had been.

"What about you, Edward? Where will your new start be?" the doc asked.

"I reckon I'll go where Trudy and Stanley settle. I'd like to rebuild in Jasper Springs, but I'll like grand-babies even more."

"Is there a lawyer in Jasper Springs?" Stanley asked.

If one more person discussed plans for a happy future she might scream out loud.

Surely they realized that their protector's future might only consist of the next several hours and that she had no future at all without him.

"There used to be a fine lawyer. But not since the Kings declared their own law."

From what they were saying, the poor fellow hadn't lasted a month before the Kings killed him for stand-ing up to them.

Next, the conversation turned to weapons. What they would take with them in the wagon and what Boone would keep here.

Her mind wandered morbidly until she heard Stan-ley's voice.

"Given that I haven't finished seeing to Boone's free-dom," Stanley announced, "I've decided to remain be-hind when the rest of you go."

Well, she truly could not love the lawyer more if he were her blood-and-bone brother.

"I appreciate that, but you'll be needed to protect the women and the children."

"Edward and Dr. Brown will protect them. I'm with you."

She didn't want to return her attention to the room's reflection, but couldn't help herself.

"You're a good friend, Stanley." Boone was smiling, falsely, she believed, but smiling nonetheless. "But you're about to become a married man. You've got responsibilities."

And Boone was not a married man!

"As do you, my friend," Stanley murmured.

She spun around. Heat flushed her face while she stared Boone down. A blow to the gut could not feel worse. How was it that he put more value on another's marriage than on his own?

The ache in her chest nearly doubled her up. Worse, words failed her. Without her best weapon to aid her, there was nothing left to do but dash out the front door and race for the sanctuary of the loft.

Stars that had been visible moments ago disappeared behind a mass of heavy clouds.

She wiped tears from her cheeks.

The storm was coming faster than anyone had expected.

Boone tore out of the house in time to see the barn door slam with such force that it bounced open again. He ran across the yard feeling the first drops of icy rain hit him in the face.

Lightning blasted a hilltop in the distance.

Rushing into the barn, he bolted the door against the rising wind. "Melinda!"

He didn't see her but he heard her weeping.

The wrenching cry cut him to the quick. If there was

one person in the world he did not want to hurt, one above all others who did not deserve it, it was his sweet, brave bride.

Hustling up the ladder rungs two at a time, he came over the top to find her laying facedown on their straw bed.

Kneeling beside her, he touched her hair where it curled down her back. She had no way of knowing the number of times he'd imagined giving her pleasure on this bed. Never once had he wanted to bring her tears.

Curse him for being the one to cause this anguish. He gathered her up, bent his head over hers, rocking.

"Honey, I'm sorry, so very sorry."

"Why is Stanley and Trudy's future more important than ours?"

It felt as if he'd been gut shot seeing the anguish on her face, the way her arms hugged her middle instead of him.

Because they had one, he thought, but figured that was something she didn't need to hear.

"If the way we feel about each other was the only thing that mattered, life would be a mite easier." He kissed the top of her head and pulled his arms tighter around her. If only he could shut out the world as easily as he'd locked the barn door. "I never expected to love you so much—

"Hell, that's a bald lie. I reckon I should have known it could happen from the first. You were so beautiful, Melinda. So perfect, that I couldn't figure out what a lady like you was doing at my trial. I haven't been able to accept you and me together and it's because I was afraid of it ending this way."

"Why, Boone?" Her voice cracked on a sob. Her despair, the hitch of her shoulders, plowed into his heart because his Melinda never cried. "I don't understand why it has to end at all."

"I won't say why, but I reckon I don't need to."

She shoved away from him. Wriggling out of his embrace, she knelt on the bed, her fists curled on her thighs.

"You are not going to die!" Her breath came in fast, hard gulps. "Don't send me away. I'll fight. So will Stanley."

"I know you want to, but my attention would be on protecting you. I'll have a better chance on my own."

"You won't! I'm not helpless and I don't need protecting. I'll do what's needed. Just because I've never killed a man doesn't mean I wouldn't do it."

"Brave words. I believe you mean them. But I've seen men who are used to killing hesitate. A half a second is all it is between life and death. You've seen it."

"I won't hesitate."

"Look." He reached toward her then let his hand drop when she turned her cheek away from his caress. "I'm not saying you won't be called upon to fire your gun, just that it won't be in my defense."

"There are three men to watch out for Giselle and the baby. Even Trudy is a fair shot."

"Trudy hits one can out of ten." He folded his arms across his chest, hoping he looked more commanding than he felt. "If you believe the men can shoot any better, you're fooling yourself."

She looked up, silently staring at the rafters—or an abandoned bird's nest, he couldn't be sure. Hell, she was probably looking at his cold, dead body.

A sudden deluge of rain hit the roof. It slammed against the walls, made the mule stomp in his stall and bray.

"Honey, those innocent lives mean something. Think of the baby. She deserves her shot at life. I know you believe that."

Melinda covered her upturned face with her hands. He thought she might be praying. He hoped she was praying, for him, for them all.

With a huff, a sigh, she lowered her hands. She stared at him, resignation tugging her mouth down at the corners.

"I'll do as you ask, Boone, because I love you and because, as much as I hate it to be so, you are right."

Thunder pummeled the roof hard enough to sprinkle dust from the rafters down upon their heads.

"I want one thing in return," she added once the pounding rolled toward the east. She wiped the tears from her face, sniffed. "If I'm to be a widow, don't leave me a virgin. I want— I need my husband."

She was asking him to cross the one line he had vowed that he would not. The line that he had crossed so many times in his mind.

"When this is over if—"

"If you leave me untouched, it never will be over for me."

"I'm a dirty outlaw, Melinda, not nearly good enough for you."

All of a sudden she started unbuttoning her dress. It was unlikely, but he thought she was cussing under her breath. Heedlessly, she tossed petticoats and whatever those other frilly things were, around the loft.

"What's that you're saying?" he asked.

"A string of curse words."

Angry curse words, if he heard right.

While he watched, spellbound, she stripped down to her skin.

"How dare you say you fell in love with me the first time you saw me! That I was perfect! Look at me, Boone Walker! Look past this!" She circled her hand in front of her face. "Can't you see me? I'm a woman like any other. Knock me off the damned pedestal!"

Breathless in her rage, her undeniably-perfect-in-every-way chest heaved with exertion and emotion. A fine sheen of sweat glittered on her skin.

A woman like any other? No.

"Why are you smiling?" She fired the question at him.

"You aren't a woman like any other, at least not like any I've ever watched undress. But then I've never had one take off her clothes with such…" He gestured with his hands, following the path of her clothing. "Abandon."

"None of them were your legally wed wife. No doubt they had more time than I do. But since you've brought them up, did any of them ever tell you that you were not good enough for them?"

He shook his head, feeling that he'd been backed onto a twig suspended over a vast chasm and that it was cracking. How was a man to fight the greatest temptation of his life when his woman armed herself with a naked body, an extremely seductive naked body?

"Because it wasn't true!"

"They were whores. They didn't care."

"I care, Boone." She canceled the distance between

them by grabbing a hank of his hair in her small, fair fist. She pulled him toward her. "That man you think wasn't good enough for me is gone. The woman you held in such false esteem, she never existed."

She drew him to within an inch of her lips.

"Make love to me, Boone."

"What if I leave you with a child to raise on your own?"

"I will not allow you to leave me."

"No…" He'd do his damnedest not to die, especially since she was offering him so much to live for. "I don't reckon you will."

A frizzle of electricity skittered over the barn roof. A blue-white blaze illuminated the loft at the same time the thunderclap exploded across the paddock.

Already on hands and knees, Boone crawled forward. Melinda fell backward onto the straw. She reached up, touching the back of his neck to pull him down.

He resisted for a heartbeat, but only that.

This moment seemed a miracle. Life, he was coming to believe, was full of them. But the amazing thing was that he, Boone Walker, had been granted one.

Taking her hand from his neck, he kissed it then set it over her heart. He lifted up, his weight balanced on his knees.

Straddling her hips, he tugged his shirt off over his head. He shoved down his pants and drawers, wriggled out of them then tossed them with the same carelessness as Melinda had tossed hers.

The difference was, along with his boots, he tossed over the old Boone, the unworthy one.

A new man—the one Melinda had recognized beneath the lies even when he hadn't—this one was going to have his wife.

Skimming his flesh over hers, he breathed in the scent of her skin where her hair fell away from her neck.

She gripped his hips, her fingers digging into his butt while she pressed him close. Her belly was hot velvet against his erection.

"Slow down, honey." Not that he wanted to. Everything in him wanted to ride her hard and fast. "You're new to this."

"I've dreamed if it often enough." Her breath beat against the hollow of his throat, thick, labored. "I can't imagine I was far off the mark."

"It might—"

"Hurt? So I've read."

She nipped his ear, tangled her fingers in his hair and pulled him into a kiss that kicked his heart. Knowing that in spite of what she said and what he hoped, the first time for them might also be the last.

She must have felt him doubt, hesitate.

"No," she whispered over the steady drum of rain above their heads. "This isn't the end."

"We will have tomorrow, honey," he whispered. "I reckon I just needed my wife to set me straight on it."

Sweet, lazy seduction would have its time.

But not now.

While the storm broke around the barn, Melinda demanded his surrender.

This was one life sentence he would no longer fight.

He nuzzled the side of her breast with his cheek then closed his mouth over her nipple. Her fullness cushioned his teeth, the swollen berry at the tip twisted against his tongue.

She lifted her hips against him, impatient.

"Almost," he answered and then pressed his pelvis against her belly to still her.

With his thumb and finger, he twisted the nipple he had just suckled, watching the moisture from his mouth glisten in a flash of lightning.

Rising to his knees, he lifted her hips, spread her thighs, stroking, kneading. He wondered if feeling her smooth, firm flesh under his hands would always be this soul-shattering.

It would, of course, because he was touching Melinda and, from this day on, he accepted that she was his.

His heart pounded, his pulse beat in his fingertips when he stroked her swollen feminine crease. She took in a slow breath, let it out in a moan.

For once his Melinda seemed to have no words, but her eyes spoke clearly enough. It was time and past to make her the wife of his heart, of his body.

In a half crouch, with one hand under her buttocks, he nudged her with the head of his penis.

Had this been a leisurely wedding night, if time had been on their side, he would have entered her slowly.

But this was not, and his wife knew it. She arched, taking him inside her.

Her languid expression sharpened, her pretty eyes widened, but only for an instant.

She blinked in long, slow surrender then fastened her gaze on him while he rode her.

He couldn't look away, she would not let him. Even in the moment when he lost himself, in the moment when she throbbed around him, even then their eyes held, seeing the future in each other.

He would live through the coming hours. In this moment of surrender, she handed him her heart. In return, she took his life.

Chapter Fourteen

Had she not been anchored by Boone's big, hard body sprawled on top of her, Melinda believed she would have floated away.

With her eyes closed she savored the delicious pulsating in her womb. The languorous feeling radiated to her fingers and toes, making her feel weightless but at the same time one with the bed and the man.

"I never imagined," she sighed.

"I didn't, either." He rolled off her but hugged her to his chest so that they lay face-to-face. His breath warmed the top of her hair even as the chill of the room began to settle upon them.

"Really?" He didn't? "Even though you've done this many times? Does that mean I've erased the others from your memory completely?"

"What others?" He pinched her behind then cupped her face in his hand and lifted her chin. Stroking his thumb across her cheek, he looked into her eyes. "This is the first time I've made love to a woman who is my wife—first time to a woman I love."

"Well, then, you were as much a virgin as I was."

She liked the thought even though, by the facts, it was not true.

"Are you hurting?"

She shook her head but not so vigorously as to dislodge the tender touch of his hand on her cheek. "Deliciously sore."

"I reckon I should kiss it and make it better."

"Really? People do…" Her voice failed because he had begun to blaze a trail with his mouth that started with a suckle of each breast then a lingering lick over her ribs to her belly—well, my word, he really did intend to—

"Oh," she said. No, that really was not a word but a sigh.

His tongue was smooth, caressing her intimate spot with heat. Viking-blond hair falling loose over his shoulders tickled, shivered across her thighs. He was so very male, which made her feel so very female.

And as much as she wanted to think about this newborn womanliness, her thoughts were quickly succumbing to sensation.

When she was nearly to that point of shattering delight, he stopped, lifted his head. Exposed, a delightful shiver blew across her aching flesh.

Coarse chest hair rubbed her belly, her chest. Heat rolled off her in waves. How curious that the sizzle made her shiver.

The stiff hair of Boone's chin grazed her neck. The other stiff part of him, the one that finally made her his wife, claimed her again.

She thrust her hips taking him deep within her. And, yes, it did hurt; a twinge and nothing more. The ache dwarfed in comparison to the joy of joining bodies and lives.

No sooner had she adjusted to the womanly twinge than it was gone. Boone pushed up, his hands braced beside her head. She twined her fingers in his, gripping hard. Fascinated, engulfed, she watched his belly flex while he pumped into her, withdrew then entered her again.

She moaned his name, possibly called him husband, or lover, but certainly hers. Then in an explosion of bliss, she clenched around him.

He buried his face into her neck. It felt damp, with sweat or tears—probably both.

After a few moments of savoring the scent of him, the strength of his arms around her, she wanted to drift into a doze, but Boone sighed against her ear.

"What time is it, do you think?"

"It's forever o'clock, of course."

Billbro whined from below and woke Melinda from a deep sleep. With all that had, and was about to happen, she would not have believed it possible to even close her eyes.

She reached for Boone but touched empty space.

Forever o'clock had come and gone.

According to Boone's pocket watch, which lay open on the makeshift table, it was now a glaring eleven-thirty.

She sat up then snapped the watch closed.

Certainly he had left it there for safekeeping and nothing more. She would not entertain the possibility that he meant it as a remembrance—a physical reminder of who he had been.

Not that.

From below she heard his boots cross the floor then the barn door open. Boone spoke a few words to the dog. From up here she couldn't tell what they were.

She dressed quickly then swiped up the watch and carried it down the ladder.

Boone sat on an overturned barrel. The lamp beside him on the floor softly illuminated him. With his elbows propped on his knees, he gazed at something he turned in his fingers.

He didn't look up. She stood, one foot on the floor, one poised on the last ladder rung.

The deputy's badge gleamed from the polishing Boone was giving it.

She couldn't speak, move or even find her breath. She'd known this hour was coming, but suddenly here it was. No more a vague event happening in the future.

Her husband was arming for battle.

"Boone," she whispered across the dimly lit space.

He glanced up. With a half smile, he pinned the badge on his pocket.

"Does it look wrong?"

She shook her head.

He reached for her and she dashed to him. He pulled her onto his lap.

"Feels kind of funny." He kissed her hair. "I spent a lot of years on the wrong side of what this represents."

"Oh," she said, leaning back to get a better look at the dimly glowing metal. It smelled of fresh polish. She noticed that he had hammered out the dent. "I think you look heroic."

"I'm just a man with a job to do. But I want you to know something. That line between right and wrong,

I'll do my damnedest to never cross it again. You don't need to worry. I'm no longer that man."

"I never worried about the kind of man you are. I have faith that you will do a splendid job as deputy." She gave him a great hug around the neck and breathed in the warm, male scent of his skin. "Imagine the stories we will tell our grandchildren!"

"As long as the stories begin from this point on. Don't know what they'll think about their pa having been an outlaw."

"They'll be proud, is what. You'll be an example of how a person can be redeemed."

"Pray with me for a minute, honey."

Boone held both of her hands in his. Foreheads together, Melinda silently asked for protection, for Boone and for all of them. She also asked that her husband might do what he needed to do without killing anyone.

She knew the moment he was finished asking for guidance because he gently kissed her.

"I love you, Melinda. Never forget it."

"I'll make sure to remind you, even when we are old and doddering."

"Can't see you doddering." He shook his head. "Even if you do dodder, you'll still be the most beautiful woman around."

"Watch what you say, deputy! I know how to shoot. I've been taught by the best."

"A fact is a fact."

"I hear someone coming." She gripped his shirt-front, kissed him until she was breathless. "I love you, Boone."

"Melinda," he whispered against her hair as the barn door squealed open.

* * *

Boone shrugged into his coat and stepped outside of the barn. For the most part, the storm had moved on, leaving a depressing drizzle in its place.

Giselle, kneeling on the wagon bed and cradling Diana under her coat, waved to him. He acknowledged her farewell with a tip of his hat. When he did, water dripped from the brim to further dampen his coat.

Trudy rushed up to him for a quick hug before she joined Giselle in the buckboard. Edward, coming behind her, shook his hand.

"If there are words big enough to thank you for getting me out of the fire, I don't know what they are. And not only for that, but you took me and my girl in when we had no place else to go. You are a rare man, Boone Walker," he said then followed Trudy, helped her into the wagon and mounted a horse.

As soon as Edward settled in the saddle, Boone saw him place his rifle across his lap. His fingers curled tight on the stock.

Except for the pat of drizzle on mud, the night was silent, somber. Folks kept their thoughts to themselves.

Just as well since they were probably thinking he was about to die.

That was a possibility—but not the only possibility. For the first time Boone had plans for his life that didn't involve drifting from one hovel of a town to another. All of a sudden he had a woman to love, roots to grow and babies to be brought into the world. Wrongs to try to set right.

No, he was not riding toward his death. He was riding toward his future. The trouble was, between here and there, he'd face some nasty opposition.

Standing beside the wagon team, Doc and Stanley stood in quiet conversation. Doc stood, his arms across his chest, nodding his head.

With a glance up at Boone, Stanley crossed the paddock toward him.

"I'd like to reargue my point that I ought to stay with you."

"I'm proud to call you friend, Stanley. Hell, if it wasn't for you I'd be spending my life in a cell." Boone clapped Stanley on the shoulder. "And I might need your help, just not here with me."

"What can I do?" Hadn't the small lawyer grown a couple of inches? He'd swear the man used to be shorter. "I'll help however I can."

"If the worst happens, take Melinda back to Montana." Boone had to clear his throat; it felt as though a walnut had become lodged in his Adam's apple. "If it doesn't happen, I'd like you to stand with me when I give her a proper wedding."

Smythe must have swallowed a walnut, too, since he didn't answer. He simply nodded and let his gaze slide toward the barn.

After a long, silent moment when they should have been saying goodbye but were not, Stanley turned and walked toward the wagon. He tugged on the mule's reins, making sure the animal was tethered securely.

With a last glance at Boone, a nod, he climbed up the buckboard and sat beside the doc. He gathered up the reins.

They were ready to go—all except for Melinda. She had yet to come out of the barn.

Hell's curses. If he had to go in and fetch her, it might be a long while before he brought her out.

He was saved from having to face the temptation when she walked out leading a horse behind her.

She wore a frilly hat with a silk flower tucked into the lace band. The brim drooped in the rain, the pink bud quickly wilting with the moisture.

It looked as if she was going to walk past him without lifting her gaze from the muddy ground.

Hell, she did walk past him without a glance or a word.

"Melinda?"

She stopped, dropped the reins, then spun around.

In a leap, she was in his arms.

"I couldn't tell you goodbye," she cried. He wrapped his arms around her middle and lifted her. She pressed her face into his neck. "I think if I try I'll go to pieces."

He breathed in the scent of her hair, felt the fresh chill of the raindrops clinging to her hat.

"There are no goodbyes between us, honey." He set her back on her feet, cupped her face in his hands then bent to kiss her. "Go on now. Get on your horse and go with the wagon. I'll follow when I'm finished here."

"I'll see you soon, then." She nodded, squeezed his shoulder and shoved out of his embrace.

Her back looked stiff, walking away, as if she held it that way by the greatest of will.

Halfway she turned, touched her throat then raced back. She squeezed him around the middle.

"I'll be watching for you, Boone." With that, she ran for the horse and mounted up.

The wagon moved out of the yard and he was left alone. He watched it rattle down the road feeling bereft.

But only until a blur separated from the dark mass and charged for him.

"There's a good dog." Boone hugged Billbro's neck. "I'm grateful for your company, Deputy."

The dog-wolf sat, his wagging tail making tracks in the mud.

"How would you feel about coming to live with me and Melinda in Montana? I hear it's real pretty." Billbro whined so he ruffled his tall, furry ears. "I do believe that means yes. Would you like to know a secret, fella? One that not even Melinda knows? Sure do hope she approves because I sure as hell have my mind made up."

He took a breath. Saying this out loud made it fact, no longer something suggested by the small voice in his mind. The deputy cocked his big head.

"I know it seems unlikely, but I want to become a preacher. You're right. I'll need to clean my language up some—more than some—but I'd need to do it for the young'uns anyway."

Right now he didn't know the first thing about how a man became a preacher, but he figured since the Good Lord had given him the idea, He'd figure out a way for it to happen.

The quiet suggestion had shocked him the first time it had come to him, but once entertained, he hadn't been able to shake it. That small voice of conviction was one he used to ignore, but now things were different.

Somehow over the course of the night he'd gone from feeling his goal impossible to seeing himself comforting souls instead of doing them wrong.

He might finally do something to make his mother proud. She'd sure spent enough hours reading to him from the Good Book in an attempt to get him to mend his ways.

"Can you hear me, Ma? I'm going straight." He felt something brush his cheek. Could have been a breeze but—

The wolf licked his hand.

"Yeah, I think it was her, too. So, boy, I reckon I'll begin as a ranch hand at Moreland Ranch, if my brother will have me, just until I get the hows and whys of ministering figured out.

"Hey! I didn't know wolves licked folk's faces. That mean you think I can do it? I reckon it does and I appreciate it. But if any of this is going to happen, I need you to catch up with the wagon and keep Melinda safe."

The deputy gave a low woof then spun and loped after the wagon. Boone watched until the dark swallowed him up.

The old Boone had never minded being alone. This Boone was unsettled by it.

That's one way he knew that the outlaw was gone.

Ten minutes passed while Boone stood in the drizzle listening, fearing that he would hear the crack of gunfire coming from the direction the wagon had taken.

He had no way of knowing for sure what mayhem the Kings intended or when they intended to perpetrate it, but he knew it would be soon and it would happen here.

There was something about the feel of the night that wasn't right. Evil was riding in and it wouldn't be long before it got here.

Boone checked his pistol again. He knew the chambers each had a bullet, but he needed to do something to keep his hands occupied while he thought about what to do.

Staying here and waiting for an attack didn't seem

wise. He'd rather ambush his enemies than have them ambush him.

But where the dickens was he supposed to go? The ranch would be best, but they could as easily be in Jasper Springs as at the ranch.

He wouldn't go to town and risk someone being injured if he could figure a way around it.

And he desperately did want to find a way around it. Life, he had learned in the past couple of weeks, took more turns than a blowing tumbleweed.

He'd been an outlaw, had figured on being such for the rest of his life. The next thing he knew he had been hoodwinked into marriage and forced to represent law and order.

Now he wanted to be married—would do anything to stay that way. As far as upholding the law went, he wanted to do it and not simply as a way to gain his freedom.

Maybe the biggest revelation for the new Boone was that he wanted to uphold more than the law of the land. There were those commandments he'd learned at his mother's knee, the very ones he'd scoffed at his whole life. He'd let Ma down, ignoring them and living wild. But if that brush against his cheek wasn't just the wind, she knew how sorry he was.

He couldn't pinpoint when he'd left the criminal behind and become the man that Melinda had seen all along. But here he was, standing in the rain hoping that the lawman he was at the moment would not be forced to do anything that the preacher he hoped to become would regret.

"Truuuudyyyyy…" a singsong voice called, carrying

through the darkness. Lump wasn't in the yard yet but he was close. "Oh, Truuuudyyyy!"

Here it was, the time of reckoning. If there was one varmint creeping around in the night the others could not be far behind.

At least he was saved from puzzling over where to go. The stage had been set. This is where he would take a stand. Live or die in defense of the wagon, which had not gotten nearly far enough away.

Hoofbeats clopped into the yard. Distant gunshots cut the darkness.

The fools announced their arrival like a trumpet would announce the coming of a royal presence.

While he ran toward the barn he listened to the direction and pattern of the shots. One blast came from a shotgun. A pair of pistol shots echoed from the same direction. Three more riders, three shooting guns. All of the noise was coming from the road leading to town.

Relief washed through him but mingled equally with dread.

Relief because the wagon was not traveling that road but cut a path across the homestead in the opposite direction.

Dread because he was the only one standing between the Kings and his wife.

Boone dashed for the loft. Scrambling up the ladder, he lunged for the window and crouched beside it.

Lump, bawling Trudy's name without letup, rode up to the front of the house. He stared at it for a moment then led his horse around the back.

A movement caught Boone's attention, not coming from the direction he expected it to.

Another rider charged into the yard, her lacy bonnet dangling down her back.

In horror he watched Melinda slide off her horse at the same time Leland King galloped into the yard.

Melinda'd had every intention of staying in the wagon. Then, fifteen minutes out, she'd heard gunfire.

It had come from the east—from the homestead. Clearly, the wagon was not being followed.

But unless Boone had help, it would be. If their protector was overcome, they all would be, as well.

No one would be safe unless the Kings were dealt with at the homestead.

Boone would not be happy about her decision, but she's spun her horse around and urged it toward the homestead at a full run.

Charging into the yard, she didn't see Boone. She slipped off the horse, shouting his name.

"It's a pleasure to see you again, Mrs. Walker."

Startled, Melinda turned.

The snake charmer sat upon his horse, his forearm resting across his saddle horn, an indulgent smile upon his handsome face.

"As it is to see you." Melinda felt reassured by the weight of the gun in her skirt pocket, but she didn't dare pull it out and begin firing. Even if she did not hesitate, he would be faster. "Our last meeting was interrupted in such a distressing way. I trust the dog didn't wound you too terribly. I would be devastated if that were the case."

His jaw tensed but the false smile continued to slither across his face.

Dread shot a chill up her neck. Where was Boone? Had Leland beaten her here, taken him by surprise?

"Don't give it a thought. It was well worth the cost of making your lovely acquaintance."

He made no move to dismount but rather stared down at her. No doubt behind the wink he just stabbed at her, he was frightened of encountering Billbro.

She was almost relieved to hear hoofbeats coming out from behind the house, if only to end this cat-and-mouse trifling. Putting on a charming front was more than she was up to.

It would be ever so much more productive if she could simply draw her gun and fire it.

"Can't find my Trudy gal anywhere."

Productive and satisfying.

Lump circled into her line of vision. He reminded her of a maggot, all white and squirmy.

"Take this one instead." Leland grinned at his brother. "She's more a woman than that other one, anyway."

"Not instead—but before—then at the same time." The maggot licked his lips. "You and me together, Leland?"

"Together, little brother. But it's a shame, really." Leland shook his head slowly from side to side. "Pure loveliness put to such dastardly use."

The pair of them began to circle their horses, sweeping around her in an ever-tightening circle. She clenched her fists, raised her chin and squared her shoulders because she was so very frightened. Instinct told her that running would only make things happen quicker, before she had time to devise a plan of escape—if there was one.

"I'll tie the girlies to that post over yonder. One on each side to make sure they don't get away. We can just mate around and around, like they's one but with twice as many lady parts."

"When one wears out..." Leland's laugh echoed across the yard. "We've still got the other."

Lump's horse trotted from her line of vision. Leland reappeared, his eyes grazing her, his expression speculative. He drew his pistol and pointed it at her face.

"Where's your husband?"

Her shoulders nearly slipped with relief but she held them firm. If Leland had to ask where Boone was, he hadn't killed him.

"That scoundrel left me high and dry. One would think I meant no more to him than a flea."

Lump reappeared.

"Where's my woman?"

"Clearly, Trudy did mean more to Boone than a flea. He took her with him. They rode west hours ago."

"Is that why you were just hollering for him?" Leland circled once more into her line of vision.

Blast! She had been doing that. It was unlike her to miss such a detail.

"Not for. At! Put yourself in my place. You can only imagine how angry I am."

He didn't believe her. Although she suspected that Lump did because he began to turn his horse's head toward the west.

Suddenly, Efrin and Buck galloped into the yard. They joined the circle. The four of them revolved around her at a distance of only twenty feet.

The steady clop of sixteen hooves in the mud, going round and round, was unnerving. She wanted to scream, to roll up in a ball and cover her head.

Instead she reached into her pocket and curled her fingers around her weapon.

Instantly, Efrin and Lump drew their pistols, pointed them at her. Laughing, Leland wagged his polished gun at her. Even in the dark she saw its wicked gleam.

Buck sat tall in his saddle with a shotgun across his lap. He wasn't looking at her but at his oldest brother.

"Where is Walker?" Efrin demanded.

"I don't know." It was the truth, she didn't know.

Efrin fired at the mud. The hem of her skirt stirred when the bullet brushed it.

Even though it was past midnight, she was not swallowed up by the dark. She was as exposed as a hatchling tumbled from its nest.

The brothers followed Efrin's lead, taking shots that exploded in the mud and put holes in the ruffle of her skirt.

Without warning, something hit her back. A vision of mud rushed at her face. A heavy body crushed the breath out of her.

Boone! Nearly suffocating from the weight pressing her down, she squirmed, elbowed him in the ribs.

He lifted up on his forearms, giving her the space to drag in a gasping breath.

"You fools are under arrest. Throw your weapons on the ground." Melinda felt Boone's order rumble against her back.

Efrin laughed, but nervously. Leland chuckled. Lump and Buck remained silent.

After the false humor ran out, they resumed their deadly game of sniping.

Peeking out from under Boone's armpit, she saw red

flashes erupting from the tips of the King's pistols. Mud splattered on Boone from the impact of the bullets.

The outlaws were toying with them. Taunting them with the certainty of imminent death.

The game changed when Boone drew his gun and fired back.

She plucked the pistol from her pocket, took aim on Lump then pulled the trigger. Missed. Hitting a moving target was a far different thing than knocking a can from a post.

Panic closed her throat because she and Boone were sedentary, stuck in the mud. It was unlikely that she would be the first wounded, not with her husband a living bulwark on top of her.

But only living for the moment.

She pointed her gun again, this time at Efrin because he had reined in his horse to grin down at them, to make sure they knew that the shot he was sighting on Boone would be the lethal one. With her finger on the trigger, she drew a bead on his heart.

All she had to do was squeeze. The man would be dead. One less villain intent on murder. She could do it. She took a breath, stuffed down the natural revulsion of—

Efrin blew backward out of his saddle. He hit the ground. Rolling and groaning, he crawled toward the open barn door.

Boone had warned her about that half second of hesitation. Had it been up to her to bring down Efrin, Boone would have been killed.

"I'm going to stand up," Boone's voice rasped in her ear. "When I do, run for the house."

An instant later the pressure lifted from her back. She pushed up from the mud, ran.

Boone must be backing up behind her. She heard his gun firing.

She felt a thud hit her boot along with a flash of heat. She would have to see later if she had been wounded. It didn't hurt but, she'd learned from Lantree, that sometimes shock blocked pain.

With a backward glance she saw Lump slide off his horse, flail on the ground holding his belly. His screech was unnerving but stopped when he went suddenly still.

Rushing up the front steps, she tripped on her skirt. On hands and knees she scrambled toward the door. Wood splintered around her but she made it inside.

"Boone!" she called into the dim interior. There was no sound, no voice or rustle of clothing to indicate that he had followed her inside.

Rushing to the window, she pushed aside the curtain.

She saw him in profile, standing on the porch. His rifle lifted to his shoulder while he fired into the darkness.

In the distance she heard a mule braying. Too great a distance, she feared, to help Boone.

Chapter Fifteen

With Melinda in the house, the front porch was the worst place he could be. While shooting at him they might easily hit her.

He leaped over the porch rail, ran to the center of the yard, his rifle at the ready even though his bullets were spent.

Buck and Leland circled him.

A mule brayed but was still some distance from the house.

Watching the brothers go 'round and 'round, their murderous intentions evident even in the dark, he hoped that Stanley would be delayed.

Smythe had given a lot to secure Boone's future; it wouldn't be right for him to have to watch his client die. To watch his friend cut down.

But with no ammunition left and two killers eyeing him, that was likely to happen.

Not that he meant to roll over and allow it to occur without a fight. For the one thing, Melinda was watching through the window.

At the least, if he could disable Leland before he

went down, it would give Melinda and Stanley a fair shot at Buck.

"Throw your weapons down. Raise your hands in the air," he demanded but couldn't figure why they should do it.

With things going in their favor, the Kings quit shooting. No doubt to prolong his execution. They were having far too much fun, whooping and cackling, to let it end quickly.

"I believe I'll reload instead." Buck made a show of lazily opening the chamber of his shotgun, casually inspecting each bullet as he dropped it in. "This one here's for your shoulder. This one? It's for your knee. Ah, here's one for your gut and—"

The show of bravado turned out to be a mistake because a snarling, snapping blur of angry canine burst out of the darkness.

Buck's horse reared, unseating him. The animal took off across open land before his rider had his foot clear of the stirrup.

Buck was visible for a moment while being dragged into the darkness. It took a mite longer for his screams to fade into the distance.

Billbro raced for the house and Melinda.

Leland aimed his gun at Boone's chest, pulled the trigger. An impotent click erupted instead of a bullet.

Leland tried to reload, but Boone was damned if he was going to wait for that.

He charged, dragged Leland from the saddle.

Locking his arm around King's neck, he slammed him down, heard him grunt when they both hit the ground. Boone knocked the gun away with a backward blow of his hand. It sailed into the dark.

Leland was strong; giving back all that Boone gave him. A blow to the gut for one on the face. A knee to the back for an elbow in the ribs. They were equally matched and his opponent showed no sign of tiring.

Amid the grunts, curses and the slaps of fists on flesh, Boone heard the front door open.

"Get back!" he shouted. But short of Melinda tripping on a rock in the dark, she would rush to help.

He'd need to bring Leland to heel now. The trouble was, his enemy was every bit of the scrapper that Boone was, and he had the advantage of being a remorseless killer.

But Boone was defending someone he loved.

On the fringe of his awareness, he dimly heard the dog barking.

Leland took the advantage when Boone tripped on a rock and went down. He fell upon Boone, shoved his jaw up and to the side, forcing his gaze upon the porch.

Melinda was trying to come down the steps but Bill-bro blocked her way.

Seeing his wife's face, he knew she was screaming, but all he heard was the clamor of battle. Odd, that it was silent and roaring all at one time.

All of a sudden something stung his neck. A warm trickle dripped down his throat. Hell, Leland must have a blade!

With his head being crushed into the mud, Boone's gaze was locked on Melinda's horrified expression, on the dog turning away from the porch, charging toward him with saliva and blood dripping from his muzzle. On Stanley's frantic dash across the yard.

The hell if this is how he was going to die, murdered in view of those who loved him.

With a prayer for strength, he shoved his knee into Leland's belly and bit the hand holding his jaw. The movement only made the prick on his neck feel like a burning gash.

Then the knife was no longer at his throat. He scrambled out from under King's weight in time to see the blade arch toward the lawyer's back.

Boone buried his balled fist in Leland's throat, but too late. The knife's arch was only deflected.

A crimson splotch blossomed from under Stanley's coat at the shoulder.

Leland lay in an unconscious heap. The deputy stood over him, watching with bared teeth in case the man was fool enough to come to.

Boone lifted Melinda off her feet and, even with his breathing fast, labored from the fight, wrapped her in a great hug. She could not squeeze him back tight enough.

Sometime during the clash, the wind had come up and blown the storm east. She had not even been aware of the change until the breeze stirred her hair.

When she opened her eyes and glanced past Boone's shoulder, she saw their moon-cast shadows as one on the mud.

"We're alive." Otherwise they would not be casting shadows. Boone's skin wouldn't smell damp with sweat. Her belly would not be dizzy with joy.

"I'd better see if everyone else is." Boone set her on her feet then kissed her one more time before he turned to see to the grim business.

"Wait!" She touched his arm then his throat. There was a fair amount of blood but the wound was not as bad as it might have been. "It's not so horrible."

Stanley was alive. More than alive, really. He was actually beaming as he poked at the sticky red stain on the shoulder of his coat.

"You won't be so pleased if I need to stitch it up," she warned him. "Let me fetch a lantern from the house and we'll see."

She could go in the house to take care of Stanley's needs, but even with the outlaws disabled, she did not want to leave Boone alone with them.

"You know how to apply sutures?"

She shrugged. "I've seen it done."

All of a sudden Stanley's bravado faded.

"There, Boone's just brought a lantern out of the barn. Let's have a look-see out here." The dog-wolf trotted between her and Stanley while they walked toward the barn, wagging his great tail then stopping to shake the leftover raindrops from his fur. "Oh, and he's dragging Edwin King behind him."

"He doesn't look dead."

Lamentably, the dark side of her nature observed, he did not. What he did look is spitting angry that Boone had tied him up and propped him against the barn.

He did not appear regal by any standard. He looked to be who he really was: a wicked man. If she imagined it just right, she could see his black heart sputtering in his chest.

Next, Boone tied up Leland and dropped him beside his brother. He was only now beginning to moan and come to awareness.

Last, Boone secured Lump with a coarse rope. Dragging him across the mud, he deposited him beside his brothers.

"Not a mortal wound, but it will change his life," Boone announced.

Seeing the three of them helpless—their evil contained—Melinda was able to relax for the first time in... oh, she couldn't think of when. Probably since Judge Mathers had proposed this misadventure.

Melinda snuggled under his arm while they looked down on the disabled criminals. She hugged him tight.

"You did it, Boone. You captured them without killing a single one. Not, of course, that they didn't have it coming." She was so proud of him she felt as if she might burst out of her soggy dress. "You're a free man."

"I will be." He pressed her shoulder to pull her even closer. She felt his lungs expand against her side. "I've still got to go after Buck."

"Not without me." Stanley tested his shoulder by rolling it in a circular motion. He grinned. "Only a scratch."

It had to be more than a scratch. No doubt he was pleased as punch, the threat of stitches not withstanding.

Lump must have just noticed the severity and the location of his own wound and realized for the first time that he would be neutered, because he began to squeal. The high-pitched screech probably hurt Billbro's ears because he set to howling.

"Shut your face!" She was certain that Leland intended to shout at his brother, but with his throat half crushed all he managed was a croak.

All at once Efrin's gaze sharpened, he sat up straight. Curiously he began to smile—no, not smile, smirk. "Shoot 'em, Buck! Every disrespectful one of them."

Boone spun around, shoving Melinda behind him.

Peeking out from behind his arm, she spotted Buck

limping into the lamplight, his shotgun gripped tight in his fist.

"Sittin' there all trussed up like a hog, and you're still giving orders, big brother?"

"Shoot her first. Then once he's licking her brains off his face, slit his throat."

Buck chuckled, shook his head. "The devil take you, Efrin."

Boone moved her more fully behind him. She pressed her face against his back and squeezed her eyes shut.

She heard a rumble of sorts but could not begin to identify what it could be. Her roaring heart, distant thunder...

She knew when Buck raised his shotgun because Boone tensed, his muscles shifting for a lunge.

The shot exploded. She saw Efrin's head slam against the barn wall.

Dead beyond a doubt, he slumped over.

"Had it comin'. All those years of ordering me around like I was his trained rat." Buck turned his satisfied smile upon Boone. "'Course that don't mean I ain't going to kill you, anyway, even though I do admire an outlaw with your balls. I'll take no pleasure in it, though. Not for you, your lady or the little man. Getting rid of you folks is just something I gotta do to protect myself and my brothers."

The odd rumble got closer. So close that she was beginning to make out shouting voices. Angry, shouting voices, she was certain of it.

There! In the distance, she saw torches bobbing in the dark. The bearers were running. And there were so many of them.

Buck turned when a large man yelling curses broke

away from the rest. The fellow waved something in his fist, but in the dark she could not tell what the object was.

Openmouthed and clearly empty-brained, Buck watched the man rush him. At the last second he must have gathered his wits because he raised his shotgun and pointed it at the attacker's belly.

Boone leaped, tackled Buck at the feet and yanked him off balance. While he was still falling, the attacker slammed Buck in the head with a shovel.

"That is for trying to lead my boy to sin!" The butcher raised the pointed end of the shovel over Buck's throat. "This is for threatening to cut off my hand!"

Boone pushed away the tool on the down stroke.

Melinda recognized the child as the King's messenger boy. He stood behind his father, his head hung in shame.

The man, who could only be the butcher, yanked his son out from behind him.

"I discovered what was about to happen here when I caught my hotheaded boy bragging about it to his friends. Me and the rest of the folks figured if we were ever going to take back Jasper Springs, it had to be now, before they murdered the only one who ever stood up for us." The butcher shoved his boy in Boone's direction. "You have something to say to Mr. Walker."

"I—I'm sorry. I promise I won't grow up to be like you, sir."

The butcher cuffed his offspring on the ear. "You better grow up to be just like him."

"But he told me—"

"Boone Walker is a hero, never forget that."

"I won't, Pa. You have my word. So do you, Mr. Walker."

With a gentle pat to the boy's cheek, the butcher turned his attention to Boone.

The rest of the group stood behind their leader. The reflection of their torches cast an eerie red glow on the mud.

"This town owes you a debt. Don't make no difference to us what the rest of the country thinks of you, you have a home here. We'll watch out for you."

A lump swelled in Melinda's throat. Even with her husband's reputation the stuff of nightmares, the people of Jasper Springs offered refuge.

Well, naturally they would. They had come to know the Boone Walker she had known from the beginning.

"That's kind of you all, but my wife and I are going home. As soon as I deliver these outlaws to Judge Mathers in Buffalo Bend, we'll be on our way."

One would think that the town marshal would be present to take the criminals, but he was not.

"If you'll take my prisoners to the jail, I'll collect them in the morning."

"It would be an honor—Deputy?" Someone answered, apparently noticing the badge. A murmur began, starting at the front of the crowd and rolling to the back. Their confusion about who Boone was, was understandable. "A great honor."

Heads nodded in agreement. One by one they came forward to shake Boone's hand, offer their thanks.

The butcher and another man tossed the living Kings, belly-first, onto horses and secured them, the same as they did to the dead man.

A few moments later the yard was empty.

"Trudy will be worried, so I'll be on my way." Mounting the mule, Stanley turned in the saddle. "I'll meet you in Buffalo Bend."

Stanley rode out of the circle of lamplight.

Together, she and Boone stood listening to the mule's hooves clop away.

The wind was cold, their clothing wet, yet they stood for some time, facing each other and simply smiling.

"We have a future, Mrs. Walker." Boone lifted a damp strand of hair away from her face, brushing the arch of her cheekbone with his thumb. "What shall we do with it?"

"Make love all night in our first home." Odd how a humble loft, barely big enough to walk around in, could feel like home, but it did.

She took his hand and turned toward the barn, but he stopped her.

"Melinda?" He cocked his head at her. "Did you ever feel like living here was beneath you? Stanley thought—"

"Stanley has changed a great deal since I met him. I have not."

"What if I can never give you a grand home?"

"I don't need one. Cozy is cozy wherever you find it. When you think about it, it might be harder to find cozy in a large, drafty place. I don't care about how big our walls are, just as long as there's room for our babies to sleep."

He smiled and seemed different now that everything was over. A new spirit shone out of him.

"You know that I don't want our marriage annulled? That you are mine forever?"

"I know, Boone. I always have."

"There's one more thing. I want to be a preacher."

He looked apprehensive. Did he want her approval or did he wonder if she would declare him insane?

"You'll be perfect!" And he would. "Not everyone understands what it is they were meant to do. I'm so very proud of you."

He hugged her tight, sighed against her hair. "So what's the price you put on my head a while ago?"

She let go of him and backed toward the barn. "There're only a few hours left until morning, husband, which I don't intend to spend sleeping. If you want to know your value, you'll have to catch me."

With a wink, she spun around and ran for the barn. Boone chased her, laughing.

After all that had just happened, maybe it was wrong to feel so elated. A man had lost his life right in front of her eyes, after all.

But Boone had not. The good one had triumphed and the evil one had perished.

And life had suddenly opened up, bright and shining.

It had been less than a month since Boone had sat in this courthouse, but it seemed a lifetime ago.

The guard was the same fellow, but this time he wasn't hired to keep Boone from running, rather for his protection.

While the judge had signed the document granting him his freedom—even overturned his original verdict, in the public eye he was still the scourge of everything decent.

"I wonder why the judge has called us here?" Melinda tangled her fingers up in his, squeezed them hard. Her hand felt damp and he guessed she was nervous.

He was, too.

Having turned the outlaws over to face justice, he had expected to leave Buffalo Bend right away. Melinda was nervously anxious to go to Kansas City and introduce him to her mother. Then Judge Mathers had insisted they stay a couple of days longer.

A couple of days where they had been confined to a hotel room with a guard posted outside the door.

As it turned out, the confinement was far from a hardship.

Boone had hoped the guard in the hall was not of a prudish nature. A honeymoon was not a restrained occasion; not a quiet one, either.

He had spent the hours of seclusion getting to know every inch of his wife's pretty body, how it responded to a stroke, a kiss. They'd explored long, slow hours of gentle lovemaking, as well as the fast, hard joining of bodies.

This sort of a sexual union was as new to him as it was to her. The man he used to be had simply hurried the act to complete a physical need. In the marriage bed he was learning the joy of giving and taking love.

A chair scraping on the floor of the judge's chamber brought his attention back to the here and now.

He noticed that Melinda was staring at him, her cheeks flushed. One thing about a wife, he'd learned, was that she had an uncanny knack for knowing her husband's thoughts.

He'd learned a few other things, as well. Yep, he reckoned that the pretty pink coloring in her cheeks was not due to shyness but to answered longing.

He wished the judge would hurry and tell him what this delay was all about. He was anxious to take his wife and be on their way to Montana.

Cautiously on the way. A document would hardly protect them from an overeager lawman or bounty hunter.

The doorknob to the judge's chambers turned with a squeal. Boone felt Melinda's quick inhalation.

Smythe came out first. The judge strode out behind him, hands clasped behind his back. He only hoped Mathers was not about to offer another bargain.

"No need to stand," the judge declared, waiving his hand. "I'm not in robes."

It was darn hard to sit, though, not knowing what was going on.

Garbled voices came from outside the window. It was early for saloon patrons to be gathering.

"Keep them out for a few more moments, Mr. Guise," Mathers told the guard.

It was hard to guess what those murmuring voices could mean, but Stanley was grinning, so it must be all right.

Before he said a word, Mathers shook Boone's hand. "I still can't figure out how you managed it, Walker. Again, you have my thanks—the thanks of everyone in Jasper Springs."

Mathers nodded to Melinda, sent her a warm smile. "As do you, Mrs. Walker. From the looks of things, I feel it will be acceptable to destroy the marriage annulment I have prepared?"

"Is that it?" Boone pointed to a sheaf of paper tucked under the judge's arm.

When Mathers nodded and handed it to him, he ripped it in two. Then he passed it to Melinda who tore it into a dozen pieces.

"Now there's the matter of the reward." Mathers patted the pocket of his shirt. His hand made a tapping sound on a bulge under the fabric.

"Money?" he asked, hope warring with doubt. He had not considered a reward. A few dollars would be a boon to a new family man.

Mathers handed him an envelope. "Three thousand dollars."

Hell's curs— Blazing blessings, he meant. Not just a family man, but one with a nest egg.

There was one more thing he didn't want to leave here without, though.

"Many thanks, Judge, but what about the dog?"

"I hate to lose a good deputy, but if he stays or goes, I reckon that's up to him. But if he does go, I'll need twenty of those dollars back."

Without a thought Boone dug into the envelope and handed Mathers forty. It felt odd, but good to make a legitimate purchase.

He had no doubt that the deputy would follow Melinda. Apparently the power of her charm extended to the canine species.

All at once the voices outside stopped and a dozen or more footsteps shuffled across the boardwalk.

"I reckon we ought to stop by the bank before we leave town."

"I wish I could convince you to take the job of sheriff in Jasper Springs, Walker. The folks there want you."

"I was fortunate, Judge. I arrested the Kings without having to kill any of them. But lawmen aren't always that lucky. I reckon the day would come when I'd be called upon to do it. I've got my sights set another way."

The judge nodded, smiled. "Smythe, as the last duty to your client, would you send in the reporters?"

Dang nation! Men with photographic instruments spilled through the doorway, as well as five with pencils and notepads. At the front of the crowd was a woman with a hundred questions that she tried to ask all at once.

"Is it true that you were falsely convicted? That you aren't even a killer? That you were forced to marry? That—"

A photographer waved for him and Melinda to stand still. A bright flash illuminated the room.

Melinda motioned vigorously for Stanley to come and stand with them. With the three of them standing shoulder to shoulder, the flash erupted again.

"Is it true," a man asked, dabbing the point of his pencil on a paper pad, "that you saved a whole town single-handedly? And without killing a man?"

"It seems far-fetched," another reporter said, wagging his head and frowning.

"I can understand why you think so." Melinda folded her hands at her waist, smiled then walked away from him and Smythe to greet the doubter.

While the photographers continued to take pictures of him and his lawyer, the rest of the reporters gathered around Melinda.

Hang it if they didn't look like a hoard of bees buzzing around a pollen-laden flower.

"I will be the first to say that it looked as though we were all going to die. Why, I doubt that even the baby would have been safe from that horrid King gang."

The scratch of pencils across paper stilled.

"There was a baby?" the woman asked, her eyes wide in surprise.

"Of course. And, really, little Diana is the first one to owe her life to Boone Walker. Let's all sit down, there's so much to tell we'll all end up exhausted if we stand."

Melinda sat in a chair. The reporters sat on the floor at her feet, expectant little bees gathered around their queen. Naturally, the photographer captured the image.

"So, there we were, being chased by the Kings, all except for Leland, the one known as Copperhead—for some reason they gave themselves the names of snakes. Well, Leland had already been brought down by Deputy Billbro, who is part wolf, part dog. But, sadly, the Copperhead was not down for good. We'll get back to him in a bit. So the person they were really after that day was Dr. Brown who was in the back of the wagon delivering baby Diana who was breach…"

"They'll give me hero of the year award by the time she's finished with them."

"Probably, but then you would deserve it." Stanley shrugged, nodded.

All this hero talk made him uneasy, but it did serve a purpose. Better to be hailed in the public eye as a hero than a villain, he reckoned.

"When are you going to marry Miss Trudy?" Boone asked to divert the talk from things heroic. It only took a glance at Smythe's smitten face to know it would be soon.

"About the time this show is over and you and your wife can meet us at the church. An hour, maybe?"

It made his stomach churn for a moment, thinking of setting foot in a church. But given his chosen profession, he reckoned he'd have to get over feeling unworthy.

Maybe he could do it. It had been several days since he'd cussed. He reckoned it was a start down the good path.

"Then, there we were, the four of them circling us with

their horses—I declare they looked just like vultures—and Boone lying on top of me, once again using his body to protect me…"

"I expected to say a few words on your behalf, Walker," the judge said, coming to stand beside him and Stanley. "Looks like your wife will have you the hero of a dime novel before you set foot out of town."

Since there was still a good bit of the story to tell, Boone sat on the floor with the others. Looking up, he fell in love with Melinda even more than he already was.

Reunions
Kansas City, December
Mama

The fancy fringe on the roof of the elegant rented buggy swayed madly in the icy wind whipping down the road. Up ahead the plaque for the Kansas City Ladies Cultural Club squealed on cold, iron hinges.

Billbro, taking up the whole of the backseat, didn't seem to mind the falling temperature, but Melinda snuggled against the warmth of Boone's big, warm body. It was only midafternoon, but all she could think of was sitting in front of a blazing fire. Hopefully beside Mama.

She wasn't certain what her reception would be. She was as likely to be rejected as to be welcomed, given the way she had left home against her mother's wishes.

No one could hold on to an ill temper the way her mother could.

"I reckon we might have snow for Christmas." Boone tugged her tighter to him. "Still nervous, honey?"

"I feel as jittery as the decoration on this buggy that you paid so much to rent."

"I'm not bringing you home in a buckboard. Scary enough meeting a mother-in-law for the first time as it is."

She tipped her face up, felt the nip of cold on her nose, then kissed his cheek. "She will be impressed."

"Enough to overlook my past, I hope."

"And mine." She found Boone's free hand under the blanket spread across their laps. "Living in the wilderness was never her dream for my future."

"Marrying an outlaw couldn't have been, either."

"If she's heard of you, she'll not be happy. But a minister as a son-in-law, there is some prestige in that."

Up ahead on the boardwalk a couple struggled in the wind. The man dragged a fair-size Christmas tree behind him. The pair must have found the struggle amusing because they were laughing.

For some reason the sound warmed her. Her nervous stomach eased a bit.

She focused her attention on the happy woman as their buggy rolled up behind them.

It was shallow of her, but she found comfort in the stranger's clothing. Her coat was red with a white ruffle at the hem and cuffs. A sprig of mistletoe hung from her bonnet by a green satin ribbon.

Her step was buoyant. Naturally, whose would not be given that the man beside her gazed down at her as though she were the most precious person alive.

The woman's face was hidden in her fur-trimmed hat, but Melinda felt the lady must be smiling clear to her toes.

Melinda guessed this because, as they came alongside the couple, the woman picked up her skirt and twirled.

She didn't seem to mind that a pair of strangers were rolling by and seeing her petticoat exposed to her knees.

Her feet tapped a happy jig.

Melinda's foot tapped in time to the stranger's dance even while her heart constricted. The past fell away and she saw her mama dancing just this way.

Exactly this way, the steps were so familiar.

Like Mama of old, this woman was overcome with the joy of being alive. She didn't seem to care what anyone thought about it.

The buggy rolled past the couple. She turned on the bench, not wanting to lose sight of the lady who reminded her of Mama in years gone by.

Now she saw the woman's face full-on. Her cheeks were pink, her eyes blazing blue.

Melinda's stomach flipped. She had a sensation of falling, stopped only when Boone squeezed her hand.

"You all right, honey?"

"Stop the buggy!" She stood while the wheels were still moving. Boone yanked her down. "It's Mama!"

"That's your mother?"

"No, not my mother—Boone, that's Mama."

The buggy halted several yards beyond the couple. She tried again to scramble down but Boone leaped over the side and lifted her gently to the road.

"It's Mama, but before."

Melinda rushed up the boardwalk steps. Behind her she heard Boone's boots clicking on the wood.

When her mother's eyes grew wide in recognition Melinda stopped, still not sure who she was facing. Mother? Mama? Both of them? She wasn't certain she could walk the distance separating them to find out.

Then she felt the heat of Boone's chest against her back, the weight of his hand on her shoulder.

"Do I show?" she whispered, touching her belly.

"Only with your clothes off." His voice puffed against her ear, leaving a white cold vapor behind. "But I reckon your mother already knows, see her smiling?"

Yes, she had noticed her mother's downward glance to where Melinda's fingers covered her bean-size baby.

And Boone was right! Even though she had no way of knowing that her wild girl was a married woman, she was smiling.

"Mama?"

The woman she had missed for too many years opened her arms wide. Melinda rushed into them.

Mama's cheeks were damp. So were hers.

It was hard to breathe or to think or to even believe. How could the mama she had lost be restored?

"I'm so sorry, baby."

"Why would you be? I'm the one who left home so—"

"No… I left you." Mama took Melinda's face in her hands, looked deeply at her. "I came to realize some things while you were away. I left you. When my little girl needed me the most, I left her. Please forgive me."

Vaguely she heard Boone and Mama's companion speaking, not clearly, though, because of the wind howling coldly along the ground.

"I love you, Mama!"

Melinda wrapped her mother in a hug. Mama hugged back. They remained heart to heart for a long time, saying things that words could not.

At last Mama held her at arm's length.

"You always did have too much life in you for this stale, old town. I don't blame you for leaving. I should have taken you all away after your father died. But it seemed a daunting thing to do alone, and I never had your spirit."

She was aware of Boone putting the tree in the back of the buggy but her full attention was on the miracle of having her mother back.

"How are my sisters?"

"Bethune is stodgy. A librarian. She claims to be happy in her library with her dusty books. Prudence has a beau. A good man who will make her happy." Mama clasped her hands in front of her still trim waist. "You'll be staying for Christmas?"

"New Year! Mama, I've got so much to tell you it will take more than a few days."

"You men go along home." Mama blew a kiss to the man she now recognized to be Mr. Portlet, the neighbor who had come to Mama's rescue when the butcher had come pounding at the door. "My daughter and I are going to catch up with things while we walk."

Mama looped her arm through Melinda's as they walked, watching the buggy move down the road, the tree bouncing off the backseat.

"So, who was that great big handsome man with you? I must say, he's ever so much more…well, more than anyone in this town."

"My husband—Boone Walker—he's wonderful in every way. He's going to be a preacher."

"You and a preacher? Melinda." Her mother laughed out loud. "I should not be surprised that you continue to surprise me."

"Well, he used to be an outlaw, but we'll talk about that later. So, Mama, who is the man with you?" She knew who he was, of course, but who was he to Mama?

"My husband. You remember our neighbor, Mr. Portlet?" Mama winked, her smile indicating that Melinda would know what she was smiling about.

And of course she did.

"You look so happy, Mama." Melinda squeezed her hand.

"Really, I've never been happier. What about Rebecca?" For an instant a shadow crossed her expression. "I hope she did well in spite of the way I treated her."

"Well, Mama, if you think my husband is handsome, you will think Rebecca's is, too. Boone and Lantree are twins, except Lantree is a doctor. They have a beautiful baby girl."

"I couldn't be happier. Maybe someday I can let her know how I regret things and that, really, I did care for her."

"I have news." Melinda stopped walking because she had daydreamed so many times about how she would tell Mama about the baby and wondered if she would be happy. "I'm expecting a baby."

Mama covered her mouth but screamed joyfully, anyway.

"I thought so! The way you touched your middle so lovingly."

"You're happy?"

"Deliriously so. I'm walking on clouds."

Yes, and she had been ever since Melinda had first spotted her.

"Do you recall our happy dance, Melinda? The one we did when you were tiny?"

Melinda lifted her skirt high. She shuffled her feet.

Mama echoed the movement.

"Aren't you worried that folks might be watching through the windows?" she asked.

"I'm going to be a granny!" she called to invisible listeners. "Even though I'm far too young!"

They danced down the boardwalk, kicking up their heels, tapping their toes and twirling their skirts.

The celebration didn't end until they whirled up the front steps, Mama into her husband's arms and Melinda into Boone's.

Montana, March
Lantree

A thaw in early March made it possible for Boone to take his bride and leave the small house in Billings where they had sheltered for the winter.

He liked the bustling new town but didn't care much for Coulson, the dying one next to it.

Interesting how the towns, side by side, resembled his life. The old dying one full of wickedness; the new burgeoning one full of hope and new beginnings.

Emotionally, it hadn't been easy to hole up for the hard months of winter, not when Moreland Ranch was only eighty miles away.

Eighty hard miles this time of year, he'd been told. While he might have attempted the journey alone, he would never subject his wife to it.

All through the long days and nights of snowy weather, he had longed for the reunion with his twin nearly as much as he'd dreaded it.

He'd spent a lot of years doing a lot of things to make his brother ashamed. Beginning with abandoning

Lantree the night of the killing and ending with robbing
the saloon where he had been captured and arrested.

There was little chance that Lantree would have
any respect for him. When he finally met his brother
face-to-face would there be even a ghost of their former
affection?

Melinda had assured him that his brother loved him
deeply. That might be true since he had hired Smythe to
represent him. Then again, it could be that he had hired
the lawyer out of family obligation.

There was every chance that his brother deeply resented
him. It was hard to imagine any man being pleased
to open his door and find an outlaw standing there.

He and Melinda had discussed sending a telegram
to let Lantree and Rebecca know that they were coming,
that he was a free man, and about their marriage.

With all they had to tell, it would have made for a
mighty long wire. Plus his wife was set on sharing every
detail of their good news in person.

He had no doubt that Melinda's reunion with her
cousin would be joyful, with hugs, kisses and tears. As
for what his own reception would be? He had no idea.
What he did know is that he would spend a lifetime making
things up to Lantree if that's what needed doing.

"We're nearly home." Melinda rose in her stirrups,
pointing down the slope of the hill they had just topped.
She glanced across at him, eagerness moistening her
eyes and casting them a deeper blue.

"Do you see the big house down below? There's
smoke coming from the chimneys! Boone I think they're
at home!"

It was hard to imagine that they would be anywhere

else. From all he'd seen, they'd passed the nearest neighbor at noon. It was now getting toward sundown.

Besides, the weather was taking a turn for the worse. He doubted Lantree would take his family farther than the front porch.

"We'd better get a move on, honey. A snowflake just hit your nose."

She laughed and wiped it and a stray, happy tear away.

By the time they rode into the yard, the sun had set. Lamps glowed softly through the parlor windows. Seen through a dusting of falling snow, the room held an aura of quiet peace, of contentment.

Moreland Ranch seemed a place that had only existed in his dreams.

But the vision greeting him through the window was something he had never even dared dream of. He felt Melinda's gaze settle on him. Knowing his wife as he did, he was certain that she wanted nothing more than to leap from the horse and rush inside. But she waited, watching him watch his brother.

Lantree sat on a large chair with a tall, lovely woman snuggled on his lap. It looked as if they were reading a book of some sort. It was a cozy scene with the fire brushing the pair of them in shades of soft orange.

The woman—Rebecca, she could only be—rocked a cradle beside them using one long, bare toe.

Lantree set the book aside. The pair of them laughed then Rebecca's fingers settled on her stomach with a caress. Lantree covered her hand with his. They shared a smile.

Melinda would not have seen the brief gesture since she was looking at him.

It was going to be like the Fourth of July with all the

emotional fireworks that were going to go off when she found out there was another baby on the way.

"Don't worry, Boone." She leaned sideways in her saddle to caress his shoulder. "This is going to be a wonderful moment."

And it was time to face the moment, whatever it was.

He dismounted then rounded Melinda's horse and helped her down. He braced his arm at her back, not only to keep her from slipping on the quickly icing steps, but for the great comfort of holding on to her small body, of clinging to her reassuring spirit.

They crossed the porch together. When he lifted his hand to knock on the door, Melinda stopped him.

"Do I show?" Her eyes alight with hope, she feathered her fingers across her belly, cupping what would soon be a lovely bulge.

"A bit more than yesterday." He kissed her forehead then her chilly lips.

He lifted his hand once more to knock but Melinda threw open the door and charged inside, dragging him by the coat sleeve, out of the cold and into the warmth.

"Becca!"

With a screech, Rebecca Walker pushed out of Lantree's lap. She dashed across the room to catch her cousin up in a hug.

Watching his brother rise, unsmiling from his chair, Boone was dimly aware of the women crying joyfully all over each other.

Barefooted, Lantree slowly crossed the room to where Boone stood riveted in the doorway. A gust of wind howled across the porch and blew a flurry of snowflakes inside.

For some reason, a lamp shade trembled.

Without speaking, Lantree spread his arms. Before Boone could blink, he was folded in his brother's sturdy embrace. Public exoneration meant nothing compared to this silent pardon.

After a long moment he became aware of life returning around him.

A bird screeched from inside the house. He heard a man's voice saying, "Miss Melinda, praise the Good Lord you've come home to us safely!"

He ought to make the man's acquaintance, but he was caught up in this long-dreamed-of moment. This was meant for him and his brother alone.

"You're all right?" Lantree asked, looking him over from head to toe then deep into his eyes. He swore that his brother was delving into his soul, looking for shadows of the past.

"I'm all right." Thanks to Melinda, he could stand in front of Lantree and say that. "And you're a doctor?"

"It was a twisted road but, yes, I am. That and a cowpoke." Lantree wiped a bit of moisture from one eye, shook his head on a long breath. "Hell and damn, I can't believe you are standing in my living room."

"I want you to know that I'm no longer an outlaw." That was something that needed to be said before anything else. "Even in the eyes of the law. Because of you and Mr. Smythe, my verdict was overturned. I'm a free man."

From the other side of the room he heard the women's voices happily chattering. Melinda was probably relating all the news from Kansas City. The best of which was about her mother marrying Mr. Portlet and, being a changed woman, sorry for how she had treated them, especially Rebecca.

There was more talk than that, about how Mr. and Mrs. Portlet were coming to visit in the spring, but being involved in the moment of reunion with Lantree, he registered only a word here and a "By the saints!" there.

"I wasn't sure what to think of the little man," Lantree said. "But I reckon he did well."

There was another silence between them. Not lack of communication, though. For a moment they were simply seeing each other, feeling each other's presence.

"I need your forgiveness," Boone managed to say at last. "For running away—leaving you to deal with everything. For all the years of worry I caused."

"Hell and damn. You're here, you're safe." Lantree clapped him on the shoulder. "It's all I ever wanted."

"You should know—most of what they said about me wasn't true—but not all of it."

"Oh!" A short, round fellow hurried across the room flapping a book in his hand. Now he understood why the lamp shades shook. "We know that, sir. Every evening we gather about the fire and read about you and our Melinda."

All of a sudden Melinda was there beside him, snuggling under his arm, hugging him around the middle.

"How much of that account is true?" Rebecca asked. Looping her arm through her husband's, she arched a brow at Melinda.

"I related it myself." Melinda shot her cousin a grin. "Nearly every word is gospel."

Lantree glanced between Boone and Melinda, his expression suddenly anxious. "The part about the two of you being married? That's true?"

Melinda straightened her shoulders, arched her back. She stroked her hand lovingly across her belly. She swayed to and fro, her eyes snapping with joy. "That part is gospel."

Rebecca gasped, covered a scream. She copied Melinda's stance and patted her stomach.

As he'd expected, the fireworks began in the form of screeches, hugs and tears. The green bird caterwauled along with them.

At one point during the ruckus the front door opened and three men came in, brushing snow off their shoulders and stomping it from their boots.

"Saw some horses in the—" An older man with white hair strode into the room ahead of the others.

"Grandfather!" Melinda ran for the old fellow and gave him a stranglehold of a hug. "Look whose come home. And I'm having his baby. Oh, we're married, of course."

"Say, Tom, he looks like the boss!" A red-haired young man nudged the man who must be Tom in the ribs.

"Hard to tell whose Lantree and whose not," Tom agreed. "He's got to be one of them since they're standing together."

"Tom and Jeeter," Melinda said. "Won't you meet my husband, Boone Walker?"

"A great pleasure, sir." Jeeter, who Boone knew to be one of the ranch hands from Melinda's stories of Moreland Ranch, offered his hand in greeting. "If half of the things they write about you are true, I'm pleased as peaches to make your acquaintance."

"Most honored, Mr. Walker," Tom added, pumping Boone's hand vigorously in greeting.

"Welcome to Moreland Ranch, son." The old fellow clapped him on the shoulder. "If it's a job you need, I'd be pleased to have you. You and Melinda can settle into Lantree's old cabin."

"I'd appreciate a job, Mr. Moreland." Boone had been nervous about asking. Now with it being offered so freely, a sense of belonging began to grow inside him.

"It's Grandfather or nothing, none of this 'Mr. More-land' from you, young Boone."

He'd never had a sense of belonging to a place, or this natural bonding with strangers. If this feeling of instant kinship was anything to go by, he'd dig his roots deep into Montana soil.

Hershal Moreland—Grandfather—wrapped him in a hug, pounded him on the back then stepped back wagging his head.

"Now, girls, what's this I heard about a baby?"

Melinda and Rebecca both burst into tears at the same time.

He felt a prickle behind his own eyes and wondered if his brother felt the same thing.

Six hours later in Rebecca and Lantree's former cozy cabin

Melinda yawned, stretched out in the bed then crossed her leg over her husband's muscular thigh. Coarse hair tickled the inside of her knee.

"They did look surprised when Billbro scratched at the door, but not as surprised as when you told them that you were going to be a preacher," she said.

"It wasn't in the dime novel."

"Do you really want to live here, Boone? We could go anywhere."

She hoped he wanted to. This is the place she imagined raising their babies. Here with Rebecca, Lantree and Grandfather, but she would go with him wherever he saw their future.

"I reckon I'll get the hang of rounding up cattle after a time."

"You'll be brilliant."

"Helpful, anyway." She felt his chuckle shimmy the bed. "Here's what's really got me excited. With all the folks settling here, a preacher won't have trouble finding work." Boone stroked her naked back all along her spine. It sent a delicious shiver from her scalp to her toes. "I'm for staying, just as long as you keep me warm on these freezing Montana nights."

Not much of a chore, that. She rolled on top of him, leaving room between her belly and his for the baby. She spread her hair in a curtain around his head and shoulders. Enclosed in the intimate space, she gazed down at Boone. He smiled up at her. She lowered her mouth. Boone lifted his.

"I wonder what time it is, honey. You must be tired…"

"Not so tired. It's my favorite time of night, in fact."

"What time is that?" He kissed her long and hard and then he grinned because he well knew her answer.

"It's forever o'clock, of course."

* * * * *

*If you want to find out about the other Walker twin,
look out for*
WED TO THE MONTANA COWBOY

COMING NEXT MONTH FROM

H HARLEQUIN®

ℋ ISTORICAL

Available March 22, 2016

WESTERN SPRING WEDDINGS (Western)
by Lynna Banning, Kathryn Albright and Lauri Robinson
Spring wedding fever comes to the Wild West in this collection of three
short stories celebrating the season of new beginnings!

FORBIDDEN NIGHTS WITH THE VISCOUNT (1830s)
Hadley's Hellions • by Julia Justiss
After suffering the loss of her beloved husband, quick-witted
Lady Margaret Roberts has sworn off the pursuit of passion. That is,
until she meets Giles Hadley...

THE WIDOW AND THE SHEIKH (Regency)
Hot Arabian Nights • by Marguerite Kaye
Intent on his quest to reclaim his throne, will Prince Azhar give in to
temptation and pursue a dalliance with enticing English adventuress
Julia Trevelyan?

BOUND BY ONE SCANDALOUS NIGHT (Regency)
The Scandalous Summerfields • by Diane Gaston
On the eve of battle, Lieutenant Edmund Summerfield and mysterious
Amelie Glenville spend the night together, but their scandalous actions have
one inescapable consequence...!

Available via Reader Service and online:

RETURN OF THE RUNAWAY (Regency)
The Infamous Arrandales • by Sarah Mallory
Can courageous fugitive Raoul Doulevant be the one to give Lady
Cassandra Witney the home she has been yearning for?

SAVED BY SCANDAL'S HEIR (Regency)
Men About Town • by Janice Preston
Respectable Lady Brierley has buried the secrets of her broken heart. But
when her childhood sweetheart, Benedict Poole, returns, her safe world
threatens to unravel!

HHCNM0316

REQUEST YOUR FREE BOOKS!

HARLEQUIN®

HISTORICAL

Where love is timeless

2 FREE NOVELS PLUS 2 FREE GIFTS!

YES! Please send me 2 FREE Harlequin® Historical novels and my 2 FREE gifts (gifts are worth about $10). After receiving them, if I don't wish to receive any more books, I can return the shipping statement marked "cancel." If I don't cancel, I will receive 6 brand-new novels every month and be billed just $5.69 per book in the U.S. or $5.99 per book in Canada. That's a savings of at least 12% off the cover price! It's quite a bargain! Shipping and handling is just 50¢ per book in the U.S. and 75¢ per book in Canada.* I understand that accepting the 2 free books and gifts places me under no obligation to buy anything. I can always return a shipment and cancel at any time. Even if I never buy another book, the two free books and gifts are mine to keep forever.

246/349 HDN GH2Z

Name	(PLEASE PRINT)

Address	Apt. #

City	State/Prov.	Zip/Postal Code

Signature (if under 18, a parent or guardian must sign)

Mail to the **Reader Service:**
IN U.S.A.: P.O. Box 1867, Buffalo, NY 14240-1867
IN CANADA: P.O. Box 609, Fort Erie, Ontario L2A 5X3

Want to try two free books from another line?
Call 1-800-873-8635 or visit www.ReaderService.com.

* Terms and prices subject to change without notice. Prices do not include applicable taxes. Sales tax applicable in N.Y. Canadian residents will be charged applicable taxes. Offer not valid in Quebec. This offer is limited to one order per household. Not valid for current subscribers to Harlequin Historical books. All orders subject to credit approval. Credit or debit balances in a customer's account(s) may be offset by any other outstanding balance owed by or to the customer. Please allow 4 to 6 weeks for delivery. Offer available while quantities last.

Your Privacy—The Reader Service is committed to protecting your privacy. Our Privacy Policy is available online at www.ReaderService.com or upon request from the Reader Service.

We make a portion of our mailing list available to reputable third parties that offer products we believe may interest you. If you prefer that we not exchange your name with third parties, or if you wish to clarify or modify your communication preferences, please visit us at www.ReaderService.com/consumerschoice or write to us at Reader Service Preference Service, P.O. Box 9062, Buffalo, NY 14240-9062. Include your complete name and address.

HHI5

SPECIAL EXCERPT FROM

ⒽHARLEQUIN®
TM

ℍISTORICAL

Julia Trevelyan knows Azhar al-Farid is forbidden to her—duty must come first for the desert prince. But how can she resist the power of the sheikh's seduction?

Read on for a sneak preview of
THE WIDOW AND THE SHEIKH,
the first book in **Marguerite Kaye**'s
sensational new quartet, **HOT ARABIAN NIGHTS**.

"You do care, no matter how much you deny it."

Azhar stepped out onto the terrace, indicating that she should follow. "It is incumbent upon me, Julia, to behave honorably, that is all."

"As a prince of royal blood, you mean?"

"Yes, but also as a man."

"That, I would never doubt. You could easily have left me at the oasis, but your conscience would not let you, and for that I will always be eternally grateful. To the man, not the prince."

It was dusk, and though they were in the middle of a palace, in the middle of a city, it was that time of the evening when a stillness, a silence, fell over everything like a cloak. Azhar slid his arms around her, pulling her toward him. There were only a few layers of cotton and silk between them. His hand slid down to rest on the small of her back. "Julia?"

Her stomach knotted. She ran her fingers through the short, soft silk of his hair. "Azhar?"

"We are not on a camel now."

"No, we are most certainly not on a camel…"

"So I wondered if it might be possible that the moment might be…?"

"Propitious?"

"Precisely," Azhar said, dipping his head toward her. "Very, very propitious. And very well chosen, in my humble opinion."

Her eyes drifted shut as his lips caressed hers, sending shivers of delight over her skin. He kissed her slowly, flattening his hand on her back to mold her to him, as his lips shaped themselves to hers. He kissed her as if he was tasting her, as if he was savoring her. The combination of the twilight, the pent-up heat of the desert sun glowing on her skin, the alluring desert man holding her tightly against him, the seductive shimmer of her desert clothes, the persistent flicker of desire that had lingered all day, waiting to be ignited, made her stomach flutter, and it made the blood sparkle in her veins. She ran her fingers up his back, relishing the sensation of fine silk rippling against the knot of his spine, and their kiss deepened. His tongue touched hers, and Julia let out an odd little sigh of delight. And then, as slowly as it had begun, the kiss ended, fluttering to a stop.

Don't miss
THE WIDOW AND THE SHEIKH
by Marguerite Kaye,
available April 2016 wherever
Harlequin® Historical books and ebooks are sold.

www.Harlequin.com

JUST CAN'T GET ENOUGH?

Join our social communities
and talk to us online.

You will have access to the latest
news on upcoming titles and special
promotions, but most importantly,
you can talk to other fans about your
favorite Harlequin reads.

Harlequin.com/Community

Facebook.com/HarlequinBooks

Twitter.com/HarlequinBooks

Pinterest.com/HarlequinBooks

THE WORLD IS BETTER WITH

Romance

Harlequin has everything from contemporary, passionate and heartwarming to suspenseful and inspirational stories.

Whatever your mood, we have a romance just for you!

Connect with us to find your next great read, special offers and more.

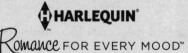